ACCLAIM FOR ANDREW KLAVAN

". . . the focus is on action, and there's just enough left unresolved to tempt readers onward."

—*Kirkus Reviews* on *MindWar*

"A fantastic read. Fast-paced and wildly imaginative, *MINDWAR* is a cinematic cyber thriller with more twists than a circuit board."

—John Dixon, author of *Phoenix Island* (inspiration for the CBS-TV show *Intelligence*)

"This book will appeal to anyone who is looking for a fast-paced adventure story in which teens must do some fast thinking to survive."

—*School Library Journal* review of *If We Survive*

"Klavan turns up the heat for YA fiction . . ."

—*Publishers Weekly* review of *If We Survive*

"A thriller that reads like a teenage version of *24* . . . an adrenaline-pumping adventure."

—TheDailyBeast.com review of *The Last Thing I Remember*

"Action sequences that never let up . . . wrung for every possible drop of nervous sweat."

—*Booklist* review of *The Long Way Home*

". . . the adrenaline-charged action will keep you totally immersed. The original plot is full of twists and turns and unexpected treasures."

—*Romantic Times* review of *Crazy Dangerous*

"[Klavan] is a solid storyteller with a keen eye for detail and vivid descriptive power . . . *The Long Way Home* is something like 'The Hardy Boys' crossed with the 'My Teacher Is an Alien' series."

—*Washington Times*

"I'm buying everything Klavan is selling, from the excellent first-person narrative, to the gut-punching action; to the perfect doses of humor and wit . . . it's all working for me."

—Jake Chism, FictionAddict.com

"Through it all, Charlie teaches lessons in Christian decency and patriotism, not by talking about those things, or even thinking about them much, but through practicing them . . . Well done, Andrew Klavan."

—*The American Culture*

"This is Young Adult fiction . . . but the unadulterated intelligence of a superb suspense novelist is very much in evidence throughout."

—*Books & Culture*

MINDWAR

ALSO BY ANDREW KLAVAN

Nightmare City

If We Survive

Crazy Dangerous

THE HOMELANDERS SERIES

The Last Thing I Remember

The Long Way Home

The Truth of the Matter

The Final Hour

MINDWAR

ANDREW KLAVAN

THOMAS NELSON
Since 1798

NASHVILLE MEXICO CITY RIO DE JANEIRO

Published in Nashville, Tennessee, by Thomas Nelson. Thomas Nelson is a registered trademark of HarperCollins Christian Publishing, Inc.

Thomas Nelson, Inc., titles may be purchased in bulk for educational, business, fund-raising, or sales promotional use. For information, please email SpecialMarkets@ThomasNelson.com.

Publisher's Note: This novel is a work of fiction. Names, characters, places, and incidents are either products of the author's imagination or used fictitiously. All characters are fictional, and any similarity to people living or dead is purely coincidental.

Library of Congress Cataloging-in-Publication Data

Klavan, Andrew.
MindWar : a novel / Andrew Klavan.
pages cm. -- (The MindWar Trilogy ; 1)
ISBN 978-1-4016-8892-9 (hardback)
1. Cyberterrorism--Prevention--Fiction. 2. Undercover operations--Fiction. 3. Video gamers--Fiction. 4. Suspense fiction. I. Klavan, Andrew. II. Title.
PS3561.L334M56 2014
813'.54--dc23

2013050887

Printed in the United States of America

14 15 16 17 18 19 RRD 6 5 4 3 2 1

MINDWAR

LEVEL ONE:
TUTORIAL

1. STAR FIGHTER

RICK DIAL STREAKED through the vastness of space, starlight and gunfire blazing all around him. The seat of his battlecraft shook beneath him as he pressed the button to unleash another deadly barrage from his two forward guns. He caught one glimpse of the pilot of the Orgon ship veering in toward him from starboard, then his shot struck home. There was an orange blast of flame and scrap metal. When it was over, both the Orgon ship and its pilot were gone.

That was the last of the guardians. Rick righted his battlecraft and zoomed in toward the mothership, which now hovered in the endless darkness undefended. He held the Fire button down. His forward guns bucked and spat death in a continual rattle. The black wall of the mothership frayed, chipped, and then burst apart. The landing bay was laid open to the vacuum of space.

As Rick guided his craft in toward the interior landing strip, he could see the insectile Orgon crewmen screaming in terror as they were swept from their battle stations into the infinite emptiness around them. He kept firing. The last parked crafts of his alien enemies exploded, killing whatever crew members were still on board.

With that, it was over. None of the giant bug-like creatures were left. The landing bay was clear.

Rick slowed his craft into a sleek glide and headed toward the centerline. He touched down effortlessly. The moment he did, words flashed on the television screen:

Starlight Warriors

New High Score! New Record Time!

Rick nodded with grim satisfaction. He laid the game controller aside on the sofa and reached for his crutches.

2. A HALF LIFE

WITH THE RUBBER pads of the aluminum crutches wedged under his arms, Rick swung himself across the dark room to the door. He paused by his workstation there. Reached down to touch the keys of his Mac. The monitor woke and glowed in the shadows. There was a new e-mail—another note from Molly.

For a moment, he let himself remember her. The light brown hair tumbling down to frame the high cheekbones on her robust, delicately freckled face. The tall, shapely figure. The smart, strong gaze. He remembered the last time he had kissed her—four months ago—the feel of her lips. The last words he had spoken to her, face-to-face:

I never expected this, Molly.

He meant he had never expected a romance between them. They had always just been friends with a lot in common. She was the child of a local college professor, like he was. She was an athlete, like he was . . .

Or, that is, like he used to be.

An acid bitterness went through his heart and Rick forced the memories away. He deleted the e-mail without reading it. Molly had not given up on their relationship—not yet—but she would get the message sooner or later. He'd make sure of it.

He opened the door and, propped on his crutches, swung out into the hall.

He squinted as the morning light hit him. He was surprised how bright it was. He hadn't seen it in his bedroom, not at all. His mother had set up the new bedroom for him on the ground floor so he wouldn't have to negotiate the stairs anymore with his busted-up legs. He kept the curtains in there pulled shut twenty-four/seven. He didn't want anyone to look in at him from the sidewalk. He didn't want anyone to see him sitting there playing his video games hour after hour after hour—sleeping the days away—doing nothing—a useless cripple.

He swung himself down the hall to the kitchen. He could smell eggs cooking, bacon, too. It suddenly occurred to him he was hungry.

His mother was at the stove with her back to him when he came in. She didn't turn around—probably didn't hear him enter over the crackling of the eggs in the frying pan and the bacon sizzling. But Raider saw him—his kid brother, Wade, eight years old. Raider was sitting at the round kitchen table in the corner. When he saw his big brother come in, he lit up like a Christmas tree. Big, big smile on his round face, blue eyes bright and beaming. That was typical Raider: no matter what happened, he could always find a reason to grin. Kid probably had some kind of weird psychological condition or something.

"Hey, Rick!" he said. He sounded as glad to see him as if they'd been apart for months instead of a few hours.

At the sound of Raider's voice, Rick's mom turned and looked at Rick over her shoulder. She smiled, too, but she wasn't as good at it as Raider. No matter how hard she tried, Rick could see the sorrow in her eyes. He could see it in the way the corners of her mouth always turned down. Her face—round like Raider's—was pale and saggy. No makeup. No energy. Not at all like she used to be, like she was in the old days—the old days being five months ago, before Rick's father tossed their twenty-year-old marriage in the garbage and ran off, no one knew where, with some old flame of his.

"Well!" Mom said, trying to put some feeling in her voice. "You came out of your room!"

Rick only nodded. He hobbled to the refrigerator.

"Will wonders never cease?" his mother went on. "Who knows? Maybe you'll even shave."

"Let's not get ahead of ourselves," Rick muttered. "I just got hungry, that's all."

"Mom's making eggs!" said Raider, as if he were delivering news that World War III was over and the good guys had won.

"Wow," said Rick, but his voice was expressionless. Leaning on his crutches, he pulled open the refrigerator door and snagged a bottle of orange juice. Carrying it clumsily by the bottle neck, he thumped his way back to the kitchen table.

"I'll get you a glass!" said Raider—and he was off on the mission before Rick could stop him. He practically ran to the cupboard. Grabbed the glass like it was the baton in a relay race. Came barreling back to the table to set it down beside the juice bottle.

"Thanks," Rick managed to say. He set his crutches against the wall and dropped into a chair.

The kid kept hanging over him, though, all hopeful and eager. For what? What did he think Rick was going to do for him? Toss the football around with him in the backyard? Teach him some gridiron moves like he used to? All that was over now. He couldn't be that kind of big brother anymore—a hero a younger brother could look up to and imitate. Those days were finished. The kid just never learned, that's all.

"Hey, I know: maybe you could get some exercise today," Raider suggested helpfully. "The doctor says if you exercise enough, you'll get the strength in your legs back, then you won't have to use the crutches anymore."

Rick poured himself some juice and drank. "Aw, what do doctors know?"

"Uh . . . doctoring?" said Raider.

Rick smiled in spite of himself. It was impossible not to like the runt.

"Sit down and eat your breakfast," said their mother. She set a plate with eggs, bacon, and toast on the table for Raider.

"Rick can have those," said Raider. "He's hungry. I'll get the next batch."

"Sit down and eat, punk, or you'll get the Crutch of Doom," said Rick.

"Not the Crutch of Doom!" cried Raider in mock horror. But he sat down and started eating his eggs.

Rick and his mother exchanged a look. She lifted her chin at him—a little gesture of thanks for not being cruel to his kid brother. She knew it was hard for Rick to be nice to anyone anymore. And she knew Raider worshipped the ground Rick walked on. Or hobbled on.

"I'll make some more for you," she said and moved back to the stove.

Rick's eyes hung on her retreating figure for a moment. Her sad, slumped figure, still in her bathrobe, her graying hair uncombed, all out of place. She never looked like that when Dad was still here . . . but there was no point thinking about that anymore, was there? Those days were over, too. Dad was gone.

His eyes moved away from her—but it didn't matter where he looked. There was something in every direction that brought the situation home to him. Over there in the corner of the kitchen counter, for instance, there was a glass bowl full of unpaid bills. Rick could see the red writing on them: *Second Warning. Urgent Notice. Final Warning.* Soon the debt collectors would be after them, calling at all hours, ringing the doorbell, hounding them. Or the electricity would be turned off or the bank would come to take the house away. Maybe all those things together.

His gaze moved on—and he could see through the kitchen doorway into the dining room beyond. There on the sideboard were photographs, snapshots in frames. He couldn't really make them out from where he was sitting, but that didn't matter. He knew what was in them. They were pictures of his dad and mom with their arms around each other, smiling happily at the camera, their two sons nearby. And pictures of him,

Rick, proud and straight and strong in his football uniform, holding a ball, striking a quarterback pose, looking like the local hero he was, ready to head off for Syracuse and a full scholarship and college glory . . .

Was that only a few short months ago? It was. A few short months—and another lifetime. He'd been the big man at Putnam Hills High School then. Six-foot-two, broad-shouldered, muscular. Captain Hunky, the girls called him, on account of his sandy-blond hair, his even features, and his intense blue eyes, full of feeling. Good grades. More friends than he could name. As many girls as he could handle. And on the football field? A star, pure and simple. The quarterback, Number 12. His teammates, his Lions, would have followed him anywhere. No matter how far down they were in a game, no matter how outmatched, if Number 12 said to them, "Don't worry. We're going to win this," they didn't worry and they did win it. They knew that nothing could stop the man under center when he was on his game. Even on the rare occasions when Rick got sacked, when some 250-pound lineman barreled into his midsection and laid him out flat on his back, even then, when some lesser quarterback might have lain in the grass for thirty seconds or so watching the twinkling stars and twittering birdies dance around in the air above his dazed head, Rick would leap to his feet while the defender was still doing his sack dance. He would spit in the hash marks defiantly and swagger back into the huddle—and the whole team would swagger with him. Because he was Rick Dial—he was Number 12—and they would follow him anywhere.

Rick turned his eyes from the snapshots.

She oughta throw that stuff away, he thought. She ought to throw away every photo taken before Dad left and before the accident turned him, Rick, into the cripple he was. Why wallow in what they'd had and lost? Why not just forget the past and deal with the facts as they were now?

He was still gazing in the direction of the pictures, gazing into space, when his mother plunked a plate of eggs, bacon, and toast in front of him. He thanked her and lowered his head to begin to eat, but he could feel her, still standing over him, looking down.

"Raider's right, you know," she said softly after a moment. "It wouldn't kill you to get some exercise. You ought to go outside at least and get some air."

"Don't start, Ma, okay? I just want to have some breakfast," Rick said.

"You can't spend every day playing video games and nothing else."

"Sure I can. It just takes a little effort, that's all." Rick concentrated even harder on eating his eggs, but all the same he was aware his mother was still there, still looking down at him.

"Rick . . . ," she began.

A hot gust of anger went through him. He'd had enough. He tossed his fork down on the plate hard enough to make it clatter. He started to look up. He was about to tell his mother to back off and leave him alone, quit nagging him all the time. But before he could speak, he caught a glimpse of Raider. He saw the way the kid was staring at him, the freckles on his round cheeks standing out as he turned pale, the smile draining out of his eyes as he realized that yet another argument was about to start, and that his big brother—his lifelong hero—was about to disappoint him again.

Rick got control of himself just in time. He didn't want to torture the kid. Or his mother either, for that matter. He loved them both—more than he could say—it was a warm, pulsing ache inside him. He loved them, but they just didn't understand. He just wanted to be left alone, that's all.

He looked up at his mother, into her damp, sorrowful eyes.

"Okay," he said with a sigh finally. "Okay, Mom, sure. I'll take a walk. Or a limp. Whatever."

Mom managed a tight-lipped smile. She nodded at him. "Good," she said. "You don't want to be on those crutches your whole life, after all."

What difference does it make? he thought. *No matter how strong my legs get, they'll never be strong enough. I'll never play football again, not like before. I'll never be what I was going to be. So why bother?*

But—because he really did love her—he willed himself to keep his mouth shut. As his mother finally turned away from him, he looked across the bright kitchen at the window over the sink. He could see outside into the sunlit morning. He could see through the branches of the cherry tree to the front yard, and beyond the front yard to the street. He could see beams of sun falling on the scene and patches of blue sky above.

At least it's a nice day for it, he thought. And he thought:

His mom was right—a walk probably would be good for him. It wouldn't kill him anyway.

He put his head down and picked up his fork and continued eating his breakfast. He did not look up at the window again.

So he never noticed the green van parked out there, beyond the cherry tree, beyond the lawn, across the street against the far curb. He never even saw it.

But the people inside the van—they saw Rick. They had a camera with a powerful zoom lens trained on his window, and they watched him on the video screens they had set up behind the van's driver's seat.

And they waited for him to come out.

3. CRASH DAY

RICK STEPPED OUT of the house. As he moved down the front walk, he was slumped over his crutches like a marionette hung from a hook. He barely lifted his eyes from the concrete paving stones. He moved past the lawn toward the sidewalk with a slow, jerky shamble. With three days' growth of beard, with his hair overlong, flopping down into his eyes, with his flannel shirt hanging untucked over his worn-out jeans, he looked like a panhandler searching for pity and spare change.

He came to the end of the front path and continued hobbling on his crutches down the sidewalk.

His street, Oak Street, was lined with modest houses, lawns, and trees—oaks and maples overshadowing the pavement, their leaves turning bright yellow, bright orange, and red. This early on a Saturday morning, there were a couple of families heading out to the mall or one of the reservoirs—a woman walking her dog—but mostly it was quiet. Cars stood still in driveways and on the street, parked by the curb.

Including the green van—which Rick still didn't notice—and the people inside, watching him, tracking him, taking his picture.

It was a short walk to the corner, but it took Rick a long time, nearly ten minutes. Partly because of the weakness in his legs—because he had to pause to rest every couple of steps—partly because he just didn't care enough to hurry. By the time he reached the intersection with Lincoln Avenue, he was breathless and sweating under his shirt despite the pleasant chill in the fair October weather.

He paused where he was, standing under the yellow leaves of a broad maple, scanning the quiet streets of the small town. Putnam Hills, New York. A nowhere place a couple of hours north of New York City. Nothing special. Good fishing in the local reservoirs. Hills for hiking and limestone caves for exploring. And the sprawling campus of the university where his father used to work.

Rick wondered if it was too soon for him to turn around and go home. Would his mother be annoyed with him if he came back through the door only minutes after he'd left? Or would she finally leave him in peace, let him return to his video games without nagging him? As he considered the question, his eyes swept over the scene—and paused as he saw a panel truck rattle by the corner of Lincoln and Elm.

The sight of the truck made him grimace. Something sour came into his stomach. It was a truck just like the one that had plowed into his silver-blue Accord four months ago—and it was just at that corner, just there.

It happened less than a month after his father had done his disappearing act. The beginning of June, a week after graduation. Summer was coming, but a cold rain was falling hard out of a slate-gray sky that day. Rick was driving to meet Molly for a run at the indoor track at the college, but his mind wasn't on it. He was wrapped up in his own angry thoughts. Daydreams about facing down his father. Shouting at his father, nose-to-nose. Telling the old man what a hypocrite he was. To have pretended all these years that he was a God-fearing person of decency and integrity, faithfulness and honor—and then to just walk off, to just dump his wife, their mother, to just abandon *them*, his kids, because some old girlfriend came back into his life. To disappear with nothing more than a note of explanation. As Rick drove through the rain, he kept thinking of all the things he wanted to scream into his father's face.

While he was thinking that, his car passed through the intersection. He barely slowed for the Stop sign. Without warning, he heard the scream of an oncoming horn. Startled out of his own thoughts, he looked up. For one split second of pure shock and terror, he saw the front grille of the panel truck driving toward his window.

That was the last thing he remembered. After that, there was only the hospital. The surgeries. The pain.

Standing on the corner now, Rick shook his head. Enough of this. His walk down memory lane was over. He was going home, going back into his room, back to his video games, no matter what his mother said. He had forgotten how much he hated coming out here. Out here where the memories were waiting. Where the very air seemed to taunt him with his bad luck, with all that he had been and would never be again.

Working his crutches in a circle on the sidewalk pavement,

he turned around—and was startled to see a woman standing inches away from him, blocking his way.

She was in her thirties, compact and trim, with short black hair and hard, serious features. She was wearing a black suit—black jacket, black slacks—with a blue blouse beneath, buttoned to her throat. Her face was hard, expressionless, all business.

"Hello, Rick," she said in a low, deep voice. "My name is Miss Ferris—and this is Juliet Seven."

Rick stared at her for a second, thinking, *What?* Then he became aware of the green van that had somehow pulled up to the curb beside him. A moment later, he also understood that when the woman said "This is Juliet Seven," she was indicating someone standing behind him.

Clumsy on his crutches, Rick turned to see there was, in fact, someone behind him now. A man—a tremendous man—bigger than Rick—who seemed for all the world to be made out of wooden blocks. His head was square, his torso a rectangle; his arms and legs were huge rectangles, too.

Juliet Seven? The guy was a monster!

The monster's face was as blank as the woman's face—at first. Then, he grinned.

"How you doing, Rick?" he said—and he jabbed a syringe into Rick's neck.

Rick had time to gasp. To think again, *What . . . ?*

Then fog and dark closed in around him. His eyes rolled up in his head and he caught a glimpse of the sky as it fell away from him into spiraling nothingness.

4. THE ASSASSIN'S CREED

MURDER WAS JUST a job to Reza. Someone paid him to kill and he killed. It didn't matter who gave him the money. It didn't matter who had to die. He didn't think about it much. He just did what he was paid to do.

Today, it was a Russian. The man was staying at a small hotel in a white town house in Earl's Court, a busy corner of London. He had phoned for a car to take him to a restaurant across town in Soho. The car showed up at 6 p.m., just after dark. Reza was the driver.

The Russian got in the backseat. He was talking on a cell phone. "I understand," he said into the phone in English, "but we can't trust his methods." He shut the car door and gestured to Reza in the mirror: *Get going.* Reza nodded and put the car in gear.

He drove about a quarter of a mile, then turned the car into a pleasant and secluded little alley off busy Cromwell Road.

"Excuse me," the Russian said. He was speaking to Reza though he was still holding the cell phone to his ear. "This isn't the right way. Where are we going?"

Reza brought the car to a stop. Turned in his seat. Smiled politely. And shot the Russian twice in the chest with a silenced 9mm pistol.

The Russian slumped where he sat, dead. His hand fell to his side, still holding the cell phone. Reza could hear a voice chattering on the other end of the line.

Reza left his gun on the seat of the car, got out, and walked away. He came out of the alley and blended with the crowds of pedestrians on the busy city street. Earlier, he had parked an old Citroën nearby—his escape car. He reached it, got in—and escaped.

An hour and a half later, he arrived at a small airfield outside the city. A Piper jet was waiting for him on the tarmac, its single engine already running. Inside, his old friend Ibrahim was waiting for him. The two men sat across from each other, comfortably ensconced in tall blond-leather armchairs. They were the jet's only passengers. A stewardess brought them each a gin and tonic.

"Look at your face, Reza," Ibrahim said, shaking his head. He was a squat, tubby man with a round face and a thin mustache. He was dressed casually in gray slacks and a colorless windbreaker.

Reza—a slender man with lean, sharp features—lifted his hand to stroke his chin. "What's the matter with my face?"

"It has no life in it anymore. No passion. No faith. You used to fight for a reason. For a cause. You used to fight for the God. Now . . ." Ibrahim shrugged. "You're empty inside. I can see it."

Reza didn't answer. He sipped his gin and turned to look out the window as the jet taxied to the head of the runway. The aircraft paused for a moment, then fired forward and raced into the wind. A moment more, and its wheels left the earth and it shot skyward.

Ibrahim was right, Reza thought, watching the distant skyline fall away, watching the night sky fill the windows. It was true: He *had* lost his passion. He *had* lost his faith. He had once believed the God was on his side, that the God would help him to win his battle against all those who did not believe. Then came the New York mission, and everything had changed.

He had been one of a small group of men living in Brooklyn. They had developed a plan to set off a number of bombs in Grand Central Terminal at rush hour. Hundreds of people, maybe thousands, would have been killed or maimed. The entire city—the entire United States of America—would have been crippled with terror. Reza had never doubted he would succeed. The God would make sure of it. The God would be with him every step of the way, helping him to destroy the infidel.

But that's not the way it happened. Instead, the American FBI had infiltrated his group. Three of his brother bombers had been killed in a gunfight. Five others had been arrested. Only Reza had escaped, unharmed.

Unharmed, but not unaffected. As Ibrahim said, his faith was gone. He believed in nothing now. He fought for nothing. He sold his skills and killed for money. And yes, he was empty inside. But the truth was: he didn't care.

"What you need, my friend," Ibrahim said now, raising his voice over the noise of the jet, "what you need is a new god to believe in. Or, at least, a man who is as powerful as a god, a man who can give you what you want: the cities of America on fire. Her people in chains. Her rivers running with blood."

Reza turned from the window and looked at his friend. "Is that where you're taking me? To meet such a man? My new god?"

Ibrahim raised his glass as if to make a toast. "You don't believe me," he said. "But you'll see."

They flew for four hours. When they began their descent a little after midnight, Reza judged they were somewhere off the coast of Africa. As the jet sank lower, he could make out dark patches in the white-capped ocean: islands, unlit, probably uninhabited. He didn't ask where they were. It didn't matter to him.

They landed on a dirt airstrip in the middle of a dense jungle. Reza could see the black shapes of the trees against the starlit sky. A long limousine met them on the tarmac. They rode together in the backseat. There was nothing to see out the windows but deep darkness.

"Have you ever heard of a man who goes by the name of Kurodar?" Ibrahim asked after a few minutes.

Reza gave a small start of surprise. "I saw him once. In Afghanistan. Someone pointed him out to me. A small, ugly little Russian. They acted as if I was supposed to be impressed."

"You should have been," said Ibrahim, his round head

bobbing up and down. "You should have been. He may be small and ugly. He may even be Russian. But he is a great genius."

The limo went through a gate in a barbed-wire fence, past guards armed with automatic rifles. It came to a stop outside a building. It was hard to make out in the darkness, but the building seemed faceless, a large, square white structure with few windows.

Ibrahim led the way inside, showing his identification to the rifleman at the entrance, pressing his eyeball to the scanner that opened the inner doors.

The two men moved shoulder-to-shoulder through an enormous lobby, empty except for the thick, round pillars that held up the ceiling. They reached a silver elevator at the rear. Ibrahim pressed his thumb into a sensor, and the elevator door slid open. Reza followed the squat man into the box. The door closed immediately and the elevator started down. It seemed to descend for a long time.

When the elevator door opened, Reza found himself in a long, windowless corridor lit by cold, blue-white fluorescents. As he walked beside Ibrahim through yet another checkpoint, Reza found himself beginning to feel excited. It was a startling sensation: the first excitement he had felt in a very long time. *America on fire,* he thought. *Her people in chains. Her rivers running with blood.* After all the failure and frustration, was it possible that his dream could still be realized? If there was a man who could give him that—yes, he would fall down and worship him.

They had reached a final door: a heavy slab of steel like the door of a bank vault. The rifleman stationed there nodded at them. Ibrahim punched a code into a keypad, then put his eye to one sensor and his palm to another. With a loud grinding noise, the huge door slid slowly open.

Ibrahim stepped back and made a theatrical gesture toward the room beyond.

"Enter, and find your faith," he said.

Reza hesitated a moment—then moved through the entranceway.

He came into a cramped, shadowy chamber. He stood before a chaos of screens and wires, panels and flickering monitors. It took a moment before his mind could make any sense of it, before he could see and comprehend what was there in front of him . . .

Then Reza—even Reza—a man who had killed more people than he could remember—who had waged war and practiced torture and committed every manner of atrocity—even he staggered back a step, choking down his disgust at what he saw. The slimy white-and-purple thing strapped to the chair in the center of the room. The pulsing arteries connected to plastic tubes. The shuddering wires linked to the naked brain. The open torso. The flashing screens. The huge, staring eyes . . .

"Behold your new god," said Ibrahim.

Reza stared in openmouthed horror.

He could not tell where the man ended and the machines began.

5. A JUST CAUSE

THE DARKNESS AROUND him was so complete, it was a moment before Rick realized he had awakened and opened his eyes. He could see nothing—nothing at all. He closed his eyes tight and opened them again. No difference. Just darkness. Frightened, his heart beating hard, he sat up. With one hand, he felt a stark metal surface beneath him. With the other hand, he reached out into the blackness to see if anything was there. Nothing. He felt nothing.

Dizziness and nausea swept over him. He stared and stared in every direction. In every direction . . . darkness. Nothing.

And then—out of nowhere—right in front of him: a train appeared! An enormous, sleek-nosed, silver bullet of a locomotive speeding toward him through a gray dawn.

It was so sudden, so impossible—and Rick was so startled—he couldn't react. Frozen in terror, he watched, helpless, as the train raced at him head-on, growing larger and larger. Only at the last moment, as the huge machine filled his vision, did Rick try to dodge it, throwing his body to the side in a desperate attempt to get out of the way.

An instant later, with an awful sound—a metallic shriek that seemed to come from everywhere around him—the train leapt off the track. Sparks flew, blindingly bright. The great silver locomotive heeled over and its side scraped against the earth, throwing up a gout of friction fire. Rick, lying on one shoulder, watched helplessly as the machine skidded wildly, as its coupling buckled, as its rear cars whipped around in his direction.

Then the whole scene vanished.

Just like that, the train was gone. The darkness was everywhere again.

Blinking, gaping, totally confused, Rick sat up, looking this way and that.

"That was in Canada, outside Vancouver, eighteen months ago."

Rick caught his breath. He turned toward the voice. What he saw was impossible. A man was suddenly standing a few feet away from him, completely visible, completely illuminated even in the surrounding dark. It was as if the man were lit by a light inside him, as if he were made of light.

Rick closed and opened his eyes again, thinking the illusion would disappear, as the train had. But the man was still there. He was real. It made no sense.

The man was middle-age, maybe fifty, maybe older. He had silver hair and a craggy face pulled downward in what seemed a permanent frown. His bushy silver eyebrows hung over deep-set eyes that had no humor in them. He was dressed in a gray suit and a white shirt and a black tie. When he moved toward Rick, he seemed to glide through the air, his footsteps soundless. The way he did that—and the way he was all lit up in the blackness—was truly weird.

"Who are you?" said Rick. "Where am I?"

"My name is Commander Jonathan Mars," said the man. "I'm the director of the MindWar Project. You're in an underground facility, not very far from where you live."

"MindWar . . . ?" Instinctively, Rick reached up and touched his own face—to make sure he was real, to make sure he wasn't dreaming. "You drugged me. That woman . . . that giant guy—he stuck a needle in my neck . . ."

"We had to get you off the street, somewhere safe, secret, quickly. We can't be seen."

"We . . . ? Who . . . ? What am I, like—your prisoner?"

"No. You can leave. When we're finished."

Rick felt another wave of nausea. It was the drug, he realized—whatever they'd pumped into him. It hadn't worn off yet. "When we're finished with what?" he said warily. "What was that? That train I saw? Was that real?"

"It was a hologram," said Jonathan Mars. "A three-dimensional movie of a train derailment that occurred a year and a half ago. In Canada, as I said. And yes, it was very real. Eighty-three people died, in fact. The official investigation discovered no cause—none at all. No mechanical malfunction, no driver error, nothing wrong with the tracks. It all seemed to happen for no reason whatsoever."

Rick shook his head, trying to clear his mind, trying to think. "I don't understand. Why are you telling me this?"

"It was only when some of the top computer technicians in North America examined the train's guidance systems that they discovered an almost undetectable disturbance in the train's ATO, its automatic controls. Somehow, someone had done the impossible. They'd hacked the guidance computer from the outside and run the train right off the rail—almost without leaving a trace. That's how we discovered the Realm—the MindWar."

With that, Commander Jonathan Mars vanished. Just like that, just like the train. Without warning, without a sound, he was simply gone.

Confused and disoriented, Rick sat through another moment of utter darkness. Then, suddenly, people appeared all around him. Men. Grim-faced men in suits and ties. They were sitting in chairs on every side of him, like an audience in an amphitheater. And at the center of them, right in front of Rick, standing at a podium that had appeared out of nowhere, was a small, ugly little man. Hunched, spindly. A face like a cross between a skull and a toad.

Rick was about to say something to him when the man began speaking. He was in the middle of a sentence, reading something off the podium. Making a speech. Rick realized: He wasn't real either! He was a hologram, too. All of these people were just some kind of three-dimensional movie.

The frog-faced little man spoke in a deep, droning voice that had some sort of accent. Russian, Rick thought.

". . . my system takes the Brain-Computer Interface to a new level," he was saying. "By surgically connecting the default network of my brain to advanced computers of my own design, I will be able, in effect, to daydream a Realm into existence. Through that Realm, I will be able to move at will, to enter, disrupt, and destroy the enemy's defense systems; his industries; energy grid; water supply; information networks; transportation; finance. All these depend on computers and the Internet, and I will be able to enter those computers and bring them down merely by imagining it to be so! The train wreck in Canada was just a test, just a sample. With your support, with your funding, I can be fully operational quickly. I will be able to wage a MindWar against the United States that will bring that nation to complete ruin in little more than a year."

On the word *year*, the man at the podium—and all the men sitting around him—vanished as quickly as they had appeared. They snapped off like a lightbulb, leaving Rick in total blackness again.

"That man goes by the name of Kurodar." Rick nearly jumped when Jonathan Mars appeared out of nowhere again, gliding toward him soundlessly, the one bright spot in the darkness. "That—his name—is almost all we know about him. He seems to be Russian, about sixty years old. And a genius, clearly. That's the only time he's ever been filmed. He came out of hiding to address the Axis Assembly, the gathered leaders of every tyranny on earth. What he told them was true. With their funding, he can finish imagining this—this MindWar Realm of his—into being. And with it, he'll be able to control and destroy our most sensitive systems: turn our weapons against us; shut off our electricity; close our industries; foul our water supplies—all with little more than a single thought. People will die, Rick. Lots of people. Millions of people. This country as we know it will vanish into chaos and bloodshed."

Jonathan Mars was standing directly in front of Rick now, only a few feet away. A thought occurred to Rick, and he lifted a hand and reached out to the other man. He placed his fingers against Mars's chest—and his fingers went right through him, right into his body, touching nothing, nothing at all.

"You're a hologram, too!" Rick said, amazed. "You're not real."

"I'm real. I'm just not here in the room with you. I'm being projected from another location."

"And why . . . ?" Rick shook his head again, trying to dispel the last fog of the drug. "Why are you telling me these things? All this stuff about Kurodar, about how he's trying to destroy everybody. Why are you telling *me*?"

"Because we want you to stop him," said Jonathan Mars.

"Me?" Rick actually laughed out loud. Now he was sure: This had to be some kind of joke. Or a dream or a hallucination. It had to be. "A mad scientist is trying to destroy our computer systems and you want *me* to stop him? What do I know about this stuff? I'm an athlete, man. I was, anyway. When it comes to computers, I know how to send e-mails and watch videos and that's much pretty much it."

The hologram of Jonathan Mars glided away from him, moving through the darkness in its eerie soundless way. When Mars turned, the bushy silver eyebrows had gathered on his face like thunderclouds; the eyes beneath flashed like lightning.

"Have you ever heard of a video game called *Dragon Soul 3*?" he asked.

Another laugh broke from Rick. This was now officially the

craziest conversation he had ever had. "*Dragon Soul 3*? Yeah, sure, I know it. I play it all the time."

"In fact," said Commander Mars, "you hold the highest score in the world."

"Really? I didn't even know it had a score. I just like the sword fights."

"Well, it has a score and yours is the highest anywhere. Anywhere. We've actually trained people to play the game. Professional gamers. Soldiers. Army Rangers. Navy SEALs. Some of our finest, best warriors. They've never matched your score. They've never come close."

At first, Rick was pleased to hear this. Highest score anywhere. Not too shabby. "I guess I really got into it for awhile," he said modestly.

"I guess you really got into *Starlight Warriors*, too. No one's ever topped your score in that either. Or in *Zombie Apocalypse 5: The Return*."

"*Zombie Apocalypse*. Yeah, that was a cool one," Rick murmured. He was glad the dark was so deep because he felt his cheeks getting hot, and he knew he was blushing. Now that his first pride in his gaming achievements had passed, he was beginning to feel something else—he was beginning to feel embarrassment. The reason he had scored so high on all those games was because for the past four months, ever since his accident, he had sat holed up in his room doing nothing but fiddling with his Xbox. "I guess I've been kind of housebound lately," he said. "I've had a lot of time to play." It sounded like a lame excuse, even to him.

Commander Jonathan Mars, his craggy face still harsh as a storm, said, "You've been hiding away in your room like a toddler in a sulk. Bitter over your missing father and your broken legs. Too weak-willed to rise above your troubles. Doing nothing with your life but playing video games. And with your quick wits and your athlete's reflexes and quarterback skills, you've become very, very good at them very fast. Congratulations," he added with dry sarcasm.

Rick squinted through the dark at the hologram-man. His feelings were confused. He knew what Jonathan Mars said was true. He *had* been hiding away, sulking, bitter. Weak. But hey, what business was it of his? What business was it of anyone's?

Rick started to get angry. "What, have you been spying on me?" he said. "Watching me through, like, secret cameras or something?"

"Yes," Commander Mars thundered back at him. "That's exactly what we've been doing."

"Oh great!" said Rick. "Great. And then you drug me? You kidnap me off the street? Bring me to this underground prison here?"

"Yes."

"Well, that's . . . That stinks. That stinks! You have no right to do that! You have no right to do any of it!"

"That's true," said Jonathan Mars. "Now: Are you going to help us save the country or not?"

Rick's anger burned hotter. He was frustrated by Mars's stern, unshakable calm—and that made him angrier. And he was humiliated to find out they'd been watching him while he sulked in his room and wasted his days with endless gaming—and that made him angrier, too. He had the urge to jump off this . . . seat . . . this table . . . whatever this metal thing under him was . . . He had the urge to jump off it, and clock this guy a good one on the chin. The only problem was, if he jumped up without his crutches, his legs would collapse under him. And the only other problem was that Mars wasn't even here: he was just a three-dimensional movie—and a fist would pass right through him. So Rick stayed where he was, frustrated, humiliated, and enraged.

And Jonathan Mars, still calm, still stern, went on speaking. "Because Kurodar has imagined the Realm into being, it's a place of human dimensions. It has fields and forests, castles and towns: it's a place where Kurodar can feel comfortable, where his imagination can move freely." Mars put his hands behind his back and floated toward Rick again. "But that means you can move in it, too. Our scientists have developed a system that will put you inside—a digital version of you, anyway, a digital analogue of your mind, your spirit. You'll be able to spy on the Realm's secrets, outwit its security bots, locate its weaknesses. You might even be able to deflect its attacks. The Axis wants a MindWar. We'll give them one."

The man's words began to cut through Rick's anger. He was starting to understand.

"You mean, it's like you want to put me inside a video game," he said.

"Something like that," said Jonathan Mars. "But with two significant differences."

"Like what?" said Rick.

"Like it's not a game—and you only get one life. We'd be linking the most intimate part of your brain to a system of computers. What happens to your digital form will happen to your body. If you get cut in there, you'll bleed. If you get killed in there, you'll die. And if you stay in the Realm too long, the strain on your brain systems will cause your mind to disintegrate, leaving your body here in a vegetative state forever. Don't make any mistake about this, Rick. We're asking you to risk everything. Go into the Realm, and you may never come back."

With those words, Commander Jonathan Mars was gone. His disappearance was so quick and silent that for a moment Rick sat staring at the emptiness, the impenetrable blackness, as if he expected the man to come back, to go on speaking.

What happened instead was this: There was a thick, metallic clunk, like a great switch being thrown. The lights came on—bright and blinding at first, so that Rick threw up his arm to protect his eyes. When his eyes had adjusted, he looked—and what he saw was somehow even stranger than the holograms and 3-D movies that had surrounded him before.

He was in a small chamber—little more than a closet. It had seemed large to him because of the images he'd been seeing: the train, the audience, the speaker, Mars floating from place to place. Now in the light he saw its blank, white walls pressed close around him. There were no windows, no doors, no way out. No furniture except a shiny steel cot attached to the wall—the metal thing on which he was sitting.

Rick felt panic starting to rise inside him like an icy whirlpool. He wasn't claustrophobic exactly, but he didn't exactly like tight spaces either. Had Mars abandoned him here? Was he going to be left here alone, confined in this tiny cell until he cracked and agreed to play along with whatever Mars wanted?

No. The very next second, there was a soft clicking noise, a quick hiss of air. A rectangular portion of the wall swung open. A door. An exit into a hallway. And there were his crutches, leaning against the wall on the door's far side.

Carefully, Rick slid off the cot, holding on to the edge of it to support his weight so his rubbery legs wouldn't fold up under him. He shuffled along, flinching with the pain, until he reached the wall. Then he braced himself against the wall as he went on shuffling, grunting with the effort, to the doorway. Here, leaning against the frame, he snagged the crutches and got them wedged under his arms.

There. Now he could get somewhere.

He looked up. He was in a narrow hall, its white walls lit as brightly as the cell. The corridor ran in only one direction and had only one exit: a door at the far end. Rick swung down the hall on his crutches until he reached it. It was already ajar. He shouldered his way through and came into a chamber on the other side.

It was like stepping into the bowels of a great machine. The room was big, and every inch of it was crowded with electronic equipment and monitors. Lights and graphs and meters were flashing and rising and falling all around him. Men and women in dark suits sat at keyboards before lit screens, where red and blue and white indicators flickered and images shifted and audio speakers let out small electronic buzzes and bleeps, while numbers flitted across long electric strips.

On the far wall, implanted right into the wall, surrounded by lights and monitors and sensors, was what looked to Rick, for all the world, like some sort of coffin, a glass box standing vertical, lined with silvery foil and stuffed thick with wires.

Standing beneath that raised coffin was the woman who had confronted him on the street near his house. What was her name again? Miss Ferris. She looked just the same as before. Stone-faced. Emotionless. Planted there with her arms crossed on her chest as if she were waiting for him. Beside her stood the block-man with the bizarre girl-name—Juliet Seven—the giant who had stuck the needle into Rick's neck.

Rick came toward them hesitantly. No one else in the room paid any attention to him. No one even glanced up from any of the monitors as he hobbled by. Only the woman, Miss Ferris, continued to gaze at him with that blank expression of hers. And Juliet Seven—the block-man—watched him approach with a slight and somehow dangerous-looking smile.

Rick stopped in front of Miss Ferris. She stood silent. He lifted his eyes from her face to the coffin set into the wall.

"What is that thing?" he said.

She glanced up at the glass box for a moment. Then she answered him in her clipped, toneless voice. "That's the portal, Rick."

Rick's throat went dry. He licked his lips. He had to work hard before he could swallow. "The portal," he repeated softly.

The woman nodded. "The portal into Kurodar's Realm. The portal into the MindWar."

6. THE CALL OF DUTY

AS SOON AS Rick came through the door of his house, his mother was there hurrying down the hall to meet him in the foyer.

"Where did you get to? You've been gone for hours! You didn't answer your phone . . . I've been calling and calling you. I was worried."

Rick looked at the floor. He couldn't meet her eyes. "Well . . . You said you wanted me to get some exercise . . ."

When he did glance up, he saw an odd expression on his mom's face. Her head was cocked to one side, and she was . . . well, she was practically studying him, studying his features. It felt as if she was trying to read his mind—as if she *was* reading it. After a moment, she nodded, as if she understood everything, as if she knew everything he was trying to hide.

Rick felt embarrassed, exposed. He didn't want to keep secrets from her, didn't want to lie to her about Jonathan Mars and the MindWar Project and what they were asking him to do. But before Miss Ferris had sent him home in the green van, she had spoken to him very clearly:

Don't tell anyone about us. Whatever you do. Not your

mother, not your brother, not your friends. Not for our sake—for theirs. Anyone who knows about MindWar could be in serious danger.

He was trying to think of a way to answer his mother, something neutral he could say that wasn't an outright lie, when Raider saved him charging down the stairs like he was some kind of miniature avalanche.

"Hey, Rick! Did you take a walk? Did you get some exercise? You were gone a long time! I'll bet you got a *lot* of exercise. That'll make you stronger! I'll bet you'll be able to walk without the crutches really soon!"

Rick seized on the excuse to look away from his mother. "Hey, punk! What're you doing here? It's Saturday. Don't you have baseball or something?"

"I'm done already. You were gone such a long time I already played and came back! That's great you got so much exercise—isn't it, Mom?"

Mom put her hand on the kid's shoulder, but she kept her eyes on Rick. The knowledge in her gaze made Rick uncomfortable.

"Sure," she said carefully. "Sure, it's great, Raider."

"Well . . . ," Rick muttered. He needed to get away, get out from under his mother's scrutiny. He worked his crutches and swung down the hall to his room.

Raider came after him, scurrying along at his heels like a puppy.

"You gonna play video games, Rick? Can I watch? I won't say anything! I just like to see it . . ."

The anger, frustration, and confusion of the day welled up in Rick. He stopped suddenly in the hallway so that Raider went tumbling past him. He pinned the kid with a stare and was about to unleash all the fury he hadn't been able to unleash on Jonathan Mars.

Would you be quiet for one lousy second? Would you leave me alone? I can hardly think with you chattering at me all the time! Stop acting like I'm your hero! Can't you see I'm not anybody's hero anymore? I can't even walk!

The words were in his throat, on his tongue, but he saw Raider's eager face, and he bit them back. He didn't have the heart to smash the kid's spirits. Instead, he just barely managed a smile and said, "Later, kid, okay? I gotta get some rest. After all that exercise, you know?"

"Right! Sure! Of course," said Raider eagerly. "All that exercise, sure, you gotta rest! Maybe later."

"Yeah," said Rick. "Yeah. Maybe later."

He managed one more half smile, then hobbled the rest of the way into his room and elbowed the door shut behind him.

Relieved to be alone, he let out a long sigh. He stood still in the shadows. The curtains were closed, as he'd left them, as he always left them. And the room was dark, as always. He could just make out the shapes of the sofa, the computer, the TV—the furniture of his world.

Leaning on one crutch, Rick reached over to the wall unsteadily and flicked the light switch. The light came on and he saw the room clearly. What a mess. It was embarrassing. Clothes, underwear, socks lying all over the floor. Dirty dishes on the writing table, crumpled paper towels lying on them amid bread crumbs. He hadn't cleaned the place in days and wouldn't let his mother come in to clean it for him. There was a grungy blanket bunched up in one corner of the sofa—because he didn't bother to pull out the sofa bed anymore, just fell asleep where he was whenever he got tired of playing games. Even the air in his room was dirty somehow, thick and musty, because he hadn't opened a window for . . .

Four months. The thought stabbed into Rick's midsection like an accusing finger. He'd been living like this for four months. In this room, in this squalor. Sitting on that sofa, staring at the television set, playing his games. Ever since the accident.

You've been hiding away in your room like a toddler in a sulk. Bitter over your missing father and your broken legs. Too weak-willed to rise above your troubles. Doing nothing with your life but playing video games.

Jonathan Mars's words came back to him, and he thought: *Aw, shut up. Who asked you? First you spy on me. Then you kidnap me. Then you insult me . . .*

And he could almost hear Mars answer back:

That's true. Now: Are you going to help us save the country or not?

Rick shook his head to make the inner voices stop. He made his way to the sofa. He laid his crutches aside and sank down onto the cushions. He picked up the Xbox controller he'd left lying there only a few hours before. As his fingers played absently over the buttons, he looked across the room at the rectangle of the TV. For a moment, he felt a tremendous urge to grab the remote control and turn the set on, to turn the Xbox on, to stop thinking and worrying—and to drug himself instead with the animated battles of *Starlight Warriors* or *Dragon Soul* or *Zombie Apocalypse.* The games were the only thing that killed the pain he felt—the pain of losing his father, of watching his mother grieve, of losing his football career and his scholarship and his future.

But now, he laid the controller aside. He leaned forward. Propping his elbows on his knees, he screwed the heels of his palms into his eyes, trying to rub away the exhaustion and confusion.

When he dropped his hands, he looked at the mess around him. And again, he heard the words of Jonathan Mars:

It's not a game—and you only get one life . . . Go into the Realm, and you may never come back.

Why should he do it? he thought angrily. For whom? For what? Hadn't he lost enough already? Hadn't his mother lost enough? Her husband had already left her, what would she do if her son was killed . . . ?

Rick needed answers and he needed help finding them. In the old days, he would have asked his father, but he couldn't very well do that now, could he? In the old days, he might have prayed and asked God for guidance, too. But he wasn't going to do that either. That religious stuff—the Bible and praying and the rest—that had always been his father's big thing. And now that it turned out his father was a phony—a liar, a hypocrite . . . Rick didn't want to do any of the things he did. So he just sat there, confused. He felt completely alone.

There was a soft knock at the door. Rick looked up, surprised by the hope that rose in him.

"Who is it?"

The door cracked open and his mother peeked in.

"I brought you a sandwich," she said. "You must've missed lunch."

"Thanks," said Rick, trying to keep the disappointment out of his voice. Why should he feel disappointed? Whom had he been expecting?

His mother came in, both hands full, a sandwich on a small plate in one, a glass of milk in the other. She negotiated her way through the clothes lying all over the floor and set the food down on the end table beside the sofa, clearing a place by gathering the dirty dishes already there. She hesitated. She stood above him, looking at him as if there was something she wanted to say.

Rick waited. There were times—a lot of times—when he wished she would leave him alone, but right now, he felt plenty alone already.

"Is something bothering you, Rick?" she asked. "Is there something I can help you with?"

He looked up at her. He yearned to tell her everything. But he heard Miss Ferris, her cold voice:

Anyone who knows about MindWar could be in serious danger.

After a moment, his shoulders slumped; he shook his head no.

His mother waited another moment, as if she thought he might change his mind. Then she nodded and moved to the door, carrying the dirty dishes with her. But before she got there, she paused. Turned back.

"I forgot to tell you," she said. "Molly called while you were out."

It was not what Rick wanted to hear. Just one more thing to worry about. "Oh yeah?"

"She just wanted to ask me how you were feeling. She says you won't answer any of her calls or e-mails."

"I don't really feel like talking to her right now," Rick said. "I wish she'd just take the hint."

"Well . . . maybe she actually cares about you."

Rick grimaced. "She cares about the football star I used to be."

His mother made a gesture with her chin, as if to say she understood. "I know that's what you're afraid of," she said. "But that doesn't make it true. You might let her come by and visit, at least."

He made the same grimace again. "Molly's an athlete. She was the top volleyball player in high school. We used to run together, hike together. What's she gonna do with me now? Sit around and watch me limp?"

His mother gave a small smile. "You know, your father always said . . . ," she started.

But a fresh surge of anger went through Rick and he snapped at her, "Yeah, well, my father's not here is he?"

His mom fell silent for a long moment. Finally, she said, "No. No, he's not. But you are."

She turned and continued to the door. Opened it, about to step out.

Rick felt bad for lashing out at her like that. Why couldn't he keep his stupid temper in check?

"Mom," he said.

She stopped. She looked back over her shoulder at him, waiting.

Rick's mouth opened and closed, but no words came out. He didn't know what to say to her. Finally, he said, "Sorry . . . sorry about the mess in here."

She shook it off. "Don't worry," she said. "I know you'll clean it up. It's just taking you a little time, that's all."

She smiled at him, a tired smile, and left him, closing the door behind her.

Rick sat where he was. He looked around him at the clothes lying everywhere, and the plates and the crumbs and the crumpled paper towels. He was still angry—but now he was angry at himself. Angry because he couldn't control his temper. Angry because he was languishing in his room. Angry because . . . because he was afraid. That was it, deep down, wasn't it? He was afraid to come out of there. Afraid to let Molly see him as he was. Afraid of the Realm, of the MindWar—and afraid of refusing to go, of staying as he was.

Because when it came down to it, his choice was really pretty simple, wasn't it? He could go on like this—playing video games in that dull, druggy peace that hid his pain, or he could take up the challenge that Jonathan Mars presented.

Try to do something to help his country, to stop that ugly little Russian with the funny name: Kurodar. If he didn't . . .

People will die, Rick. Lots of people. Millions of people. This country as we know it will vanish into chaos and bloodshed.

Rick looked over at the sandwich his mother had brought him, but he didn't reach for it. Instead, he reached into the pocket of his jeans and brought out his phone. Miss Ferris had given him a number. He punched the number in. He wrote out a text. He hesitated one more second. Then he sent the message:

I'll do it.

LEVEL TWO:

ON THE SCARLET PLAIN

7. GUN

VICTOR ONE HEARD a footstep and quickly put his hand on the pistol holstered at his hip. His eyes scanned the woods around the cottage.

This was a good location, he thought, easy to defend. A clearing near the top of a forested hill. There was no way to get here by car or chopper, and no way to scale the cliff to the south. You had to come right up the slope in plain sight from the north or east, and you had to walk it. And there was no way to walk silently either—especially not now when the forest floor was carpeted with dry, crunchy autumn leaves. It was like a natural alarm system. If anyone tried to approach, Victor One would hear him coming a mile off.

Victor One was a bodyguard, twenty-six years old. A rangy six-foot-four muscleman with short-cropped brown hair and kindly, humorous blue eyes in a tanned, weather-beaten face. He was wearing jeans and a sweatshirt and a windbreaker—and the pistol in the holster on his belt. He had a modified combat rifle secreted nearby as well—so did his colleagues, Alpha Twelve and Bravo Niner, who were both stationed in the trees farther down the hill.

Their assignment was to protect this cottage—or, rather, to protect the man inside the cottage—at any cost.

The man inside the cottage was code-named Traveler.

Traveler was an odd sort of character. One of those absent-minded genius types who seemed to be living on another planet somewhere inside his own head. But over the past few months, Victor One had come to like the guy, to like him a lot. Keeping him safe wasn't just a job anymore; it was a mission. And any unfriendlies who came through that forest with evil intent were going to find out very quickly that Victor One was not the person they wanted to meet. He was a man who could take on a whole army by himself if he had to. He'd done it in Afghanistan. He had the scars—and the medals—to prove it.

Hand on his weapon, Victor One stepped backward until he was up against the front of the cottage. It was a rustic clapboard structure with a pitched roof and a metal chimney. Peeking in through the living room window, he could see Traveler sitting at his desk: a small, narrow man in his late forties, bald except for a fringe of gray-brown hair. He had a mild, thoughtful face; dreamy eyes. He had his glasses perched on top of his head, and he was gazing with a puzzled expression at a screenful of incomprehensible equations on the computer in front of him.

Victor One smiled to himself. He didn't know what Traveler was puzzled about, but it probably wasn't the equations. The professor understood that mathematical gibberish better than anyone else alive.

Victor One stepped carefully away from the cottage and

continued to peer through the forest in the direction of the oncoming footsteps. Another second or two and he made out the elegant figure of Miss Kent—Leila Kent—trudging up the hill. He took his hand off his gun and put both hands in the pockets of his windbreaker instead. Miss Kent was with the U.S. Department of State. She was one of the good guys.

The cottage door opened behind him. Traveler stepped out onto the flattened dirt in front of the entrance. He was wearing wrinkled slacks and a moth-eaten cardigan over an aging button-down shirt. He still looked puzzled.

"I can't understand it," he said. "I had my glasses a minute ago, now they seem to have disappeared."

"They're on top of your head, Doc," Victor One told him.

Startled, Traveler reached up and found them. "Ah!" he said, and he beamed with delight. "Thank you, Victor. I can't see a thing without them." He pulled the glasses down onto his nose and blinked through the lenses. "Oh, look, here comes Leila!" he said.

"What a surprise," said Victor One drily, hiding his smile. It struck him as funny that a guy as brilliant as Traveler could also be kind of dopey at the same time.

Traveler moved forward to greet Leila as she crested the hill. Victor One hung back near the house and pretended not to watch them. He judged Leila Kent to be about the same age as Traveler, late forties, but she was far younger-looking. She was beautiful, in fact, like a fashion model you might see on TV. She was tall and slender and wore a tan fall jacket belted loosely around her narrow waist. Her hair was golden—maybe she dyed it; Victor One didn't really know about such things—and she wore it short and sort of swept back. She had a thin face with high cheekbones. Victor One thought she looked very smart and sophisticated.

He also thought something else—something he would never tell anyone. He thought Leila Kent was in love with Traveler. He could see it in her eyes right now as Traveler took both her hands and kissed her cheek in greeting. She loved him, all right—which Victor One thought was sort of sad because Traveler pretty obviously didn't love her back. Traveler was a devoted family man. Practically all he ever talked about was his wife and kids. Plus he was religious, judging from the Bible he kept on his bedside table and the cross he'd hung on the cabin wall. In fact, the cross—and the framed picture of his family on his desk—was the only decoration he'd put up in the cabin anywhere. So Victor One didn't think Traveler was going to be returning Leila Kent's love any time soon. Which really was sort of sad—for her, anyway.

"How are you, Traveler?" she asked him. Victor One thought he could practically hear the love in her voice, but maybe he just imagined it.

Traveler sighed. "I'm about as well as I'm going to be until I see my wife and kids again, Leila." Leila Kent smiled at that, though Victor One thought it was sort of forced. "It's peaceful here, at least. I like the animals. There's a chipmunk who visits me at the kitchen window every morning. I find my little pleasures wherever I can."

Leila Kent squeezed his hand reassuringly. "It's almost over," she said. "We'll have you home soon, I promise." She gestured toward the cabin. "We should go inside. We need to talk."

When they were inside the cabin, Victor One remained where he was, patrolling the clearing outside the cottage, watching the woods beyond. He could hear the voices of the man and the woman inside the house. From time to time, he could even make out the words.

"We're going to have to move you," he heard Miss Kent say. "We have intel that there are killers hunting for you. They're closing in."

"Never mind me," Traveler answered. "What about my wife? What about my kids? Are they still safe?"

"We think they're safe for now. We're watching them round the clock," said Leila Kent. Then she dropped her voice and Victor One could not make out the words.

A little while later, the two of them must have moved closer to a window or something because suddenly Victor One could hear them very clearly.

"We think that Kurodar is planning to launch some kind of new attack from the Realm—something bigger than the train wreck," she said.

Traveler replied: "No. It's impossible. He can't be ready for that yet. Not for anything really big, anyway. The Realm is still months away from being fully operational."

Miss Kent said, "Maybe he can't make any kind of full assault. But our surveillance shows he's constructing some sort of outpost from which he can—I don't know—stage a raid, I guess. We think that's why he brought in Reza—the assassin I told you about: to protect the outpost in case we try to get in again."

"But why would he do that? Why would he do something small when, in a few months, he'll be able to cripple our entire defense system?"

"Because he needs to impress the Axis so they'll keep funding the project. That's why we want to attack the outpost. If we can stop him now, maybe the Axis will lose faith and the money'll dry up. Maybe we can slow the whole project down."

Victor One heard a silence inside the cabin after that—and then Traveler said, "Why are you telling me this, Leila?"

There was an even longer pause before she answered. Then the answer came, "We've asked Rick to go into the Realm."

Victor One straightened as he heard Traveler shout at her, "What? Are you out of your mind?" He had never heard the mild-mannered professor so much as raise his voice before. "You can't do that! You promised . . ."

"It's not me. The order came from Commander Mars himself. There's nothing I can do about it," Leila Kent said.

"I won't let you do this! I can shut you down. You know I can."

"Listen to me. You know what the Realm is. You know what Kurodar can do already. No communication is safe. No one can be trusted. This new development caught us by surprise. We needed to act fast and we didn't have anywhere else to go, anyone else we could ask without risking the entire program. And . . . well, it turns out Rick is perfect for the job."

"Does he know what can happen? To his mind? To his body? Does he know?"

Miss Kent's response was low. To Victor One, her voice sounded sad. "Not all of it," she said. "We didn't want to tell him the worst. But he knows it's very dangerous—and he's agreed to go."

Victor One could not hear what Traveler said then. He spoke in a rapid murmur, his tone harsh, but his words inaudible. All Victor One knew was that when the cottage door came open and Miss Kent came out, she was crying. Her chin was down and her cheeks were wet with tears.

Traveler came into the doorway behind her. His face was set and serious. Victor One could see that—in spite of his mild manners and his absentmindedness—there was something very strong about the man. Tough as Victor One was, he thought he would not want the Traveler for an enemy.

Leila Kent hurried away from them toward the tree line, but she stopped before she reached the forest. She turned around to face Traveler. She didn't try to hide the fact that she was crying. As far as Victor One could tell, she didn't try to hide the fact that she loved the man either.

"I want you to know," she said, "that I did everything I could to stop this. I never wanted to do anything to hurt you, Traveler. That was the whole point from the beginning."

But Traveler's expression did not soften. He frowned coldly.

"God help that boy in there," he said. "And if anything happens to him . . . God help us all."

He turned, went back into the cottage, and shut the door.

Crying, Leila Kent hurried away through the woods.

8. PORTAL

RICK DIDN'T LIKE to admit it, but he was scared. Really scared. All those years on the football field—all those years with huge linemen rushing at him, charging to take him down, screaming to pound him into the turf—he'd never felt fear anything like this.

Swinging himself along on his crutches, he followed Miss Ferris down the white corridor. Dressed in a dark suit indistinguishable from the dark suit she'd been wearing the last time, she walked ahead in a brisk business-like march, her emotionless voice trailing back to him.

"Our tests show you should be able to stay in for an hour this first time," she said. "We've implanted a time image in your palm so you'll be able to know when the time is up. Do not, under any circumstances, stay one minute longer than the time allotted. Do you understand me?"

Rick nodded absently as he hobbled along. He was thinking about what Jonathan Mars had told him: If he overstayed his time in the Realm, his mind would "disintegrate" and he'd be left in a vegetative state. He didn't need Miss Ferris to remind him to get out as quickly as possible.

"I said: Do you understand me?" Miss Ferris said with a cold look.

"Yeah, yeah," said Rick, trying to keep his voice steady. "Believe me, I understand."

"Good. And you know your mission."

"I know it," said Rick. "I'm supposed to scout the place out. Look for an outpost of some kind, a structure from which Kurodar might launch his next attack."

"Look—but don't stray too far," Miss Ferris said—as she'd already told him half a dozen times before. "When you get there, you should see the portal point, the place where you can get in and out. Do not, under any circumstances, move too far away from that point."

"Right, right, you said all that."

"While we won't be able to communicate with you, we will be able to follow your movements in real time on the monitors. We can map out any area you see. All we need you to do this first time is locate the outpost and get out."

She reached the door. Paused there as Rick worked his crutches quickly, trying to catch up with her. As he approached, she pinned him with her cold, expressionless gaze. "Don't go too far from the portal point," she said yet again. "Am I clear?"

Rick was glad he was breathless from working the crutches. It hid the fear in his voice. "You're clear, you're clear," he panted quickly. "You don't have to say it over and over."

She studied him for a moment, then she nodded—"Good!"—and pushed open the door.

They came into the Portal Room. Rick could feel the

tension in the atmosphere. The people at their workstations glanced up at him with serious expressions as he hobbled past them. The nervousness he saw in their eyes made him even more nervous than he was.

But Miss Ferris didn't seem to notice any of that. She simply marched across the room, past the flickering lights and graphs, past the machinery and monitors, until she was standing underneath that glass box embedded in the far wall. That glass box that looked to Rick very much like a coffin.

Juliet Seven was already there, standing beside the box with his tremendous rectangle arms crossed over his tremendous square chest. Miss Ferris stood on the other side, so that they framed the glass coffin between them. She waited until Rick reached her.

"All right," said Miss Ferris, in that voice so frighteningly devoid of any feeling. She put out one hand. "Give me the crutches and get in."

Someone in the room must have pressed a button then, because the glass lid of the coffin opened with a loud hiss. Rick felt his stomach turn. On top of everything else—like, the whole your-mind-might-disintegrate scenario—he didn't much like tight spaces. He remembered how he'd had an MRI after his accident. They'd slid him into a metal tube. It was like being buried alive—and since the machine made a lot of noise, it was like being buried alive in a rock slide. The imaging process took fifteen minutes. When they'd pulled him out, his entire body was bathed in sweat. And that was after only fifteen minutes, and only for an MRI. This . . .

He took a long, deep breath to fight down the panic that was rising in him like a cold wind. He licked his lips, which were suddenly very dry.

There was a set of three metal steps built into the wall beside the box. Rick moved to the bottom step. Then he worked his crutches out from under his arms and handed them to Miss Ferris. He stood unsteadily a moment. He had to clench his fists to keep his hands from trembling. He looked at Juliet Seven.

"I'm gonna need a hand up here," he said.

The blocky giant stepped forward and extended an arm roughly the size of an iron girder. Rick grabbed hold of it. It was hard and solid like a girder, too. Bracing himself on it, he climbed the steps until he was standing directly beside the glass coffin. He looked in at the metallic lining and the snaking wires. Then he looked back down at Miss Ferris, at her expressionless face.

"I looked up Brain-Computer Interface online," he told her. "It was pretty primitive stuff. Guys wearing electric hats that let them type letters with their minds and so on. Nothing like this. You guys sure this is safe?"

She shook her head once briskly. "No, we're not."

Rick managed a pale laugh. "Thanks for the encouragement."

"I'm not trying to encourage you," she said.

"Well, in that case, you're doing a terrific job."

"If you're worried about it, it's not too late for you to change your mind," she told him.

Something—some little touch of something in her voice—made Rick study her face more closely. Had he spotted a flash of feeling in those steely blue eyes of hers? Some sort of concern for him? Was she hoping he wouldn't do this? Hoping he'd back out at the last minute?

Then he thought: *No.* He was kidding himself. Seeing something that wasn't there. This woman was a total robot. She didn't care what he did.

He let go of Juliet Seven's arm and quickly grabbed hold of the edge of the coffin to keep himself upright. Grimacing at the pain in his legs, he turned and slowly lowered himself backward into the glass box. The metallic lining yielded to his body, letting him settle into the shape of himself. He lay there for a long second.

What happened next was very, very weird—and it did nothing to make him less afraid.

The box's metallic lining seemed to come alive beneath him. With a crinkling noise, it began to fold around him, to mold itself to him. He was wearing black jeans and a black T-shirt, and the lining wrapped itself tightly around his bare arms and pressed the rough fabric of his jeans firmly against his legs. But the lining got even tighter. It pressed into the sides of his face and curled over the top of his head. He felt like a fly that had landed on one of those Venus flytraps—as if the device were closing to devour him.

Within just a few seconds, the lining held him so tight that his arms, legs, and head were rendered immobile. It was an awful, claustrophobic feeling. He wanted to scream: *Take me out of here!* Then things got even worse. Rick gritted his teeth as he felt a stinging sensation in his scalp. It was as if the lining were sprouting needles that were injecting themselves into his skull. The pain made his claustrophobic panic rise even higher. He could do nothing but lie there, looking up helplessly, his breath coming rapidly, his heart hammering hard with fear.

Now the pitiless face of Miss Ferris appeared above him. She had climbed the stairs to stand beside the box. She was looking down at him.

"One hour," she said—for the umpteenth time. "Stay close to the portal point. Look around for an outpost of some kind. Come back. Don't be late."

"Yeah, yeah, yeah." Rick barely managed to squeeze out the words as the metallic lining seemed to grow even tighter around him. The prickling in his scalp grew even more painful.

Miss Ferris gave a brief nod. "Good luck."

She touched the box's lid—and Rick realized with a fresh gout of panic that she was about to close the box, to seal him inside the coffin.

What am I doing? he thought in a sudden rush. *What have I gotten myself into?*

Miss Ferris pressed the glass lid, and it slowly closed over him.

9. ANOTHER WORLD

AT FIRST, NOTHING happened. Rick just lay there in the glass box, held fast in the grip of the metallic lining like a caterpillar in a cocoon. He felt sweat beading on his cheeks. He heard his heart pounding, the sound of it filling his head. He saw the glass lid above him fogging with his breath, the Portal Room beyond the glass growing dim and unclear.

Oh man, he wanted out of this thing! He wanted out of here so bad! He knew he could not stand an hour of this, no way.

But then, all at once, something changed. There was a faint whirring sound, nothing more than what a fly might make buzzing by your ear. He couldn't tell if the noise was coming from outside him or from within him. But the next thing he knew, he felt a faint vibration under his skin. His vision blurred, his body started to relax.

He waited—but nothing else happened. He stared up at the lid of the coffin. The lining continued to squeeze him, continued to hold him.

Then, with a soft jolt, he felt the weirdest thing. Something came loose inside him. There was no other way to describe it. It was as if some inner-Rick had broken away from the

Rick-body that surrounded it. The buzzing noise grew distant. The vibrations stopped. He felt the glass lid, and the dim world beyond the glass lid—felt everything, in fact, except his own heartbeat—drawing away from him into some distant darkness. Or maybe it was him falling away from the world, falling and falling, down into deep nothingness.

And yet . . .

And yet, as reality flew further and further away above him—as the nothingness filled his vision—he began to see something in the center of the blackness: a gap, an opening, a cylinder of—what was it?—of light, of being.

In another moment, Rick understood what it was: it was a passageway.

The cylindrical passage hung there in the blackness above him. And Rick hung there, floating free inside his own body. Somehow, he began to understand, he had to will himself through that opening. He had to make the choice to go.

Rick did not know exactly how to pull that off—how to choose to enter the passage—any more than he knew exactly how to choose to lift his arm. He could just do it, that's all. So with the darkness closing around him, he focused his mind, and willed himself into that spiraling passage of light . . .

There was a swift kiss of noise, barely a noise at all: *pffft!* He had the bizarre sensation that he was turning into liquid, slipping through the portal like water through a straw.

Then, all at once, his form congealed again. Rick found himself standing . . . somewhere . . .

. . . where?

He looked around him. The first thing he saw—the only thing he saw at first—was a strange purple shape floating impossibly in the air beside him, a glowing three-dimensional purple diamond about two feet high and a foot wide. He watched, fascinated, as the thing glowed and pulsed and turned slowly in midair.

That must be the portal point, he thought.

That was the way in—and the way out. He would have to keep that in sight at all times, just as Miss Ferris had said.

He felt there was more around him. He looked up.

"Oh my . . . WOW!" he said loudly.

He was standing on a little hill, surrounded by the strangest landscape he had ever seen. The color of it—it was wild! The hill was red—a scarlet red so bright it hurt his eyes. A gently undulating scarlet plain flowed down from his feet, and ran toward the horizon, ending in a forest of bright blue trees. Above the scarlet plain and the blue forest hung a low sky of the deepest, most beautiful yellow. Here and there the bright colors seemed to mingle in stirring cloud-like streaks of bright orange and green.

Stunned by the rainbow-like beauty of the place, Rick turned this way and that, gaping in amazement. It was as if he had stepped into a painting or a movie cartoon. He was so mesmerized by the red valley and the blue woods and the streaked yellow sky that it took a moment before something else amazing—really amazing—suddenly occurred to him.

He was standing up! He was! He was standing free. No crutches! No pain! Not even any weakness. He looked down at his legs. He was still dressed as he had been, in a black T-shirt and jeans. But his legs were straight now. They felt fine. More than fine. They felt strong!

Rick let out a laugh. This was incredible! In-crazy-credible! He felt so . . . so good! Better than he'd felt in ages, since the accident. He lifted one foot high and wiggled it in the air, then he set it back down and lifted the other. He hopped in a circle, laughing again, a high-pitched whoop of laughter this time. He began dancing around on the hilltop.

"Whoo-hoo!" he shouted. "Whoo-whoo-whoo-hoo!"

He tucked an invisible football beneath his arm and ran across the ridge, straight-arming imaginary blockers.

"Yaaaaah!" he screamed.

He spun around at the end and rushed back, running till he reached the floating purple diamond.

He shouted, "Touchdown!"

He spiked the invisible ball into the red, red earth. He lifted his face to that weirdly beautiful yellow sky. He lifted his hands in celebration and did a victory dance. He was healed! He could walk! He could run and jump and kick and . . .

What was that?

He stopped. Still panting from his celebration, he stood still. He peered into the distance, over the flowing red plain, toward the line of blue trees where the weird forest began. Had he seen something over there? A movement? He stood, staring. There was nothing.

Then, suddenly—yes!—there it was again. A movement down by the trees. Something—no—no, it was someone—a person!—a man—had stepped out of the forest, had edged out from under the blue leaves into the scarlet grass.

Rick could hardly believe it.

He wasn't alone!

He squinted, trying to see the man better. The man was waving at him. Beckoning him. Inviting him to come down the hill, to join him by the woods.

Rick started to raise his hand in greeting to the far-off stranger—then he hesitated. Maybe he should be a little more careful. After all, who else could be in this place besides one of Kurodar's agents? Maybe this dude was one of the bad guys.

But the man near the woods did not seem like an enemy. He kept waving at him, gesturing at him to come, to come down—almost as if he were welcoming him. Rick felt like an idiot just standing there. So, finally, he raised his hand and gave a small wave in return.

The guy just gestured all the more forcefully—beckoned all the more frantically: *Come down! Come down!*

What was he supposed to do now?

Miss Ferris's voice rang in his mind:

Do not, under any circumstances, move too far away from that portal point.

Well, yes, but she hadn't mentioned there would be other people here. Was he just supposed to ignore the guy?

He began to lower his hand. As he did, he noticed for the first time that there were numbers on it—bright white numbers glowing in the center of his palm. The numbers were moving; they were counting down:

58:17 . . . 58:16 . . . 58:15 . . .

We've implanted a time image in your palm so you'll be able to know when the time is up, Miss Ferris had said.

Rick looked up from the numbers, back to the man beckoning in the distance. He wasn't that far away. He had a whole hour, after all—fifty-eight minutes. That was plenty of time to go down there and talk to the guy, find out who he was, what he wanted, and get back here to the portal point. After all, he was supposed to look for an outpost, right? He couldn't see any kind of outpost from where he was standing. Maybe this guy knew where it was. Wouldn't Miss Ferris be glad if he found someone living here who could help him? Sure she would.

Rick considered for one more second. The sudden, wonderful strength coursing through his legs—coursing through his whole body—filled him with confidence and a sense of daring. He was Rick Dial again. He was Number 12 again. What was the point of having all this power back in his body, if he wasn't going to use it?

"Oh, come on," he said out loud, as if he were in a huddle, talking to his teammates. "Let's do this."

And with that, he started down the hill toward the beckoning man.

10. JEOPARDY

HE TRAVELED QUICKLY, practically running over the red terrain. Having his legs feel so strong and healthy again was such a pure pleasure that it sent fresh energy surging through him, and made him forget any misgivings he'd had about leaving the portal point behind or about the motives of the beckoning man. A sort of red fur or grass carpeted the reddish-brown earth underneath; it felt spongy and supportive beneath his feet like some of the Astroturf fields he'd played on. It was absolutely great to go jogging over it without the help of crutches.

He looked ahead. The beckoning man was still there, standing at the edge of the deep-blue tree line, waving his arms. As Rick drew closer, he laughed out loud to see the scarlet plain become orange and golden nearer the woods, dotted with bushes and flowers in an amazing array of pastels. It was so beautiful!

He could see the man more clearly now, too—and for the first time, he could see that there was something strange about him. He did not look quite solid somehow. In fact, his form seemed to shift and sparkle, as if he were a ghost made out of particles of light. Weird.

But before Rick could think about it too much, something else caught his eye. Out to the right of the forest, beyond the vast splashes of vivid color, he could just make out a structure of some sort.

He slowed to a walk, then stopped, squinting for a clearer view. Far in the distance, there was a tower or fort, or a castle maybe, standing black and imposing against the yellow sky.

The outpost! That had to be it! And there was something—some things—moving over it. Black forms circling lazily in the air above the structure's central spire. Were they birds? Maybe. But for him to see them at this distance, they must be awfully huge birds!

What should I do now? he wondered. He'd spotted the outpost—so was his mission complete? Should he turn back? Go back up the hill to the portal point and report his findings to Miss Ferris? Or should he continue down to the woods and talk to the beckoning man, find out what he knew?

He hesitated another moment, trying to come to a decision . . .

And as he stood there thinking, he felt something shift beneath his feet. He nearly stumbled. He straightened, alert.

What was that?

Even as he wondered, it happened again. A faint wave went through the ground beneath him. He heard a soft rumble that quickly rose and faded away, as if something had passed by directly underneath him.

It was over in a moment. Rick waited, but whatever it was, it seemed to be gone. He looked to the beckoning man—the sparkling man—and saw he was waving his arm even faster, harder than before. What was he trying to say?

Without warning, another quake struck the earth beneath him. Stronger this time. The scarlet ground surged, hoisted him up so fast and hard he almost fell right over. The rumble rose to a growl, then faded to a scrabbling noise as the earth subsided and steadied and flattened out.

And then Rick understood. The sparkling man wasn't beckoning him—he was trying to warn him! Trying to get him to hurry up, to come in out of the open into the trees because . . .

Well, because why? Rick didn't know, but he thought he'd better hurry and get out of there before he found out.

His decision was made. He started running toward the blue trees, toward the sparkling figure standing in front of them. He got about three steps—and then he heard the rumble, coming from a distance this time. He looked over his shoulder. He saw the ground hoisting up, saw the rise of it rushing toward him like a solid wave. Before he could react, before he could take another step, the rumble grew louder and the surge came up directly underneath him. The shock was sharp, fast. He was thrown two steps to his right—then he tripped and toppled over onto the spongy ground.

He started to push back up to his feet, but even as his hand pressed into the red-gold turf, there was a loud shuddering, ripping noise. Frozen where he was, Rick stared as a black chasm began to open up in the ground in front of him.

It was an astonishing sight. It was as if the surface of this strange new world were being torn apart. As Rick watched, openmouthed, the crack in the earth spread toward him quickly, the noise growing louder, the black rift shooting at him across the open space, threatening to swallow him if he didn't get out of the way—if he didn't start moving, right now.

Rick rolled, trying to dodge the oncoming crevice. He felt the whole world shuddering around him, heard the scrabbling rumble filling the air. With an agonized rending noise, the earth broke apart right beneath him. He just managed to roll to the edge of it, keeping out of the way of the widening black chasm.

And then the world shook roughly and he was thrown backward. He spilled over the rim of the break and plunged into the blackness.

His arms flailed desperately. He caught hold of the broken edge of the earth with one hand. He clung to it. Hung from it, his feet dangling in the air. He had no idea how far down the chasm went below him—it was too dark to see. If he lost his hold, he might fall and fall forever.

He hung there, his hand grasping the quivering ground, his legs swinging free in the pit. He could feel his fingers slipping off the surface. He had to bring his other hand around, get a better grip . . .

No. There was no chance. The earth shook again. He lost his hold and fell.

Rick had a moment of sickening helplessness and confusion as he tumbled down. He didn't know where the bottom was or when or what or how he'd hit when he got there. Then, with a jolt, his feet touched ground. A dull pain shot through his ankle. His knees buckled. He fell and rolled across what felt like dirt.

Almost at once, he hit hard against the wall of the crevasse. The blow jarred him to his bones. For a second or two, he lay still, stunned. Then, with a groan, he pushed off the ground, climbed to his feet. Looked around.

He was standing at the bottom of the long chasm. The fissure traveled off into distant darkness on either side of him, he couldn't tell how far. He looked up. At least it wasn't very deep. With a little effort, he thought he ought to be able to climb the wall and get a grip on the surface, pull himself back up.

He was about to try it, when the earth began shaking again, quivering and bouncing beneath him even more violently than it had before. Pebbles and dust started falling from the surface of the earth above him, pattering down on his head. The air began to fill with noise again, that slithering, scrabbling, rushing noise. *What in the world . . . ?*

Rick turned toward the sound. He froze, openmouthed. His stomach went sour and his eyes went wide. He wanted to cry out, but he couldn't. He couldn't make a sound. He couldn't even move. He was rooted to the spot.

He could not believe—no one could have believed—the horror that was rushing toward him.

11. THE THING

HE SAW ITS fangs first, enormous daggers dripping some sort of viscous goo. He saw its eyes then, two bulging dimpled mounds like the eyes of a fly. He saw a whirl of hairy, spidery legs flashing over the ground, propelling the beast straight at him—and a great leathery tail whipping behind, giving it extra speed.

For another long second, Rick stood in frozen disbelief. His mind simply could not comprehend what he was seeing: the grotesque face of this impossible onrushing death.

Then his athlete's reflexes kicked in. He turned and ran.

He dashed along the floor of the chasm as fast as he could, faster than he'd ever gone over a football field. It wasn't fast enough. When he looked behind him, the hairy, drooling spider-snake thing was clawing its way toward him at top speed, getting closer to him with every second. It would only be moments before it would overtake him, before it would have him in those dripping fangs.

He had to think—and fast. He'd seen stuff like this before, hadn't he? Monsters like this? Sure he had. In video games! That's why Jonathan Mars had chosen him for this mission—because he'd fought plenty of bizarre creatures like this—and beaten them, too. Of course, in video games, you had a lot of advantages. You could do things that defied the laws of physics. You could run along walls. You could double-jump in midair. Most important, you could come back to life if you got killed! None of that stuff was true here. Here, he was going to have to use his brains, outsmart this beast somehow, and he was going to have to do it in one try, because he wouldn't get a second chance.

He had to get out of this crevasse—that was the first thing. It was his only hope of getting away. As he ran, he eyed the rim of the earth above him. He might be able to leap up there and grab the edge, climb out. He might. With a grunt, he put on an extra burst of speed. He could feel the earth shaking under his sneakers even as he ran. He could feel the wind of the spidery legs behind him. The beast was so close now, there was no room for error. If he leapt and missed—if he leapt and could not pull himself up—he'd be devoured.

The creature made a noise behind him—so close behind him, it made Rick's whole body feel weak and hollow with terror. It was a noise of eagerness and hunger, an inhuman, squealing growl.

Fear gave Rick the extra strength he needed. Running, he jumped. He reached for the surface of the earth. He grabbed it. He saw the beast out of the corner of his eye, enormous as it charged, its hairy legs reaching for him, its great tail whipping, its dripping mouth opened wide.

Rick strained to pull himself up. He threw his legs to the side, hoping to vault out of the chasm. Something touched him, something awful, coarse, and damp—something hungry. Rick couldn't help himself—he screamed.

And then he was up—up and over. Out of the chasm and rolling across the scarlet-orange ground and into a bed of flowers whose beautiful pinks and violets and pastel greens seemed crazily out of place.

He leapt to his feet. He looked around him. He saw the man—the sparkling man—beckoning to him wildly—shouting something—what was he saying?

"The woods! Get to the woods!"

Of course. The woods. That was what the sparkling man had been trying to tell him from the start. He had to get into the forest. He might be able to lose this creature among the trees. It was his best chance—his only chance—of getting away.

He looked back toward the chasm.

For a moment, he thought he had made a clean escape. He thought the awful thing would stay in its tunnel below the earth.

No such luck. A second later, the first of its hairy legs came questing up out of the hole, searching for purchase. The next moment, the beast arose and Rick saw the fangs, the bulging eyes, the hairy, squirmy body in the aboveground light as the thing began to climb up out of the fissure.

It was a nightmare. A nightmare. Only real.

Rick dashed for the forest.

The sparkling man had stopped waving and gesturing now. He was standing stock-still, staring at the spider-snake that had risen fully into sight. Rick was close enough to see the look on the sparkling man's face now—a look of absolute terror. As Rick ran toward him, the sparkling man turned on his heels and dashed toward the forest. A second later, he was out of sight among the trees.

Rick hurried to join him. The blue forest loomed tall before him as he raced across the golden grass. When he looked back over his shoulder, he saw the creature make the rest of its way up out of the chasm onto the surface of the scarlet plain. He caught a glimpse of the twisting, slithering rear portion of its body, the snake-like tail snapping back and forth. The full sight of the thing turned his stomach. He wanted nothing more than to be back at home, back in his dark room, on his sofa, with his harmless games, safe. He was so, so sorry he had agreed to come here.

The beast spotted him. It began to propel itself toward him over the ground. Clawing with its legs, squirming with its tail, it was unbelievably fast. In an instant, it had closed the distance between them, and Rick could already hear it making that hungry, eager, squealing growl again as it charged after him.

Another cry of fear escaped from Rick—but the next moment, he reached the tree line and rocketed into the forest. He dodged between the green-brown trunks of the trees, beneath their aqua leaves. The trunks were close together, he noticed. That might be good. Maybe they were close enough to block the creature, or at least slow it down.

He looked back just as the beast reached the edge of the forest behind him. The thing didn't slow at all. It simply smashed into the base of the trees full force. Rick heard a loud cracking sound. The monster had simply knocked a tree over. Rick looked up and saw the tree toppling. Its enormous blue crown was plunging down toward his head, threatening to pin him, maybe even crush him.

Rick dodged to the side—and stumbled. He fell to the ground. The tree crashed to the earth beside him, its branches whipping at his back.

But he was unhurt. He leapt to his feet again. To his horror, he saw the spidery thing push toward him, shearing away two more trees so they crashed off to the left and right, leaving only stumps standing.

Gasping for breath, beginning to lose strength, Rick stared as the beast reared up. Several of its many legs pawed the air. It roared, the white goo dripping from its fangs.

Rick started to turn, started to run—but before he could, the spider-snake made an awful noise, a disgusting, razzling cough. Some putrid fluid came spitting out of its midsection. It sailed across the forest space between them. Before Rick could even think to move, the stuff splashed over his legs and solidified, wrapping itself around him.

A web. Something like a web. A powerful white thread that extended from the creature's underside. It tied up Rick's legs—and linked him to the beast. With a yank, the spider-snake whipped Rick off his feet and began gathering the web up, dragging Rick across the earth toward its open mouth, its dripping fangs.

Rick let out a mindless roar of fury and fear. He struggled

to get free, but it was no use. The web was unbreakable. When he twisted his body around and grabbed at it, its sticky surface stung his hands and threatened to capture them as well. The forest floor scraped against Rick's back and shoulders as the beast reeled him in, as it reared up against the blue leaves, opening its mouth even wider to receive him.

As Rick's brain kicked into gear again, he looked desperately for a weapon, for anything he could fight with. There was nothing. There was only one of the trees that the creature had knocked down. It lay on its side to the right of him. As the spider-snake dragged him toward its mouth, Rick reached out and grabbed one of the tree's branches.

He got hold of a thick one. He held on to it fast. The creature pulled him. For a second, Rick was able to hold the branch and pull back, resisting, trying with all his might to wriggle free of the web.

But then the branch snapped. It came away in his hand. He was hurtling over the earth again, only yards away from the creature's fangs.

But he was still holding the branch—the broken branch, its end sharp and jagged. He used his powerful core muscles to sit up as he was pulled along. He drove the end of the branch into the web around his legs. It punched a hole through the fiber, but the web held. Rick gritted his teeth and used the branch to stab and rip at the goo again and again.

It was no good. The web tore—it weakened—but it wouldn't release him.

The spider-snake reared up even higher against the trees.

Rick cried out as he was lifted off the ground. He dangled upside down as the beast's hairy legs surrounded him. A smell more sickening than any he had ever smelled engulfed him like a fog and made him gag. The creature's mouth yawned open above him, its fangs dripping down over him. The beast pulled him upward relentlessly.

Then the web broke. Rick had damaged and torn it with the branch just enough—and now the cut substance gave way to his weight.

Rick dropped through the air. He hit the ground hard, shoulder first. The jolt brought his teeth clamping together. But he didn't let it stop him. He didn't pause. He rolled. He jumped to his feet. The creature—startled to have lost its prey just at the moment of satisfaction—let out a shriek of frustration, its legs churning the air above Rick's head, its slithering tail whipping the forest floor behind it.

Rick seized the moment. He kicked off the last of the sticky web—and darted away.

But he was losing strength now, losing speed, running out of wind. He stumbled as he ran, barely able to keep his feet. The beast, on the other hand, was just as eager as it had been at first. It recovered from its rage. It roared and began to crash through the trees behind him. Rick heard the trunks tearing and the branches cracking as the trees toppled down. Gasping for breath, he turned to see the untiring spider-snake coming on again, crashing, roaring, squealing.

And then, above the noise, a voice.

"Hey!"

He turned. He saw the man—the strangely sparkling, shifting, half-transparent man who had beckoned to him earlier. He saw him peeking out from behind a thick aqua tree.

The man beckoned again. He shouted, "This way! Hurry!"

Rick ran toward him.

12. IRON SWORD

THE AIR OF the forest filled with the squealing roar of the charging spider-snake and the crackling swish of the falling trees. The sparkling man rushed away through the forest. Rick rushed after him. The man moved with a weirdly swift darting motion that barely seemed a motion at all. He seemed instead to flash from place to place like light. One moment, he was right in front of Rick and Rick was running toward him; the next moment, he was gone, a few yards this way or that, and Rick had to spot him, then adjust his course midflight to follow.

They went deeper and deeper into the blue woods. When Rick looked back over his shoulder, he saw the furious spider-snake thing coming after him, moving even faster now as it broke a pathway through the woods. Rick, meanwhile, was almost out of strength. He looked forward—and for a second, his heart seemed to drop in his chest.

Where was the sparkling man? He'd darted away out of sight. He was gone.

No, there he is. Rick spotted the hazy twinkle of him through some branches. As the noise of the beast grew louder behind him, he shifted course and stumbled wearily toward the spot.

At last, he broke through some branches and came into a small clearing. He let out a cry of relief. The sparkling man was waiting for him there—and next to him, there was a glowing purple diamond floating in midair.

Another portal point! Another way out! If Rick could just will himself through it, he'd be saved.

"Quick! Stand behind me," said the sparkling man. His voice was as strange and ghostly as the look of him. It was a soft, hollow, echoic sound, like a whisper made of wind. Somehow Rick could hear it clearly over the crashing and roaring that filled the woods. "Hurry!" said the sparkling man.

Rick pointed at the floating diamond. "But I can get out that way."

"You can," said the man. "I can't. And if you leave now, that creature will destroy me. Get behind me, and we both have a chance."

Rick hesitated only a second. He didn't know who this guy was, but he had tried to warn him about the beast and had shown him which way to run. He seemed to be a friend—and Rick wasn't going to leave him alone here to be devoured by that awful thing. Scared as he was—desperate to get out of this place as he was—this guy seemed to be on his side, and he would not let a teammate down. He did as he was asked: he moved around in back of the sparkling man, putting him between himself and the oncoming monster.

And on the oncoming monster came! The ground shook. Trees fell to this side and that. A patch in the blue leaves darkened—and then the hideous thing crashed into the clearing. It reared up, its many legs clawing at the air, its bizarre squealing roar making the leaves around them tremble.

Rick's eyes widened as he stared up at it: at the dripping fangs, the hairy legs, the thrashing, snake-like tail. He had always thought of himself as a brave guy, a tough guy. He'd stared down charging linebackers and calmly thrown a long pass even as they swarmed toward him, ready to bury him under the turf. But now he knew: That was nothing. This was fear. Real fear. It turned his muscles to water. He felt that if he had to stare at this thing for another second, his mind would simply break apart with the horror of it.

But what happened next happened fast. At almost the same moment the beast came crashing into the clearing, the sparkling man made his move. With one gossamer hand, he reached out toward the glowing diamond—the portal point—beside him. The diamond began to pulse and brighten. It sparked—and a line of snapping, purple energy began to crackle out of it and flow into the man's outstretched fingers. The man himself seemed to become more substantial, more solid, as if he were filling up with the diamond's power.

The spider-beast reared and roared. An orifice in its mid-section opened as it prepared to spit out its web again.

But before it could, the sparkling man thrust out his other arm toward the creature. His curled fingers straightened as his fist became an open hand. And from his fingertips there shot a hot, blinding flash of purple light. Instantaneously, the light expanded into a searing wedge. Rick, squinting through the glare of it, saw it hit the beast head-on.

There was a shivering, electric explosion. There was a loud, wet bursting noise. A splatter of gluey white flew over Rick's head. Gobs of the stuff smacked into the trees and dripped thickly down from the leaves all around him.

Then the purple flash faded. The woods came back into view. At first, Rick was dazed and couldn't see what had happened. Then he did see. He saw the spider-beast—it was still there. But it was lying on its back now, clearly wounded, its midsection dripping goo, its hairy legs clawing weakly at the air, its slimy tail thrashing back and forth.

Still breathing hard, Rick panted, "It's not dead."

The sparkling man staggered to a tree and leaned against it weakly. He seemed somehow dimmer than before, his glow more faint. He shook his head. It seemed to take a lot of effort. "No," he said. "It'll recharge in a few minutes. It'll be just as strong as it was before."

"Well, hit it again, man! Kill it!"

The sparkling man's eyes closed and he took a breath. "Can't. Too weak. Every time I do that it costs me energy. You have to finish it. Finish it before you go, or it'll come back and kill me."

Rick glanced at the spider-snake lying on its back, fighting to recover. All he wanted was to get out of here—like, right now—but when he glanced over at the portal point, he saw with a fresh jolt of fear that it had shrunk almost to nothing. The sparkling man had drawn so much energy out of it that he had nearly drained it away. It was now little more than a purple dot floating in the air, too small for Rick to get through. He glanced at his palm. The time was now at 42:37. He still had time to get back to the first portal—but he didn't want to wait around too long.

He turned back to the sparkling man, who was still leaning weakly against the tree.

"What do I have to do?" he said.

The sparkling man made a weak gesture with his head. "Go to the lake. Call Mariel. Tell her Favian said we need help. That's me: Favian. Tell her."

Rick looked in the direction of the sparkling man's—Favian's—gesture. He saw a narrow trail through the blue trees and caught glimpses of silver water twinkling beyond.

"I'll be right back," Rick said.

Favian let out a tired sigh and said, "Hurry. We don't have much time before it's back on its feet."

Rick didn't need to be told twice. He hurried. Still panting from his run through the woods, he ran as fast as he could down the little trail. A few moments later, he reached the edge of a lake.

At least it looked like a lake. It was flat and had a watery quality about it, but it was silver and opaque, as if it were made of some sort of metal, mercury or something like it. It spread out a great distance, bordered on every side by trees. The silver water rippled and changed, catching the colors of the blue leaves at the edge of it and the yellow sky above. The colors blended with the soft white mist that hung over its surface everywhere.

Rick looked all around, at the nearby trees and out over

the mercurial water, but he didn't see anyone nearby. Still, he did what the sparkling man had told him.

"Mariel?" he said—quietly at first, because he felt kind of silly talking to no one. And then, when there was no answer, he said more loudly, "Mariel!"

The word echoed over the water and faded away. The forest was quiet. Nothing happened. Rick glanced nervously over his shoulder. Through the trees, he could see into the clearing. He caught glimpses of the spider-snake thrashing on the forest floor in there, trying to right itself. Its movements were getting stronger. Its grunts of pain and frustration were growing louder. The thing was recharging, recovering, as Favian had said it would.

He turned back to the lake, impatient. "Come on, come . . . ," he began to say.

And then she was there.

Rick couldn't tell—it was impossible to tell—whether Mariel grew up out of the water or the water rose up and took the shape of Mariel. In any case, she rose up in front of him, silver and rippling and changeable—and more beautiful than anything he had ever seen. The sight of her—of her long, liquid flowing hair, of her high cheeks and compassionate eyes, of her warm expression and her full, graceful figure robed in rippling mercury—struck Rick to the heart. He forgot the spider-snake. He forgot the time. He forgot the danger. He stood and stared at her, drinking her in with his eyes. He knew right then and there that he would never forget this moment, never forget this vision before him.

"I'm Mariel," she said down at him. Her voice was ghostly and echoic like Favian's, but it had a lilting musical quality to it that made Rick's heart ache.

It took him a second before he recovered his wits enough to answer her. "I'm Rick . . . Rick Dial," he said. "Favian told me to call you. He blasted the spider-snake-thing, whatever it is, but it's still alive and he's not strong enough to finish it so I . . ."

Afterward, there was some confusion in Rick's mind as to what exactly happened then. As he was still trying to get the words out, Mariel lifted one silvery, liquid arm in his direction. The next thing he knew, there was a sword in his hand. Had she given it to him? He didn't know. It was just there, suddenly, gripped in his fist. It wasn't much of a sword—as he couldn't help noticing when he glanced down at it. It was just a rude blade of rusted iron with a hilt of copper, green with verdigris, and molded into a face of some kind. Rick thought if he tried to stab anything with this thing—especially if he tried to stab that creature back there—the blade would snap in two.

The feminine spirit hovering above him seemed to read his mind. "It'll be strong enough," she told him. "Your spirit has power here—power over material things, once you learn to use it. Strike with your spirit and the sword will be strong enough."

Rick didn't really understand what she was saying—and he doubted this sword would be strong enough to strike at anything—but somehow, the strength of her presence made it hard for him to argue with her.

He nodded dubiously and said, "Okay. I'll try. Thanks."

He had to tear his eyes away from her, but he did it. And, carrying the rusted sword, he hurried back through the trail to the clearing.

Everything was changing there. The portal point had begun to grow back. It had gone from being a little dot to being a pulsing, floating diamond again. It still wasn't big enough for Rick to get through, but it was getting larger every second.

Favian, likewise, seemed to have regained some of his strength. Some of his color and sparkle had returned to him and he was able to stand up.

But the spider-snake was also growing more powerful, and quickly.

Its tail was lashing back and forth ferociously, and its legs were clawing viciously at the air. Its great body thrashed once, twice, as it tried ever more fiercely to turn itself over. Its squealing roar was rising again, and the trees around the clearing were beginning to quake as if in fear of its return. Another few seconds, and the thing would work itself upright—and go back on the rampage, killing Rick and Favian both.

Rick was scared to go near the beast, but this was no time to hesitate. He knew, if he even thought about it too much, he would lose his nerve and it would all be over.

One more look at his sword—that rusty old relic—didn't encourage him much. But Mariel's rich, lilting voice seemed to come to him through the blade, as if she were somehow part of its rusty metal.

Strike with your spirit and the sword will be strong enough.

Whatever that means, Rick thought.

But her voice gave him courage. He drew a breath and stepped toward the spider-snake on shaking legs.

It saw him approaching and raged. Its segmented legs bicycled harder in the air. Its tail pounded the ground so that the forest shook. Rick swallowed the disgust that rose in his throat as the putrid smell of the creature surrounded him. He fought down the fear rising in his belly.

Do it, he told himself. *Do it fast! Do it now!*

He stepped close to the thrashing giant's head, out of the way of its tail and legs. He was inches away from its bulging eyes and the stare of blank hatred and hunger that made him quail inside.

He was losing his nerve. He had to strike fast. He drew up his spirit like a great breath of air. He gripped the sword tightly in his fist. He felt the strength of the weapon growing somehow, as if the force of his own heart-power were pulsing through his arm into the iron.

Then, with a sudden cry, he lifted the weapon over his head and brought it down with all his might, plunging it into the beast's throat.

The cry the spider-snake made was the stuff of nightmares. It was a shriek of rage that seemed to mushroom up out of the clearing to fill the sky. The spider-snake's whole enormous body bucked—and Rick lost his grip on the sword's molded hilt and was hurled backward, his arms pinwheeling, until he smacked into the trunk of a tree.

Dazed, he stared, appalled, as the wounded creature found the strength in its agony to turn over and stand.

The spider-snake looked at Rick with huge, hate-filled eyes and bared its dripping fangs. Rick stood helplessly pinned against the tree, waiting for it to rush at him.

But then the beast gave one final shuddering groan. Its legs folded under it. Its great body settled to the ground. Rick stared in horrified wonder as purple-white electric flashes crisscrossed through the thing's form, sparking and popping and throwing off brief gouts of purple flame. Rick had to squint against the glare as the spider-snake's entire body seemed transformed into a knot of crackling energy.

Then the energy faded. Died. The air was clear. The spider-snake was gone.

Only Rick's iron sword remained, lying rusted and unimpressive on a bed of blue leaves.

13. WORDS WITH FRIENDS

"SEE? THAT WASN'T so hard," Favian said.

Rick looked at the sparkling man and they both laughed.

"Easy-peasy," Rick said.

Moving unsteadily away from the tree, he stuck out his hand. Favian—also looking weak and shaken—put his own sparkling hand in Rick's. It felt to Rick like he was shaking hands with an electric wire. It tingled on his palm.

This was the first steady look he'd had at Favian. The sparkling man was younger than he had thought, only a few years older than he was himself. He was thin, almost gangly, with an open, innocent-looking face, his hair sheared so close to the scalp it was barely visible. His eyes were big and gentle and anxious, and his mouth quirked upward in a strangely worried little smile. Close-up, Rick could see that the man's sparkly quality came from the fact that his body was made out of tiny particles of light constantly shifting, coming together and drifting apart so that he solidified and then grew transparent and almost insubstantial and then became solid again, a ceaseless motion that made him seem to float and twinkle where he stood.

He was looking a little stronger now than he had before. He nodded toward the lake trail.

"Come on," he said.

It wasn't easy to follow his flitting figure, but Rick knew the way and soon they were both back beside the metallic water.

"Mariel," Favian called in his soft, echoing whisper of a voice.

Rick looked toward the silver lake, eager to see her rise again.

Nothing happened.

"It cost her energy to come up—to give you the sword. The same way it cost me to use the power from the portal. We've each only got so much energy and each time we use it, a little more is gone. We can never replenish it completely."

Rick glanced at him. "But that means . . ."

"We're fading, yes. We're dying, Mariel and I. We haven't got very much time left."

"Who . . . who are you?" Rick asked. "How did you get here?"

Favian turned his gentle, anxious eyes on him. "I don't know. We're just here somehow."

"Well . . . you had to come here somehow. Did Kurodar create you?"

But before Favian could answer, a new voice said firmly, "No!"

Rick turned and, with a little hitch in his heart, he saw Mariel again.

She had risen back up out of the water. If she was weaker than before, Rick couldn't see any sign of it. To him, she looked just as beautiful and impressive as the first time. He gazed up at her strong but gentle features, and caught himself wondering what it would feel like to touch the metallic surface of her cheek.

"Kurodar can create security programs—lifeless bots like the spider-snake," she said. "But Favian and I—we have spirits. He can't create those. Kurodar only *thinks* he's God."

Rick nodded. "Okay. So then, how *did* you get here?"

Mariel and Favian exchanged a sad look with each other. Clearly, they had discussed this many times.

"We don't know," she told Rick. "We only know we're here—and that we're dying—quickly."

"Actually, we were kind of hoping . . . ," Favian began. "At least, I was hoping . . . Well, we've always both sort of hoped . . ."

Rick waited for him to finish.

But it was Mariel who said, "We've always hoped that someone might come for us. Someone who knew where we belonged. Someone who could take us away from here, before the end came."

"That's why when I saw you, I tried to warn you," Favian added. "That's why I tried to get you into the safety of the woods before the guardian bot came after you. I was hoping—Mariel and I were both hoping—that you might be the one to help us."

Rick opened his mouth, but nothing came out. He hardly

knew what to say. "I would help you if I knew how. But . . . you said you can't come through the portal . . ."

Favian shook his head. "We've tried. It's closed to us. We don't even know what's on the other side, but anything would be better than this."

"And I don't know any other way out," said Rick. He thought it over. Nothing very spectacular came to him. He said, "Well, look, I was sent here for a purpose. Kurodar is about to launch a new attack on my world. I'm supposed to locate his outpost and report back. When I do go back, I'll tell them about you and see what I can do."

Again, Mariel and Favian exchanged a look—a hopeful one this time. It made Rick feel a little nauseous to think they would be waiting for him, depending on him. He had no idea whether he could do anything for them or not.

"Meanwhile, we can help you," said Mariel.

"Yes," said Favian. "We don't know what Kurodar is up to . . ."

". . . but we know he's up to something," Mariel finished the sentence for him. "And yes, he's been building a new fortress."

"I think I saw it," said Rick. "That dark building off in the distance."

Favian nodded. "He only started it a little while ago. There's never been anything like it here before. We don't know what he's going to use it for, but it seems to be almost done. If you want, I know how to get you there."

Rick glanced at his palm, at the time: 29:07. He shook his head. "It's too far. My time would run out before we reached it."

"There's even more beyond it," Mariel said in her musical, resonant voice. "A Golden City, a haunted city of ghosts and creatures and dark passageways. That's the center of this place. That's where its real secrets lie. But it's too well guarded. We can't get in."

Rick ran his fingers up through his hair. "Okay," he said. "That's all I need for now. I'll go back and tell them I saw the outpost and maybe . . . maybe they'll know a way to help you."

"We haven't got long," said Favian. His anxious face seemed more anxious still. "We don't know how much time, but not much."

"Look, I'll do what I can," said Rick—it sounded lame even to him.

"I just wish you could take us back now," Favian said. "You don't know what it's like here. The creatures always hunting us, and at night . . ." His voice trailed off.

Rick nodded sympathetically—but helplessly. He wished he knew of a way to help these . . . these people or spirits or whatever they were.

"It's all right," said Mariel after a moment. The look on her face practically mesmerized him with its calm and majesty and . . . something else. Something he couldn't quite name. But it was familiar to him. He used to see it in his father's face sometimes. Faith. That's what it was. She had a look of faith. "Rick will come back," she said to Favian. "He won't desert us.

He's a hero, Favian. You only have to look at him to see it. He's the hero we've been waiting for."

"Whoa," said Rick. "Whoa. Not so fast. I'm no hero, believe me. Back in the real world, I can barely . . ."

But before he could finish his sentence, Mariel had melted away, drifting down to the lake like rain, becoming one again with the still and silver surface of the water.

Rick turned to Favian. He saw the hope in Favian's big, anxious eyes, and it pierced him. Why did Mariel have to say that about his being a hero? How could he ever live up to it? "Listen," he said to Favian, "when you see her—when you see Mariel again, tell her . . . Tell her not to get her hopes up too much, all right? I'll do my best for you, I swear I will, but . . . I'm not the guy she thinks I am. I barely know what I'm doing here myself."

The sparkling Favian smiled his worried smile. "If you say so. But I don't know, man. Mariel—she's awfully smart, like wicked smart. She knows things. If she says you're a hero, you probably are. Maybe you just don't know it yet."

Rick rolled his eyes. Just what he needed. More pressure. He had been a sports hero once, sure, but that was before the accident. And a sports hero—well, that's not like a real hero, not like a soldier or a cop or a fireman or something. In fact, when he was facing that spider-snake, he had been so terrified, he felt like his arms and legs were made of cooked spaghetti. If the Realm held anything more dangerous than that, he didn't know how he was going to handle it at all. It made him sick to think about it: even though he'd only just met her, he hated the idea of failing in front of Mariel.

"Well, like I said . . . ," he muttered. "Don't get your hopes up too much."

But Favian held up one sparkling hand. "If you're going to have a chance to do anything, you better get started. The portal should be ready for you now."

It was. Back in the clearing, the purple diamond was fully bright again, floating in the air. Rick and Favian stood before it.

"Well . . . ," said Rick. "Thanks—thanks for your help."

"Don't forget us," said Favian. "Please. Don't just leave us here. What happens to you when you die in this place, it's . . . Well, it's not good."

Rick nodded and said, "I won't forget."

He turned and faced the glowing portal point. He took a deep breath. The purple diamond pulsed and throbbed as if it were a living thing. Rick gazed into the light of it and the light seemed to surround him.

He willed himself through the light and left the Realm.

LEVEL THREE:
INTRUDERS

14. A GOD OF WAR

IN THE REALM, Reza had wings. Kurodar had given them to him: webbed wings sprouting from his shoulder blades so that he could fly. Reza loved this. He loved to fly. He loved the Realm. He loved Kurodar. More than that. It was just as his friend Ibrahim had told him it would be: he worshipped Kurodar. Why not? He used to worship the God, and what had the God ever done for him? Kurodar, it turned out, had more actual power—here in the Realm, anyway.

Here in the Realm, Kurodar had made Reza a fearful creature altogether—more than a man. His bared upper body was now uncannily muscular and strong. His skin was a kind of pink leather. His eyes were enormous and sharper than human eyes. And the savagely sharp talons of his hands could suddenly extend into sword-like weapons. His tail—well, he wasn't sure what his tail was for, but he thought it was dashingly satanic.

He was inspecting the fortress Generator Room now. He did this obsessively, every chance he got. It was the living heart of the fortress and he always wanted to reassure himself that it was still beating.

Today, he took a few extra moments at it, because he wasn't

relishing the idea of breaking the bad news to his master. He flapped his wings slowly, hovering just above the floor of one of the iron galleries that ringed the flagstone walls.

The Generator Room was three stories high, and nearly as broad as it was tall. An enormous Disperser Wheel rose out of the cellar toward the ceiling. The lines of purple energy from various nearby portal points poured into it in lightning blasts from the center of the room to its base. The wheel absorbed this energy from around the Realm and dispersed it throughout the fortress, giving Kurodar the power he needed to finish his work here, to complete the Sky Room and create more of the guardian bots who were to form Reza's army. With that army, Reza would be able to protect the fortress in the unlikely event of some sort of attack by the Americans.

Everything here seemed to be working well. The fortress should be fully supplied with power for now.

So there was no putting his duty off any longer. Reza flapped his webbed wings harder and glided out the iron door into the fortress's Great Hall.

The strange guard-bots at each door saluted him as he flitted across the central room of soaring stone and gorgeous stained glass. When he came to the entrance of the Sky Room, the guard-bots stepped aside. The big double doors swung open.

The Sky Room! What a place this was! The control center of the fortress—the launchpad of what would be their first real attack on the Americans. Reza looked up at the dome with a feeling of almost child-like wonder. It was as if the great Kurodar had created a sky of his own. Seemingly infinite black space. Starry lights so white they seemed beacons of purity and perfection. Multicolored lines of energy streaking across the vault. And thousands of minuscule rainbow-colored bots swarming like beetles around the edges, the servants of Kurodar's imagination, ceaselessly laboring to bring the master's vision to life.

The dome was held in place by fluted golden columns soaring up from the marble floor. Gigantic classical statues stood in the alcoves between them: Hitler, Stalin, Mao, bin Laden—all the heroes who had labored and sacrificed to bring humanity to perfection. As Kurodar himself was laboring now.

There he was. Reza hovered beneath him, staring up at him with a sense of awe and joy. The sight of his master gave Reza the same powerful feeling he used to have when he was worshipping the God. It was the ecstasy of submission and obedience.

In RL—Real Life—Kurodar was just an ugly little man with spindly legs, slumped shoulders, and a frog-like face. But that was in RL. Here in the Realm, he appeared in his true form: a hazy pink presence, liberated from the flesh. Pure mind. Pure genius. The god of the MindWar.

"My master," said Reza, his words full of feeling.

The hazy form pulsed, and the hollow voice answered him, "Why are you interrupting me? I have to finish the dome. There's not much time. The Traveler is already on the move."

"I know, Master," said the assassin. He took a breath. Braced himself. "I thought you should be told: there's been a disturbance in the Blue Woods. The guardian of the Scarlet Plain was activated—and the security feedback shows it was destroyed."

The hazy form of Kurodar shifted. It was hard to tell, but it seemed a note of surprise entered the master's voice as he said, "Destroyed? You're certain? Not just disabled?"

Flapping his wings to stay aloft, Reza shook his head. "According to my information, the bot was completely destroyed."

"We have an intruder then."

"Yes, my master. Possibly more than one. Should I send more guardian bots to hunt them down?"

There was a pause as Kurodar's great mind considered. Then he said, "No. They'll have left by now. The fortress guard isn't finished. If we spread them out to search, it will weaken our defenses. I'm almost done here. Keep watch—and if anyone tries to approach the fortress itself, kill them."

Reza lowered his chin in a gesture of submission. His webbed wings gave another muscular flap and he glided from the room.

When Reza was gone, Kurodar turned his attention to the dome of the sky again. It was strange, he thought. This place—this Realm—it was purely the product of his imagination. It sprang from his mind day by day, as RL had sprung from the mind of God. Here, *he* was the god. This was *his* creation.

And yet, as powerful as he was, he was afraid.

He had tried not to show it while the assassin was present, but the report from the Blue Woods frightened him. They were coming for him again. The Americans. He had known they would. He had known they would not give up. They were going to try to destroy his life's work, just as they'd destroyed the lifework of his father. He had to finish the Sky Room. Quickly. He was running out of time.

He hated this. Building the Sky Room. Building this fortress to protect it. Staging this raid when what he wanted was to launch a full-fledged attack that would leave the United States in flames. He needed to get back to his main work, the work of completing the Golden City. That was the real weapon of the Realm. That was the structure that would give him the power to bring the U.S.—Europe—all his enemies—to their knees.

But the fortress and the Sky Room were necessary. This was an emergency. The Assembly was losing faith. If he didn't show them something soon, they would cut off his funds and the Realm would go unfinished. The Canadian train wreck had caught their attention, but it wasn't enough. It had no real point or purpose.

Now he had the chance to show them something real and effective. The Traveler was on the move. The entire U.S. security apparatus was geared up to protect him. If Kurodar could defeat that apparatus, it would show the Assembly the real potential of the MindWar Realm.

On the other hand, if the Traveler should escape . . .

That was why Kurodar was afraid. The Traveler was the

one man on earth who might just be as brilliant as he was, who might just be brilliant enough to destroy his creation. The prospect of that, the prospect of defeat at the hands of the Americans, frightened him more than anything. It haunted his nightmares. Defeat. Humiliation. The idea that the same horrible fate that had overtaken his father might now overtake him . . .

He had to stop the Traveler. He had to—and he would.

He turned his attention to the dome again, and continued creating the sky.

15. RAGE

"WHAT DID YOU think you were doing? Answer me!"

The words were full of fury, but Miss Ferris's voice never altered. She spoke in that same robotic monotone as always, as if she felt nothing at all, not even her own anger. Her face was expressionless, her eyes were cool. Only the way she paced back and forth in front of him—the taut, cat-like play of her compact body under the black suit—gave Rick any indication of just how angry at him she was.

Rick opened his mouth to answer her—"I saw—" but before he could finish, she stormed on.

"Really," she said, "I'm curious. What part of my instructions didn't you understand?"

"I saw—" Rick started again, and again, she cut him off.

"'Don't stray too far from the portal point,' I said. 'Look around,' I said. 'Find the outpost. Come back.' How difficult to comprehend was that, Rick? Were the words too long for you? Too many syllables? Answer me!"

They were sitting in some kind of conference room in the MindWar Project's underground compound. It was a long, narrow room with one wall made completely of television screens, all of them blank, all black. A long glass table took up most of the floor space. Swivel recliners were arrayed around it. Rick sat slumped and weary in one of the chairs, his crutches leaning against the table beside him, as Miss Ferris paced back and forth between him and the blank TVs. The enormous security guard, Juliet Seven, stood in one corner watching the two of them, his massive arms crossed over his chest again. His block of a face was serious, but there was laughter sparkling in his eyes. He was clearly enjoying watching little Miss Ferris rip into the huge, muscular ex-quarterback.

Rick felt gutted, emptied of all energy. His hour in the Realm had exhausted him. Coming back had been even worse. When Juliet Seven had lifted him out of the glass coffin, the crippling pain and weakness of his legs had struck him like a mallet blow. For all the dangers of the Realm, it had felt incredibly good to have his legs whole and healthy again. Just one hour in that computerized environment and he'd almost forgotten what a weak and broken man he really was. Now, already, the Realm—the scarlet plain—the blue woods—the spider-snake—the sparkling Favian—the beautiful silver Mariel—and his healthy legs—seemed like a dream to him. He could hardly believe any of it had actually happened. Already, he felt his old depression settling over him like a shroud.

But still, he tried again to answer her. He opened his mouth and . . .

"Well?" said Miss Ferris coldly. "I really want to know, Rick. What did you think you were doing?"

"I saw a man," Rick finally managed to say.

Miss Ferris stopped pacing.

"What?"

"I saw a man. In the Realm. Across this scarlet plain, just outside this blue wood."

"You saw a man?"

"He was calling to me. Trying to warn me to get into the forest. I think he saved my life. Otherwise, the gigantic spider-snake would have devoured me on the spot."

Miss Ferris blinked. Rick took this to indicate surprise. Hard to tell—it was the only change in her expression.

"The gigantic spider . . . ?" she began to say. And then she interrupted herself and said, "You're telling me there was a man?"

"Sort of a man," said Rick. "Favian, his name was. He was sort of a . . . well, a sprite or something. He was transparent and he sparkled and, like, flitted around. There was a woman, too."

Miss Ferris cocked her head, like a dog who's heard a whistle.

Didn't she have any regular facial expressions? he wondered. Smiles? Frowns? Anything? Didn't she have any emotions at all? "Only she was more like a spirit. Mariel. She came up out of the water as if she were made of it. She was very . . ." Beautiful, he wanted to say, but it embarrassed him. He didn't want Miss Ferris—or that mocking blockhead Juliet Seven—to see how much the sight of Mariel had moved him.

"And did they say anything? These sprites and spirits?" Miss Ferris asked. "Did they tell you how they got there? Did they give you any usable intelligence?"

"Oh, now you're interested," said Rick sarcastically. "Now

it's not such a bad thing that I strayed away from the portal point."

"Don't be a smart-mouth," snapped Miss Ferris without any intonation whatsoever. "Do you think this is some sort of joke?"

Rick rolled his eyes and shook his head. He didn't think anything. He just wanted to go home and get some sleep. He was too tired to sit here being scolded like a three-year-old by the Ice Queen of Robotland. His experiences in the Realm may have begun to seem like a dream, but the injuries he'd suffered there were real enough. He'd awakened with scratches on his hands and arms, aches in his muscles, vivid purple bruises all over him from when the spider-snake had dragged him over the forest turf. There was one bruise on his lower leg that was nearly black. That was from when the creature's web had wrapped around him, tied him tight. He smelled bad, too. He needed a bath. He needed some rest.

"They didn't know how they got there," he said. "They didn't remember."

Miss Ferris blinked again—and who knew what that meant? Maybe she just had a bit of dust in her eyes or something. She crossed her arms on her chest and stared at him. "What did they tell you about the Realm?" she said coldly.

"They said there was a Golden City in the distance, out of sight. They said that that was the heart of the place, where the real attacks, the big attacks, would come from. But they said that right now, Kurodar was building a fortress. I could see it, out on the edge of the scarlet plain. They thought he was planning to launch some kind of smaller attack from there."

Miss Ferris nodded. It was some sort of reaction, at least.

"There's something else," said Rick.

The woman lifted her chin in a question: *What?*

Rick continued: "They're dying. Favian and Mariel. They have a certain amount of energy and it's running out, bit by bit. They asked me if I could help them." With a pang, he remembered the look of anxiety on Favian's face. *You don't know what it's like here.* And—what was almost worse—he remembered the look of faith from Mariel. *He won't desert us. He's a hero. You only have to look at him to see it. He's the hero we've been waiting for.* "I said I would try," he told Miss Ferris. Then he added, "I promised them I would try."

Miss Ferris did something odd then. She turned away—actually swung completely around so that her back was to him. Before he lost sight of her, Rick could almost have sworn he saw an expression of actual emotion cross her face. What was it? Sorrow? Anger? Fear? No, he must have imagined it, because when she turned around again, her countenance was as stony as ever. "I'll look into it," she said brusquely. "We'll see what we can do to help them. But right now, we have other problems. Juliet Seven will take you home. You need rest before re-immersion. Twelve hours is essential. Forty-eight hours is preferable."

"You are going to send me back in, then?" Rick asked her. He had been worried that she was so angry with him for disobeying her orders that she would end the mission right here and now. He realized: He *wanted* to go back in. He wanted to feel the strength in his legs again. He wanted to complete his mission. He wanted, more than anything, to help Favian and Mariel.

But he needn't have worried about Miss Ferris's anger. She seemed to have forgotten all about it, if she had ever really felt it at all. She even seemed to have forgotten she'd been in the middle of scolding him. She now simply marched away, marched right across the floor to the conference room door, with barely a glance in his direction.

Only when she reached the door, only when she had pulled it open, did she say to him over her shoulder, "Of course we're going to send you back in. You have to get to that fortress."

16. FIGHTING FIT

RICK SAT IN his room, on his sofa, staring into the night darkness. Tired as he was, he was too restless to sleep. Memories of the Realm kept flashing through his mind. He remembered running in joy across the hilltop near the portal point, when he first realized his legs were whole. He remembered Favian beckoning to him from the woods. The horror of his first glimpse of the spider-snake. His panic and fear as it chased him through the woods. Mariel . . .

He's a hero. You only have to look at him to see it. He's the hero we've been waiting for.

He looked down at himself, his crippled legs splayed out in front of him, all but useless. Mariel was wrong. Maybe he had been a hero once. Maybe he could pretend to be a hero in the Realm. But he wasn't a real hero, not anymore.

He picked up his Xbox controller. He turned on the TV. Turned on *Starlight Warriors*. He stared at the screen as his battlecraft streaked through the stars toward the Orgon mothership. His fingers fiddled with the controller in his hand. But he wasn't paying attention.

He was thinking. He was wondering about that look he had seen on Miss Ferris's face just before she turned away from him. Did she know more about Mariel and Favian than she was telling? Did she feel more than she was showing? Or was he really just imagining the whole thing?

As he wondered about it, the Orgon ships on the television set swarmed around his battlecraft, firing at will. His craft burst apart. The debris went floating off into the vast emptiness of space. A message appeared on the screen: *You are dead.*

Rick sighed. He set the controller back down on the sofa. Snapped off the TV. Sat staring into the shadows. He didn't care about the game anyway. It was nothing compared to the Realm.

Now his feeling of restlessness overwhelmed him. He had to get up, had to move. By holding on to the sofa arm, he managed to hobble his way across the room to his computer without using crutches. He sat in front of the machine, hit the keyboard, and checked his e-mail. Nothing there but spam. His old friends, frustrated by the fact he never answered their messages, had all but stopped trying to reach him. Even Fred Hayes, the running back who had been his best buddy, had given up on him. Only Molly kept on trying to get a response.

Rick went into the Deleted file and found her latest e-mail, the one he hadn't bothered to read. He opened it.

> Hey, Rick. How you doing? I tried to call you again last night but your mom says you won't come to the phone. I know you told me you're not ready to talk to anyone about what happened, but that's okay with me, it really is. We don't have to talk about it. I just want to see you. I just miss

you, that's all. You matter to me, Rick, and I thought I mattered to you . . .

He stopped reading. The words made him feel too bad. He knew he ought to get in touch with her, but he couldn't bring himself to do it. It was not that she was far away. She had gone to Shadbrook, the local U, where her dad headed the Physics Department in which Rick's father worked . . . or, that is, used to work. She was there on a volleyball scholarship, as he had been headed to Syracuse on a football scholarship. They'd been a good match in that way: he the football hero; she the power behind the volleyball team. The two of them liked to work out together, hike together, run, swim . . .

And that was the problem. What use could she possibly have for him now? Rick liked her. He missed seeing her. But what was she going to feel when she saw him like this? Pity, that's what. He couldn't bear that. He couldn't even bear to contact her.

He closed the e-mail, sending it back into the Deleted file.

Rick was about to return to the sofa, when there was a soft knock at the door.

"Yeah?" he said.

The door opened, just a crack. There was Raider in his plaid pajama pants and baseball shirt, ready to head upstairs to bed. Raider saw Rick and his face broke into an enormous grin. Why was the kid always so incredibly happy to see him? It made Rick feel guilty about hiding in his room all this time.

"Hey, Rick! I'm going to bed!" Raider announced. He

said this in such an insanely upbeat tone it sounded as if he were starting off on the most exciting journey in the history of mankind.

"Good for you," Rick muttered. Then, feeling guilty, he looked at the boy—really looked at the eager face beaming up at him. Thoughts of Mariel flashed through his mind.

He's the hero we've been waiting for.

He wasn't acting very much like a hero, was he?

"Hey," Rick said to his brother. "Listen. Before you go to bed, you think you could do me a favor?"

"A favor? Yeah! Sure!" The eight-year-old's face was wreathed in smiles at the very idea that he might be able to do something for his big brother.

"Up in my old room," said Rick. "Where my weights are. There are these two plastic pouches with . . ."

"I know them!" Raider cried. "I'll bring them down for you! Wait here!" And he shot up the stairs like a missile.

"One at a time!" Rick called after him. "They're heavy." *Weird little kid,* he thought.

He looked down the hall then and saw his mom standing in the kitchen doorway, watching him. It was strange. She hadn't mentioned the bruises he'd picked up in the Realm. She hadn't mentioned the way he'd left the house and disappeared for hours again. And yet, the way she was looking at him . . . It was as if she already knew all about it.

A moment later, Raider's footsteps came thundering back down the stairs. Without a word, Rick's mother retreated back into the kitchen.

Grunting proudly with his effort, Raider carried the weight pack down the hall to Rick's room. He slung it off his shoulder into Rick's hand.

"Now for the other one!" he announced heroically. And he took off again.

By the time he returned with the second pack, Rick was sitting on the sofa, strapping the first weight pack around his ankle and sealing the Velcro.

"Thanks," Rick said as he took the second weight pack off the kid's shoulder.

"You gonna work out?" said Raider, gaping at him eagerly. His awestruck tone made it sound as if Rick were planning to flap his arms and fly to Saturn and back. "You gonna exercise your legs?"

"Go to bed," Rick told him, annoyed.

But as he bowed his head to Velcro the second weight around his other ankle, he sensed the kid hadn't moved. He looked up and saw the eight-year-old staring at Rick's legs with a look of such ferocious determination, you would have thought it was Raider who was going to do the lifting here. Both the kid's fists were raised in front of him and clenched so tight the fingers were turning white. When Rick lifted his eyes to him, Raider gave him a taut fist pump for encouragement. *Go, Rick.*

Rick couldn't keep a smile from touching the corner of his mouth.

"Okay, okay," he said quietly. "I'll do my best. Now get out of here."

And like a shot, the kid was gone.

Rick sat back on the sofa, the weight packs strapped tightly to his ankles. *Weird little kid,* he thought again.

Then he began to try to lift his right foot.

He could not believe the weakness of his muscles. And the pain was beyond description. It was as if someone had taken a sword made of lightning and driven it into the sole of his foot, up through his knee, and into his hamstring. Rick gasped at the agony.

He got his foot about three inches off the floor. Then his strength gave out and the leg dropped down again.

That's it, Rick thought. *That's unbearable. No more. I'm done.*

Then he tried again.

The right leg went up a few inches, then fell. The left leg: up, down. The effort was so hard, the pain so great, that tears fell from his eyes and began to stream down his cheeks. He did it again. Right, then left. *I can't do any more,* he thought. Then he did another set. Right. Then left. He thought: *I used to be able to run faster than anyone else in the school. Now I can barely lift my heels off the stupid floor. No matter how hard I work out, at best, I might one day be able to walk with a limp. Maybe. This is stupid. What's the point? What's the use?*

Then he tried again—right, left—his tears streaming.

For the next twenty excruciating minutes, Rick worked his legs like that, grunting, driving himself through the pain. In the course of those minutes, he must have given up half a dozen times—and half a dozen times, he began again. His tears fell so hard he wondered if it was only the effort that brought them to his eyes. Maybe it was more than that. Maybe he was crying for his football career: lost. His father: gone. They would never come back. What was the point of this? What good did it do? Right. Left. Right. Left.

Enough, he told himself. *There's no point. Enough.*

Shut up, he answered himself. *Just shut up and lift your stupid foot.*

When he finally allowed himself to stop, he sat on the sofa, gasping for breath. Sniffling, he wiped his cheeks dry with the palm of his hand.

Well, he thought, *at least now I might be tired enough to get some sleep.*

He bent down and peeled the weight packs off his ankles. He set them on the floor by the sofa. He lifted his crutches off the floor and leaned them against the sofa arm where he'd be able to reach them easily when he woke up. He found his blanket bunched up in one corner of the room. Stretching, he reached it and pulled it toward him, shook it out.

He lay down on the sofa and pulled the blanket over him. But sleep still didn't come. He stared up into the darkness. He began to feel angry.

What am I supposed to do? he thought. *Pray?*

In the old days, he had always prayed when he went to bed. It had calmed his mind and helped him to fall asleep. But that was the old days. In the old days, he had actually believed that someone was hearing his prayers. Maybe someone was, but there was no way he was going to pray to him after all the stinking stuff God had done to him. The accident. His father leaving. No way.

But he was so tired. So tired. And somehow, he knew he would not be able to sleep until he had said something up at the darkness. Anything.

So angrily, defiantly, he said, *Hey! Guess what? I'm still here!*

And *Hey,* the darkness said quietly back to him. *Guess what? I already knew that.*

A moment later, Rick fell into a deep, dreamless sleep.

He remained asleep until a man snuck into his room and pressed the barrel of a gun into his forehead.

17. HITMAN

AT THE TOUCH of the cold steel against his flesh, Rick's eyes flashed open.

"What?" he murmured sleepily.

"Shh," hissed the man standing in the darkness above him. "Make one move and you're dead."

Confused and frightened, Rick lay still, his heart hammering in his chest as if he had awakened from a nightmare. But this was no nightmare. This was real. He stared up into the shadows, trying to see the face of the gunman staring back down at him. Bizarrely, the gunman didn't have a face. There was just more darkness up there.

"I'm going to ask you some questions," said the faceless man. "If you lie, even once, I'm going to blow your brains out. Then I'm going upstairs to have the same conversation with your mama and your kid brother, and if I don't get what I want, I'm going to do the same to them. Do you understand me?"

Rick gave only the slightest, quickest nod. He didn't want the gunman to think he was going to try anything. "I understand," he whispered.

"You don't want me to go upstairs to talk to your mama, do you?"

"No," said Rick. His eyes were wide open now, his mind fully awake. He had figured out why the man didn't have a face. He was wearing a mask. He was dressed all in black and wearing a black ski mask. "I'll tell you whatever you want, whatever I know. Just don't hurt my family."

"Smart boy," said the gunman—and to emphasize the words, he jabbed the pistol point hard into Rick's brow. Rick grunted at the pain and his heart beat even harder. "Okay," said the gunman. "Here's question number one: Where is he?"

"What?"

The man jabbed him in the head again. "I got a short fuse and a hair trigger, son. Mess with me not, you hear me?"

Rick's hands came up from his sides in a gesture of helpless pleading. "I'm not messing with you, man, I swear it. I don't know what you mean. Where's who?"

"Your old man. Your father. Where'd he go?"

"My father? I don't know that."

This time the man pulled the barrel of the pistol away and quickly rapped it across the side of Rick's face. It wasn't a hard blow, but it hurt plenty all the same. "Wrong answer, kid," he said. "Tell me now, or say, 'Bye-bye, Mama.'"

"No, no, no, listen to me. I don't know where my father is. I really don't. And my mother doesn't know either. He just left us. He left a note. He said he was going away with an old girlfriend of his from college."

"But you don't know where."

"No. He didn't say."

"And he hasn't been in touch. All this time."

"It's true, so help me."

"I'm having a hard time believing that, Ricky boy. I'm starting to think maybe you're lying to me. Or maybe I'm talking to the wrong Dial. Maybe your mama knows something you don't . . ."

Rick felt the gun barrel steady itself against his brow. He was pretty sure the man was about one second away from pulling the trigger. And after he'd turned Rick into a corpse, he'd head upstairs for Mom and Raider . . .

Rick had to do something, say something.

"All right," he said. "All right. I lied. I do know something."

The gun barrel relaxed a little. "I kind of thought you might," said the man. "I didn't think Mars would just leave you in the dark."

Startled, Rick hesitated. Mars? Did the guy just mention Commander Mars? The leader of the MindWar Project? What did that have to do with his father?

The gunman jabbed him with the gun barrel again. "I can't hear you, son," he said. "Speak up."

"Right," said Rick. "Right. I'm the only one who knows. My mom and Raider don't know anything."

"Stop babbling. Where is he? Tell me or I'll drag you upstairs and kill your family in front of your eyes. Do you believe me?"

"Yes," said Rick. He did, too.

"Then start talking."

Rick was about to do just that. He was about to say anything, tell any crazy story he could think of to keep this guy from going nuts with that pistol. But before he could get out a word, he saw something out of the corner of his eye—something that made his stomach turn to acid.

A line of light had appeared at the bottom of his closed bedroom door. Someone had come into the hall out there. A moment later, a floorboard squeaked.

Then a little voice called to him softly: "Rick?"

Raider.

Rick stared up into the darkness. The man in the mask lifted his free hand and pressed a finger to where his mouth should have been: *Shh.*

If Raider comes through that door, this nut's going to kill him, Rick thought. *He'll kill us both.*

Another floorboard squeaked in the hall.

Raider called again, from closer this time, "Rick? Is everything okay? I thought I heard something."

The doorknob began to turn.

"Raider! Go back to bed! Everything's fine!" Rick shouted.

But the kid wouldn't listen to him. The door swung in. Raider stood in the light from the hallway.

"Rick? What's going on?"

Without warning, in one swift motion, the gunman swung the pistol from Rick's head, and pointed it at Raider.

But Rick didn't need a warning. He knew what the thug was going to do before he did it. Even as the gunman was bringing the weapon around toward his brother, Rick was rolling off the sofa, hurling his big body at the creep's knees. In football, it would have been cut blocking—totally against the rules. But this wasn't football. And there were no rules.

Rick hit the guy's knees full force. The gunman toppled over, his arms flying upward. That's when the gun went off. The shot was deafening. The flame cut through the shadows. But where did the bullet go? Into the wall? The door? Into his little brother's body? Rick didn't know.

His legs were on fire with pain as he continued his tackle. He tumbled off the sofa, bringing the gunman to the floor beneath him. The killer tried to shove Rick off, tried to bring the pistol around to get a shot at him. But Rick had the man's arm gripped in his two hands now, had his wrist, was struggling to tear the weapon from his fingers.

Fighting to keep the gun, the thug kicked a sharp heel into Rick's shin. Rick cried out in agony. The thug shot his elbow back into Rick's mouth. Rick felt his lip split painfully, but he wouldn't let go, wouldn't release his grip on the gunman's wrist. He twisted it. The gun came loose. Rick ripped the weapon from the man's grasp.

But at the same moment, the gunman used all his strength to hurl Rick off him. Rick flew backward, crashing into the sofa. He roared again as the fiery agony flashed through his legs.

Rick caught a confused glimpse of the room. The shadows were lanced by the yellow light from the open door. Where was Raider? Was he wounded? Was he dead? Rick couldn't see him. And where was the gunman? Rick had lost him in the confusion of the fight.

But there he was. Rick saw him now. The thug had jumped to his feet. He was running toward the light from the open door.

And then, suddenly, the light went out. An enormous

rectangular shadow loomed in the doorway, blocking the thug's path. In the craziness of the moment, it was another second before Rick recognized Juliet Seven.

The thug tried to stop himself from running into the great block of a bodyguard, but he was moving too quickly. He stumbled forward—within Juliet Seven's massive reach.

And Juliet Seven punched the thug in the face so hard that even Rick flinched at the bone-crunching sound the big fist made when it landed.

The thug's body went so loose it looked as if he had turned to string. He fluttered to the floor and lay still.

The lights came on. Rick looked around wildly, in a panic. The masked gunman lay unconscious on the floor. Juliet Seven loomed enormous and rectangular in the doorway.

But where was Raider?

"Raider!" Rick shouted. "Raider, you okay? Are you hurt? Are you shot?"

"He's all right," said Miss Ferris coolly. She stepped around the massive wall that was Juliet Seven. She had Raider lifted in her arms—in spite of the fact that she wasn't much bigger than he was. The boy's face was white. His eyes looked to be the size of dinner plates. He was pressing his lips together hard as he tried not to cry. "I've got him," Miss Ferris announced in her flat, robotic voice. "He's unharmed."

Rick nodded. With a sigh of relief, he dropped the gun. He let his head fall back to the floor. He lay there on his back and tried to massage some of the pain out of his screaming legs. Blood from his busted lip ran down over his chin.

The next moment, Rick's mom rushed into the room, pulling a bathrobe closed around her. Raider had slid down out of Miss Ferris's grip. He rushed to his mother and wrapped his arms around her. She held his head against her robe. If Raider's face was white, his mother's face was practically transparent with shock.

Her voice came out a hoarse croak. "What is going on? Rick, are you all right?"

Still rubbing his legs, still flinching with the pain, drinking the blood that dribbled out of his broken lip, Rick nodded. "Yeah, yeah, yeah, I'm fine, Ma. I'll be fine."

"Who are these people?" she said. "What's going on?"

Rick had no idea how to answer that.

But Miss Ferris calmly drew a billfold out of her jacket pocket. She flipped it open. There was a badge inside. It flashed in the light as she showed it to Rick's mom.

"It's all right, Mrs. Dial," Miss Ferris said in her steady monotone. "We're the police. We received a 911 call that there'd been a break-in here. But don't worry. Everything's all right now."

18. SECRET FILES

IT WAS RICK'S turn to be furious.

"You're going to tell me what's going on," he shouted. He jabbed his finger in Miss Ferris's direction. "You're going to tell me now, lady! Or you can take your stupid MindWar and eat it!"

They were in the conference room again. Rick was back in his chair at the long glass table and Miss Ferris was standing in front of the blank TV screens. Juliet Seven was at his station in the corner, where his enormous arms were once again crossed on his enormous chest as he watched them both, smiling with his eyes.

"We told you this would be dangerous," Miss Ferris said calmly.

"For *me*!" Rick shouted. It hurt to talk through his swollen lips, but he didn't care. "You said it would be dangerous for me! You never said people would break into my house and come after my family!"

Rick saw Miss Ferris swallow, maybe even a bit harder than usual. Just very slightly, he thought she averted her gaze, as if she were embarrassed. "We were guarding your house all the time," she said flatly.

"Oh, well, good job!" said Rick. "Except for the guy with the gun breaking in and nearly shooting me. Other than that, you did great."

"We were nearby the whole time. Your family wasn't in any danger."

Rick silently cursed the crippled legs that forced him to sit where he was. That flat, unemotional tone of hers was making him crazy. He wished he could jump up, tower over her, grab her by the front of her suit jacket, and shake some feeling into her. It was probably just as well he couldn't. He was so mad at her right then, he might have lost control and strangled her.

"That guy was going to kill me," he said, forcing himself to keep his voice steady. "Then he was going to kill my mom and my brother. Don't tell me we weren't in danger."

Once again, she swallowed hard, as if something were caught in her throat. But if she had any real sense of shame or guilt, she didn't let on. She only gave a brisk nod. She said, "You have to understand: this operation is different than any we've undertaken before—different than any operation anyone has undertaken. Normally, we would put you and your family under high-tech security. But that's just the problem. Our high technology may be completely vulnerable to Kurodar's infiltration. In fact, it may just make him stronger. We don't know. For now, we feel you're safer in your own home with a guard posted."

"Oh yeah! Real safe!"

"Look, one of them got by us, that's all. We're not perfect.

We came to help you as soon as we could, just as we did when you were attacked before, just as . . ." She stopped suddenly.

Rick stared at her. "Just as what?"

Miss Ferris, gave a quick shake of her head. "Never mind. I misspoke."

"No, no, no. Just as you did when what? When did you ever come to help me before? When have I ever been attacked before? This is the first time anyone's ever . . ."

The words died on Rick's split and purple lip. He gaped at Miss Ferris, and Miss Ferris looked back at him with a grim poker face.

"The accident," Rick whispered. The thought astonished him. "You're talking about the accident, aren't you? Are you talking about the truck that hit me, that destroyed my legs? I don't remember how I got to the hospital. Or what happened to the driver. Are you saying you took care of all that? Are you telling me that the accident . . . that it wasn't an accident? Are you telling me that truck hit me on purpose?"

"I'm not telling you anything," Miss Ferris said coolly. "I *can't* tell you anything."

Rick went on gaping at her as ideas he could barely believe raced and tumbled through his mind. "You have to," he said finally. "You have to tell me. That thug was asking me about my father. What's he got to do with this? What's the accident got to do with it? You're telling me that everything that's happened to me over these past months—it's all connected. That's right, isn't it? It's all connected to the MindWar."

Miss Ferris could not have looked at him with any less

emotion if she had been a department store mannequin. "I don't know," she said.

The anger exploded in him again. "What do you mean you don't know? I don't believe you."

"It doesn't matter," she said flatly. "It doesn't matter whether you believe me or not. I've told you everything I can."

"You've lied to me, you mean! You've lied to me all this time. And now my family is in danger!"

Miss Ferris didn't answer. She only gazed at him. Standing there in her stupid black suit. Or maybe this was a new stupid black suit, who could tell? Rick glared back, his swollen lip curling with rage. Their eyes remained locked together.

"My brother's terrified," Rick told her, his voice coming from somewhere deep in his throat. "My mother's scared out of her wits."

"I thought I took care of that. I explained to your mother that there was a break-in, that we were the police, and that we'd taken the intruder into custody."

"Right," Rick sneered sarcastically. "And that worked great, because my mom's an idiot! Because she would never think to call the police and ask for more information and find out they never heard of any break-in at our house at all. Oh wait, that's exactly what she did!"

Well, that really disturbed Miss Ferris. It must have, because she actually took a deep breath! She said, "All right. I'll fix that."

"Oh, you'll fix that."

"I'll have one of the local detectives follow up with her."

"Good," said Rick. "Because there's just nothing I like better than being tangled in a web of lies, especially with my mom."

"You signed on for this," Miss Ferris snapped back, almost raising her voice. Almost. "Commander Mars told you that you would have to keep the mission a secret."

"Commander Mars!" Rick said, disgusted. "The guy's a hologram! He's not even a real person. I'm not sure you're even a real person."

"I'm a real person, Rick," Miss Ferris answered quietly.

"Then why don't you act like one?" he shouted. "Why don't you . . . lose your temper or . . . or change your tone of voice or . . . or something? Do something. Feel something. Why don't you feel anything?"

"Because it doesn't help," she said flatly.

And again Rick thought he saw in her the slightest indication of—something—confusion—distress. Her mouth turned down in the briefest frown and her eyes broke away as if she could no longer meet his furious stare. To his annoyance, Rick found this little sign of weakness touched him somehow. In spite of himself, his anger at her started to ebb.

Who is this woman? he wondered. What was going on in her mind? He'd never met anyone like her. He'd never met anyone so absent emotion—certainly not a girl, anyway. And she was actually kind of a pretty girl, too, when you took the time to look at her. She had this perfect pink-and-white complexion and crystal-blue eyes that he might have called soft had they belonged to anyone else. Her hair was cut boyishly short, and her outfit was boyish, too, but it was all boyish in a cute girlish way that Rick liked. In fact, he sensed there was something in Miss Ferris that he would have liked altogether—if only she weren't working so hard to keep it from coming out.

"You're hiding something from me," he said, his tone a little less ferocious than before.

Slowly, she raised her eyes to meet his again. "I'm hiding all kinds of things from you, Rick," she told him. "It's a top secret operation, remember?"

"All right. I get that. Sure. But if you know something about my father, that's different. You have to tell me that."

"Really?" Miss Ferris asked him—and any sign of distress he might have seen in her had vanished. She had gone all robot on him again. "Why? So the next time someone puts a gun to your head and asks you where he is, you'll be able to tell them? We don't tell you things, so that you can't tell anyone else. That way, everyone's a little safer."

Rick swallowed. He had to admit he could see her point. But he couldn't stop himself from going on. "You don't know what it's been like in my house these last months. So just tell me one thing, all right? Just tell me: Did my dad walk out on us or not?"

In the long pause that followed, Rick began to hope she would break down and answer him. But all she said was, "I'm sorry." Then she glanced briskly at her watch. "It's been more than twelve hours. We need to get you back into the Realm."

19. PORTAL TWO

THE METALLIC LINING of the portal tightened around him again. Rick lay in the coffin-like glass box, staring up into Miss Ferris's impassive face above him. His mind was swirling with so many thoughts and questions, he could barely pay attention to her instructions.

"Get as close to the fortress as you can and find out as much about it as you can," she said down at him. "But don't push it. Don't put yourself in any danger. The cost of failure is too great. Greater than you can imagine."

Rick could barely nod in response, the metallic lining was already wrapped around his head so tightly.

"You'll notice we gave you an extra fifteen minutes to stay this time," Miss Ferris went on. "According to our brain scans, the fact that you played video games so much has made your mind well-adapted to being in the Realm."

Rick didn't know whether to be proud of this or ashamed.

"But again," said Miss Ferris, "don't push it. Before you go too far in any direction, make sure you know where the nearest portal point is, and make sure you can get back to it in time if there's any trouble. Under no circumstances are you to stay past the time we've allotted to you. Under no circumstances; do you understand me?"

Rick could only answer with a grimace as the lining seemed to creep over the top of his head like a living thing. Again, he felt as if invisible needles were injecting themselves into his scalp.

"We recorded the location of the new portal point you discovered in the Blue Woods. You should come out this time, at exactly the place from which you left."

One corner of Rick's mouth turned up. *Like a save point in a video game,* he thought.

"Good luck, Rick," Miss Ferris said.

She spoke, as always, without emotion. But, strangely, he found himself smiling a more or less warm farewell at her. With all their angry exchanges back and forth, he hadn't noticed it until now—but the fact was, crazy as it seemed, he was beginning to like this oddly robotic woman. He was even beginning to trust her, weird and secretive as she was.

She closed the lid of the box and stepped away.

After that, it was all as it had been before. His heart sped up as the glass coffin lid lowered over him. A claustrophobic sweat broke out on his temples, the droplets streaming back into his hair. The prickling in his scalp grew more painful as the lining of the coffin tightened around him even more. Then came that buzzing sound again, and the vibrations. And something in him began to release, as if he were falling asleep.

Then, just as before, he seemed to lose his grip on himself. He seemed to slip down inside his own mind, until he was surrounded by black nothingness. And again, in the center of that black nothingness, there emerged a cylinder of light.

As before, he focused his will. And with a conscious effort, he sent his spirit through that cylinder like liquid through a straw.

Once again, he entered the Realm.

LEVEL FOUR:

THE CREATURES OF THE AIR

20. DARK DESCENT

HE WAS BACK in the Blue Woods. It had happened just as Miss Ferris said it would: he had returned to the portal point in the forest clearing, near the spot where he and Favian had destroyed the spider-snake.

But even though it was his second time in, he was not prepared for the shock of the transition. In the brief time he had been back in the real world, the Realm had become like a dream to him. Now that he had returned, it was so staggeringly real. The crazy colors—the yellow of the sky through the startling aquamarine of the leaves, the silver of Mariel's lake just visible between the green-brown tree trunks—their vivid presence overwhelmed his senses. And his legs! The amazing pleasure of having his body suddenly whole and strong beneath him again—the joy of it flowed up and through him like water—like golden wine—filling a glass.

He turned this way and that, openmouthed and awestruck, trying to take it all in, get used to it again.

And, as he turned, his eyes fell on his sword.

It stood upright to one side of the floating purple diamond that was the portal point. Its rusty blade pierced the fallen blue leaves and stabbed the red earth beneath, as if someone had stuck it there for him so it would be easy for him to find when he returned.

Rick grabbed the sword by its greenish-copper hilt and held it up before his eyes. He could see now that the face of the woman molded into the hilt looked very much like Mariel. And as his fingers closed around the image, he thought he could almost feel her, feel some power from her, flowing into his arm.

Your spirit has power here—power over material things, once you learn to use it. Strike with your spirit and the sword will be strong enough.

The thought of her—the sound of her voice in his mind—the idea that he might see her again—made his pulse quicken with excitement.

He slipped the sword through the belt of his black jeans and headed out of the clearing, down the path to the silver lake.

He reached the lakeshore. Again, he was struck by how real it all was: how much it had become like a dream to him while he was gone, and how real it was now that he had returned to it. The shining silver of the water catching the yellow of the sky. The blue of the surrounding leaves. The colors shimmering and changing on the lake surface. It was all so vivid and bright now that he could look at it again with his own eyes.

"Mariel," he called—hoarsely, softly. He cleared his throat and tried again, louder this time. "Mariel."

He waited, taking shallow breaths, hoping—hardly daring to hope—that at any minute the metallic water would rise as it had risen before and form itself into the shape of her.

Second after second passed. His anticipation grew. But the lake lay still. He glanced down at the time-light on his palm.

1:12:46 . . . 45 . . . 44 . . .

The seconds were ticking away. If he was going to reach the fortress and get back here to the portal point, he would have to start moving. He couldn't wait any longer.

With a sigh of disappointment, he turned around—and cried out, "Whoa!" in his surprise.

Favian had crept up behind him.

The shifting, twinkling presence wavered directly in front of him: the gangly body, the almost shaved head, and the gentle anxious expression on his youthful face—all fashioned out of particles of light.

"She can't always appear," Favian said. "She can't afford to use up her energy. She has to choose her moments."

Rick felt himself blush. He thought Favian must have somehow seen his yearning and his disappointment. "No problem," he muttered. "You know—whatever's good." Then, to change the subject, he said: "I asked the people back home about getting you out of here. They said they'd work on it."

Favian nodded—without much hope, Rick thought. All he answered was, "We can't just stand around here talking. Time's short. We better get moving if we want to get to the fortress."

"Right," said Rick.

Favian's twinkling head bowed in a short nod. "Follow me."

And he darted off through the trees, a streak of blue light.

Rick jogged after him into the depths of the forest. Despite his thoughts of Mariel—and despite his worries about what was waiting for him at the fortress—he couldn't help but experience again the boundless pleasure of having his legs feel quarterback-strong underneath him. It was a joy just to run. Favian kept well ahead of him. Rick would catch glimpses of the sprite's sparkling presence through the blue leaves. He would jog toward him and—*flash*—the strange creature would dart off again and Rick would have to hurry after. As he ran, he noticed there were fallen trees and jagged tree trunks on every side of him. They must've been heading back the way he'd come, the way the spider-snake had chased him. This was the wreckage the beast had caused as he'd crashed through the forest.

Quickly, they reached the edge of the wood. Rick stepped out into the greater brightness of the Scarlet Plain to find Favian hovering there, waiting for him. Rick looked to his left, over the undulating red distance. He saw the black towers of Kurodar's fortress rising into the saffron sky. He saw the black shapes circling in the air above it.

"What *are* those flying things?" he asked.

"The creatures of the air," said Favian in his strangely echoic voice. "The guardians of the fortress."

"Like the spider-snake was the guardian of the plain?" Rick asked.

"Worse," said Favian. "Much worse than the spider-snake. Much more powerful. Whatever happens, we can't let them see us. I can outrun them, but you can't. And if they catch you, you won't survive."

Rick took a deep breath, feeling the churn of fear

beginning in his stomach. But before he could say anything else, Favian darted off in a sparkling streak. He was heading in the opposite direction, though—heading away from the fortress, back toward the hill on which Rick had first entered the Realm.

"Hey," Rick shouted after him. "Shouldn't we be going the other way . . . ?"

But Favian was already too far ahead to hear him. Rick jogged after him over the bright red earth.

He found Favian waiting for him again at the place where the spider-snake had torn its long crevasse into the ground. Panting, Rick pulled up at the edge of the chasm.

"This is what I thought. We can use the spider-snake's tunnels," said Favian. He seemed proud to have come up with the idea. "The way I figure it: they must have created the spider-snake in the fortress—that's where all the energy is going. So the spider-snake would have had to dig its way here. That means the tunnel should take us right up to the fortress. See? That way we can approach from underground and the creatures of the air won't see us."

Rick eyed the dark pit below him. "Well, that's—that's very logical," he said doubtfully. "And you're sure there're no mommy spider-snakes down there, right? No little baby spider-snakes or anything like that?"

To Rick's dismay, Favian's mouth fell open. "Well, I . . . I never thought of that."

"You never thought of that?" said Rick.

"No, I mean . . . I've never *seen* any other spider-snakes . . ."

This was not encouraging. "Oh man," he said. "I thought you'd know these things."

"You did?"

"Well, yeah! I mean, you're my trusty guide here, right? And with all your sparkling and flashing around and everything, I figured you had, like, super spiritual powers or something. I was hoping you were, like, all-knowing. Or at least a-lot-knowing."

Favian frowned. "Well . . . I guess I'm somewhat-knowing . . . ," he offered.

"Somewhat-knowing," Rick muttered. "Great."

He glanced up and off across the plain again toward the fortress in the distance. Those air creatures circling around looked small from here, but close-up they had to be monsters. He looked back at the pit again.

"Well, it's the best idea we've got, I guess," he said.

Favian swallowed hard. "I guess," he said. He looked as worried as Rick felt.

Rick gathered his courage. "Let's do it, then," he said. "Time's wasting."

And he lowered himself to the earth and began to climb over the side of the trench.

He hung from the ledge a moment, then dropped. As he hit bottom, he was startled to find Favian already waiting for him there.

"Man!" he said. "You gotta stop jumping out at me like that."

"Sorry," said Favian. "That's just what I'm like."

And, as if to prove it, he flashed along the ditch until he came to rest about fifty yards away.

Rick jogged after him—and his heart sank as he caught up and saw where Favian was standing. There was a hole in the earth wall of the trench, an entrance into an underground tunnel. The entrance was draped with hanging strands of spiderweb. Beyond that, there was only blackness. It was pretty much the last place Rick wanted to go.

"Maybe we should flip a coin or something to see who goes in there first," said Rick.

"No," said Favian at once. "You better."

"Me? Oh, hey, thanks."

"I'm just not very brave, that's all," said the sparkling sprite with a little frown.

"Now you tell me," said Rick. "All right. Well, here goes."

He bowed his head and ducked into the tunnel.

Utter blackness wrapped itself around him like an enormous fist. The rough, stinging web grabbed at him, clung to him. An awful feeling. It seemed the strands of it went on clinging to his cheeks no matter how hard he swiped at his face to get rid of them. And the smell . . . He had forgotten about the spider-snake's smell! It had nearly smothered him when the beast hauled him up on its web toward its mouth. The creature's horrible stink still pervaded the darkness of the tunnel air.

He heard a short choking noise and turned to see that Favian had come in behind him. His shifting, sparkling, semitransparent features were wrinkled with disgust.

"Oh, that so stinks!" he said.

"Guess you didn't think of that either," said Rick.

"I may throw up."

Rick wondered if Favian's throw-up would sparkle, too. Whatever. The guy was not turning out to be the helpful spirit guide he'd hoped for.

"I don't know how we're ever going to see our way through here," Rick said, peering into the tunnel's blackness.

Favian brightened at that. "Oh, wait: Watch this!" he said, excited. He lifted his hand. The twinkling palm emitted a soft purple glow that dimly lit the earthen walls around them.

"I recharged from the portal point while you were gone," he said. "If we don't overuse it, I should have just enough energy to light our way there."

Rick nodded. He was about to ask: *Won't that drain you? Won't that make you die more quickly?* But he understood that, despite his fears, this strange little fellow was very eager to help him. And their time really was short. So all he said was: "Let's go."

The two started into the tunnel. Favian kept his hand upraised and the purple light from his palm picked a few feet of winding earthen corridor out of the darkness. They moved slowly, trying to duck beneath the hanging strands of web and spider goo, forced sometimes to stop and drag the horrible stuff off their necks and faces.

They moved on, crouching low. Rick's hand automatically went to the hilt of his sword as he edged forward, squinting through the faltering light. Once or twice, he heard—or thought he heard—soft scrabbling noises just ahead of them, as if small creatures were running for cover as the two of them approached. He hoped they were running for cover, anyway. He hoped they weren't gathering for an attack!

On and on the darkness went, a long way. The smell was thick as smoke, but Rick found if he kept breathing through his mouth, he could tolerate it—just barely. It occurred to him that Favian was no longer flashing ahead of him as he had before. Instead, the spirit moved slowly by his side, gliding over the surface of the dirt by inches, his twinkling shoulder always near Rick's own. Rick cast a quick glance Favian's way. He understood. He could see by the look on his face that the sprite was absolutely terrified.

The thought made him grip his sword more tightly. That made him feel better, as if Mariel's strength were flowing into him.

"We'll be all right," he told Favian, trying to sound encouraging.

"The thing is," Favian said, his echoing voice trembling a little, "it just occurred to me: Lighting our way like this uses up my power. I'm getting weaker. If the creatures of the air attack, I'm not sure I'll be able to get away . . ."

Rick licked his dry lips. He wished Favian would think of these things a little sooner. "Well, we just won't show ourselves if it's too dangerous, that's all. I'm under orders not to take any chances."

"Oh, *you'll* be fine," said Favian. "You're a hero, like Mariel said. But me . . ."

The look on the sprite's face was so woeful that Rick tried

to pump him up a little. "You're doing great," he said. "I mean, I'm scared, too, you know."

"You are?" Favian said, surprised.

"Of course I am. I'd have to be stupid not to be scared. I'm terrified."

"But you just keep going anyway."

"Right. That's the whole trick to it: just keep going anyway."

Favian nodded, but he didn't look convinced. "I *want* to be brave, I really do, but . . . when things happen, it's like my body just takes over and I run away."

"You were brave enough with the spider-snake," said Rick. "You saved my life."

That actually made Favian brighten a bit. "I did, didn't I?" He shook his head. "I wish I could remember what I was like . . . you know—before. Before I came here. I was smart, I think. I mean, I think I was really smart . . ."

"I'll bet that's right," said Rick, still trying to keep his friend's spirits high. "Hey, I never would have thought of using the tunnels like this. So you're still pretty smart in my book."

"Sometimes I feel I can almost remember," said Favian, sounding thoughtful and far away. "Who I was. Where I came from. I can see faces—faraway faces, all out of focus. Eyes and smiles of people . . . people who really cared about me. Liked me. Even loved me. I miss them so much, but . . . But it's like looking through murky water, you know? I can't see them clearly. And then . . . then I lose sight of them completely . . . I just can't remember."

They traveled on in silence, peering ahead through the soft purple glow from Favian's hand.

But there was no silence in Rick's mind. It was buzzing with questions. He wanted to know all about this place. Why was Kurodar building his fortress? What was in the Golden City? And Mariel—who was she? Did she remember any more than Favian about where she came from and what she had done before?

He opened his mouth to ask about her—but before he could say anything, Favian cut him off with a sudden gasp.

The spirit had stopped in his tracks. He stood frozen, staring. Rick followed his gaze and saw . . . well, he wasn't sure what he saw because he only saw it for a second. For one second, it was caught in the purple glow emanating from Favian's hand—and all Rick could really see was that it was horrible, more horrible than anything he had ever seen before.

They had come to a juncture. Another arm of the tunnel intersected with the main passage, going off into the darkness to the right. A few yards down that second passage, there was a niche in the earthen wall. And in that niche, there was . . . some sort of nightmare.

It was wrapped up in the dripping white webbing, like a fly waiting to be eaten by a spider. In the single glimpse Rick had of it, he could see that it was like a skeleton—a human skeleton and yet . . . it had eyes! It had eyes and the eyes were staring at Rick in helpless pain and terror as if it were still aware, still feeling, as if it were not a corpse but a living being trapped inside a corpse, trapped in the unbelievable agony of eternal decay. It was as if, Rick thought . . . as if it were dead and yet . . . not dead.

"What on earth is . . . ," Rick began to say, as disgust rose in his throat.

"Don't look at it!" Favian cried. "Don't look! Come this way!"

And he flashed off down the main thoroughfare.

As the purple light from his palm faded, the horrendous vision in the niche vanished into the utter darkness. It was gone before Rick's brain could fully take in what he had seen.

Rick had no choice. He had to follow Favian or be left behind with that thing in the blackness. He hurried after the flashing spirit, hissing in a forced whisper, "Favian! Favian! Wait! Wait up! I can't keep up with you if you . . ."

Favian stopped suddenly, forcing Rick to stop before he bumped into him. Favian spun around and faced Rick, so close they were eye-to-eye. "Don't talk about it!" he said in a harsh whisper. "Don't even think about it. It's too awful!"

"But what—"

"Please!"

Rick suddenly understood. "That's what happens, isn't it? That's what happens to you if your energy runs out completely."

Favian flinched as if Rick had slapped him. "Don't! Stop!"

But Rick couldn't stop. He spoke his revelation as it came to him. "Your spirit gets trapped here. That's what'll happen to Mariel, too. And to me, too, if Kurodar and his bots get me."

Favian stared at him, the terror plain on his face. Ever so slightly, he nodded.

Rick and Favian—the human and the sprite—stared at each other in the purple glow with wide, frightened eyes.

"I will get us out of here," Rick whispered finally. "So help me, Favian. I will get us all out of here, or die trying."

"No!" Favian said quickly. "You can't die. You have to stop him: Kurodar. Whatever happens. He'll turn the whole world into a MindWar. You have to stop him, Rick."

And he was gone, flashing down the tunnel.

Rick followed reluctantly, afraid of being left behind. He found the spirit around a bend a few yards on. He was leaning wearily against the wall. The light from his hand was growing dim. His energy was clearly depleted. He just managed to gesture with his chin.

"There. There it is," he said.

Rick followed the gesture and, with an incredible burst of relief, he saw a circle of light in the distance. An opening in the earth. They had come to the end of the spider-snake's tunnel.

Rick could not wait to get out of this terrible place. Quickly, he checked the time on his palm. His stomach turned over. They'd been down here a long time, even longer than he'd thought. He watched as the lighted numbers ticked from 20:01 to 20:00 to 19:59.

"Oh no," he said. "It's really late. We'll never get back to the portal point."

"No, no, I thought of that," said Favian quickly. "There's one out there."

Rick let out a loud sigh of relief. "Thank God."

"It's just hard to reach, that's all."

"How hard?"

Favian didn't answer. He seemed too tired to answer.

"Well, we better haul it, then," Rick said.

He strode quickly toward the opening.

Favian called after him weakly. "Rick, wait, be careful . . ."

But Rick didn't slow down. He was so eager to get out of these tunnels. The darkness here—the stench—and the awful thing he had seen in the darkness—spurred him on even as the light—the beautiful light from the exit—poured over him and the delicious smell of fresh air reached him and drew him forward.

He heard Favian call out weakly behind him again, but he didn't hesitate. As he stepped beneath the exit, he put his foot directly into the dirt of the tunnel wall and reached up for the opening with both hands.

Grunting, he pulled himself up into the open air. The sweetness of that air—the brightness of the light—what a wild pleasure it was! He drew in a deep, deep breath, climbed to his feet, and looked around him.

He was standing on scarlet ground a few yards from a broad silver moat. Across the moat, Kurodar's black fortress loomed against the yellow sky. The fortress was enormous, dark and lowering, the crenellated walls running off to the left and the right for a great distance; the intermittent towers soaring into the orange mist above until they were almost out of sight. The great ominous front gate was drawn up and shut tight—and the way to it was blocked, in any case, by the moat, an expanse of silver running full around the fortress walls. The moat was made of the same mercury-like substance as the lake in the forest, but here it caught the darker colors of the walls and towers and so it seemed grimmer than the lake somehow, its shimmering movement more agitated and violent.

As Rick gazed into the silver depths of it, he saw a black reflection move over its surface. He raised his eyes to the sky.

The creatures of the air were circling high above him—so high—miles up, it seemed—he didn't think they would be able to see him, any more than the passengers in a jet plane could see the people on the earth below.

"Over there."

Favian was suddenly standing beside him. His face sagging with exhaustion, his shoulders hunched, he just managed to lift his hand to point across the moat.

Rick looked and was immensely reassured to see the floating purple diamond of the portal point on the far side of the water just beneath the fortress walls.

"All right," he said. "All right, that's good. I can just swim across, get back to Real Life through that portal, then come back here and try to get inside the fortress."

Favian shook his head weakly. "Too dangerous to swim. There are guardians of the water, too."

"Then how do we get to it?"

"I'm not sure."

"What?"

"I've never done it."

"You're kidding me!"

"I'm able to draw power from it, from this side of the moat, so I've never had to try to actually cross over," Favian said. When he saw Rick staring at him, he added defensively, "I told you it would be hard."

"You didn't tell me it would be impossible!" Rick said. "If I can't swim—and there's no time for me to get back to the last portal point—what am I supposed to do?"

"Well . . . Mariel said she would help us when we got here."

That gave Rick some hope. *If Mariel said she'd do something, she'll do it,* he thought. Still, he glanced nervously at the numbers ticking down on his palm. "She better show up fast," he said. "Where is she?"

"She travels by water. She should be here any minute."

"Okay," said Rick, trying to stay calm. "In the meantime, we'll just have to—"

But before he could finish, the creatures of the air attacked.

21. DRAGON SWORD

THEY WERE INCREDIBLY fast. Their shrill hawk-like screams—which had been inaudible when they were so far up in the sky—sounded in the distance one moment, and the next moment were filling the air, threatening, it seemed, to pierce Rick's eardrums.

He looked up toward the suddenly deafening noise and could not believe how close the nearest creature was—and what it was: a beast the size of a dinosaur with the horned leathery face of a desert reptile and webbed wings that nearly blotted out the sky. Its gray eyes were the size of cannonballs. Its mouth opened on a double row of bent and bloody teeth. The noise of its cry was like a weapon: the sound waves billowing from its mouth hit Rick like a hammer, stunning him, blasting every thought from his brain.

There was a horde of them. They were all around, swarming and circling in the yellow air above him. But even as Rick turned to see them, the nearest one plunged out of the tendrils of orange mist and dive-bombed straight toward him at full speed.

In that moment of confusion, dazed with noise and terror, Rick heard Favian cry out, "Run, Rick!"

But Rick was frozen to the spot.

Favian, exhausted as he was, flashed away like lightning—but Rick just stood there. Even with his legs in good shape, he could never run fast enough to escape that diving thing. Unable to think what to do, he stood rooted to the spot, gaping in helpless terror as the screaming sound enveloped him, as the diving dragon's mouth grew larger, nearer—opened wider and wider as the thing prepared to rip him in half with those shark-like teeth. In the instant before it struck, the only clear thought pounding at Rick's mind was: *I'm about to die!*

Then, just then, a wall of silver slashed like a shield across the narrowing gap between Rick and the diving dragon. The creature's enormous horned and lizardly head was turned aside by the force of the watery metal. It stopped the creature midflight. It threw him off course. The dragon swept past Rick like the great shadow of death—so close he felt its hot breath on him and the wind of its collapsing wings blew his hair back on his head.

The dragon fell. It hit the earth and skidded toward the moat, throwing up a spray of red dirt on either side of its huge body. Its impact shook the ground so violently Rick stumbled a step and went down on one knee.

As the creature of the air slithered around trying to right itself, Rick looked about him in a daze. *What just happened?* What had saved him?

He saw her. Mariel. She had risen from the moat as she had risen from the lake, her body forming itself out of the mercury-like substance as it rose like a wave, turbulent and shimmering, above the turbulent, shimmering surface.

Amazed by her sudden presence there, Rick remembered Favian's words: *She travels by water!*

Her lush, liquid form was turned to one side, and Rick saw that she had flung a curtain of her own substance between him and the onrushing dragon. That was the sheet of metal water that had turned aside the beast's attack. The liquid shield now dropped from the air and splashed down onto the red banks of the moat, splattering into droplets, which then slid and skittered like living creatures back into the main body of the moat.

At the same time, Mariel straightened, rising up stately—and beautiful, Rick noticed, even in her war-like mode.

"Rick," she said. She pronounced the single word so calmly that it seemed to snap Rick out of his bewilderment and draw him toward her.

He rose to his feet. At the same time, the fallen dragon thrashed itself upright. It bent its four pillar-like legs beneath its enormous body. Its tail lashed back and forth one time, the end of it coming within a yard of knocking Rick over. Then it flapped its leathery wings and leapt—and launched itself back into the air.

As it rose and banked, the tip of one wing scraped Rick's shoulder. It wasn't much of a blow, but it sent him spinning away from Mariel. He had to fight to stay upright, to regain his balance. At the same moment, there was another shriek. Another of the dragons plunged from the circling horde and dove toward him. Its scream instantly became a deafening weapon as its massive shape blotted out the world.

"Go to her, Rick!" Rick heard Favian shout. "Go to Mariel!"

Rick saw him. The sparkling spirit had fallen to his knees at the edge of the moat, to the right of Mariel. He was reaching out with both hands toward the floating purple diamond on the far side of the water, near the fortress walls. He was drawing energy out of the portal point and into himself. Rick could see the radiance pulsing out of the diamond and entering Favian's palms. He could see the spirit growing brighter as the diamond shrank away to a small point of purple light.

Don't destroy it, Rick thought. *I'm going to need that thing to get home, and soon!*

There was no time now to check the clock in his palm, but he could feel the seconds ticking away.

"Go to her!" Favian shouted again. "Now!"

Rick turned to run, glancing over his shoulder at the second dive-bombing dragon. He did not think he could reach Mariel before the creature struck him. And if he did reach her, he couldn't imagine what the water spirit could do to save him before the beast snapped him in half with a single bite.

But he tried it. He ran. He stretched his legs across the red ground toward where Mariel hovered above the silver water, her beauty and majesty part of the water, her form shimmering and reflecting the chaos around her as the water did. He ran—and the scream of the dragon enveloped him from behind. He felt its presence hurtling toward his back. He felt the wind of its wings. He felt the sound waves of its shriek pounding at him. He knew it was seconds away from catching him in its jaws.

And then Favian flashed to his side, his energy recharged. Rick saw him unleash a purple blast from his hand, just as he had in the woods against the spider-snake. That forest blast had knocked the spider-snake unconscious, but the creatures of the air were too massive, too powerful. All the same, when Favian's purple burst struck the charging dragon in the chest, it hit him hard. The dragon was stopped midflight, its long neck twisting in pain. Its four feet clawed at the air as it was hurled backward. Its wings folded, and it fell to the earth at a small distance, the impact shaking the ground again so that Rick was nearly toppled over as he ran.

But now Rick reached the moat. He stood beneath Mariel, gazing up at her. In the seconds before the next dragon's assault, a dozen impressions of the water woman crisscrossed his mind. He saw the quick-witted intelligence in her eyes. And the courage in the set of her mouth. And that look on her face again that reminded him of his father's look of faith, determined faith. He felt she was practically willing him to be the rescuer she and Favian needed, the hero they were waiting for.

The idea made Rick feel weak inside. He had been a hero once. He had walked around the school grounds with a swagger. He had been Rick Dial, the quarterback, Number 12. But those days were over. They seemed to have happened a million years ago, and he did not know how to bring that swagger back.

All this flashed through his mind in an instant, less a

thought than a half-formed confusion of feelings—yearning, doubt, weakness, the fear that he would disappoint her.

Then the screams of the dragons above him filled the yellow air, erasing everything else—everything but the sight of Mariel rising majestically out of the silver moat before him, hovering in front of the black shape of the massive fortress at her back.

"Lift your sword, Rick," she told him.

Rick heard the strain in her voice. He saw the weariness etched into her majestic features. He knew that each effort that she—and that Favian—made on his behalf was costing them energy, causing them to fade. He remembered the poor dead-and-yet-not-dead creature suffering in the tunnel . . . How long before Favian and Mariel used themselves up for his sake and became things like that?

There was another ear-piercing shriek from the sky.

"Lift up your sword!" Mariel thundered at him again. It was not a request.

Rick forced himself not to look up at the dragons, to keep his eyes on her. He grasped the copper hilt of his sword, drew it from his belt, and lifted it into the air before the silver woman rising from the moat. Fear and discouragement filled him at the sight of that pitted, rusted blade. Mariel had told him that his spirit would make the sword stronger, but he didn't have enough spirit for this. Killing the already wounded spider-snake was one thing. But if he tried to hit one of these flying monsters with this poor excuse for a blade, it would shatter into pieces.

The attacking dragons cried out again. It took all Rick's courage to stand there holding up his sword, not to turn and look, not to bolt and run.

Mariel lifted her arms, crossed them before her so that the V of her forearms framed her queenly face. Then, in a quick, slashing motion, she brought both arms down together, flinging them out to her sides. The movement hurled a gout of silver water from her body. The water splashed over Rick as he stood before her with his sword upraised. He expected the impact of the mercury-like stuff to knock him back, but instead it draped itself over him gently. It covered his body, covered his sword—and clung to them, and coated them with silver.

Now, Rick saw with wonder, the sword was no longer rusted iron but shining steel, the last droplets falling from the blade as it hardened in his hand. The weapon flashed in the sourceless light from the yellow sky. And he flashed, too: his body. Like the sword, his chest and legs and arms were now sheathed in metal. He was suddenly clothed in shining armor like one of those knights in the old King Arthur stories his father had read to him when he was a child.

He gaped at his sword, at himself . . . at his new self . . . so like one of those heroic knights of old, he somehow couldn't help but feel a little bit braver than he'd felt a second ago. A lot braver, actually. It was as if Mariel had clothed him not only in armor but in courage. Suddenly he felt as strong as . . . well, as his old self—stronger!

"It's all on you now," said Mariel in a weak, hollow, fading echo of a voice. "I can't do any more." Even as she spoke, she was gone, tumbling wearily from the air and splashing back into the flat surface of the moat from whence she'd come.

Rick saw her go, and ached at his core. He understood that it was *her* strength, *her* courage, her very substance she had given him.

It's all on you now.

He looked at his now-gleaming sword, his gleaming armor.

He thought, *Well, then, I have to try . . .*

But the words were blasted from his mind as the air was shredded by another head-splitting shriek.

Once again, the creatures of the air were upon him.

22. DRAGON SKIES

THERE WERE TWO of them this time. Rick swiveled to face them just as the pair swooped out of the dragon swarm and dove. The lead beast came for Favian. The sparkling spirit was on his knees, drained again by the energy blast he'd used to save Rick. In another instant, the dragon was on top of him, shrieking out of the sky with its huge gray eyes glaring and its leathery jaws jacked wide. Its double rows of crooked, blood-drenched teeth were about to encircle Favian's head, about to snap shut on top of him.

Favian lifted his eyes. He looked so weary, it seemed he didn't have enough strength to move, that he was just waiting there, waiting to be devoured.

But just as the giant creature beat its wings one more time to propel itself into the final attack, Favian flashed away in a twinkling. The dragon's jaws clamped together on empty air. It had only just enough time to recover before it smashed face-first into the earth. Straightening its neck, it leveled out, gliding inches over the red ground toward the moat. Another flap of its giant bat-like wings and it lifted up again, reflected in the silver water. Incredible grace for such an enormous being! Another flap of the wings and another, and it lifted its face skyward and rose.

All that took a moment and in that same moment, the second dragon came shrieking down at Rick.

It came at him at high speed. The sound waves of its scream pounded against the armor sheathing Rick's body. Its jaws spread to engulf him, dripping drool.

And Rick, his heart pounding wildly, suddenly knew what he had to do.

It was a mad idea, but it came to him so clearly that he knew somehow it was right—his only chance. It was as if his armor spoke the words into his mind, as if his sword sent the wild courage into his heart. He realized: it was Mariel, her spirit, urging him to this wild gamble for survival.

Every instinct in his body was telling him to run. Watching that horned head come at him—that open mouth—those double teeth shrieking his way—the urge to bolt was almost overwhelming.

But he drew courage from his armor, from his sword, from Mariel—and he stood his ground. This was right, he knew it. These beasts were fast—fast and big—with long necks that gave them a lot of reach and flexibility. They were built to hunt from the air and to snap their prey off the surface of the earth no matter how it tried to escape them. Maybe Favian could flash out of their way before they grabbed him, but it was already too late for Rick to escape.

So he forced himself to stand another second—and another. The beast screamed toward him. Rick drew a deep breath. He gripped his sword in both hands. His teeth clamped together with determination as he watched the drooling jaws of the dragon fill his field of vision. His whole head ached as the dragon's shriek hammered at his breastplate, making his body thrum. Defying the wild urge of his growing panic, he waited . . . waited . . .

Now the hot, rancid breath of the flying creature enveloped him. Now its jaws began to close over him. Now the beast's eyes flashed with eagerness and hunger.

And Rick thought, *Do it!*

At the last moment before the dragon devoured him, he spun out of its way.

It was a move he'd pulled at least a dozen times as a quarterback. Some tackler would worm his way through the blockers and storm forward to sack him in the backfield for a loss of yards. Just at the last moment, Rick would spin out of the tackler's grasp, turn in a full circle to get free, and run for daylight or hurl a pass to the open man. He spun like that now: pushed off his right foot, pivoted on his left, dodging out of the creature's jaws just before they snapped shut. His body turned in a complete circle. The sword, gripped in his two hands, dragged for a second behind the turn. Then he used all the power of his momentum to bring the blade swinging round after him. And he struck.

The sharp, gleaming edge of the sword hit the dive-bombing beast smack behind the ear. Rick felt the impact go ringing up his arms into his shoulders. The dragon let out an unholy cry of agony. It thrashed and twisted, rolling over in midair as it sailed past him.

Some part of it—its wing probably—Rick wasn't sure—

struck him on the side and sent him staggering backward. He fell, losing his grip on the sword. And the dragon fell, smashing headfirst into the earth.

Rick's body bounced up and down as the ground rumbled beneath the dragon's fall. Rick sat up, stunned by the blow he'd received.

And something else happened just then—something that was somehow even more frightening than the battle at hand. There was a sort of static *fritz* all around him. The whole scene—the dragons, the moat, the fortress, the red earth under the yellow sky—seemed to waver and digitalize, reality dissolving with a sickening shiver.

Instinctively, Rick looked at his palm. He had only four minutes and five seconds left before he had to get out, back to the real world. Miss Ferris had warned him: whatever else he did, don't stay too long or his brain would disintegrate. It was starting to happen, just as she'd said. He had to get to that portal point—now.

Still stunned by the blow he'd received, he moved by sheer willpower. He forced himself to his feet, looking at the fallen dragon.

The dragon was also dazed. It lay on its side, not quite unconscious, not quite able to stand. The blow from Rick's sword had opened a gash in its neck, and blood the color of mucus was gurgling down over its scaly hide.

Rick looked around him. He saw his sword lying on the red earth. He scooped it up by the hilt and slipped the blade quickly into a leather scabbard built into the side of his breastplate. With his head still ringing, his mind still foggy, he raced across the ground toward the fallen creature of the air.

He reached it. He seized it round its bleeding neck. And, without stopping to think, he jumped on top of it.

He knew this was what he was supposed to do. His only chance to stay alive. He could not fight off all these monsters. And without Mariel's help, he couldn't swim across the guarded moat. But if he could commandeer one of the dragons . . . if he could mount it, ride it into the sky . . . if he could guide it low over the water, then jump down . . . well, he might be able to land near the portal point on the other side of the moat before his time ran out.

He might. It seemed an insane plan even to him. But it was the only plan he had. He had to try it.

Again, he experienced that sickening static, that horrifying digitalization of the scenery around him. It was over in a second, but he knew it would return again and again as his time ran down and his mind went to pieces.

He thought of the living-dead creature trapped in the spider-snake's tunnel.

This had to work. It had to.

The dragon's neck was the size of a small tree trunk, yet it was twisting and alive like a gigantic snake. Its leathery skin was so rough it scraped the flesh off his hands as he desperately tried to wrap his arms around it. Its strength was such that when it whipped its head and writhed and roared, Rick felt himself flung back and forth on the creature's back like a limp rag doll. He thought the thing could easily toss him off and send him tumbling head over heels through the air.

And that was before the dragon lifted off the ground.

Because now, the dragon's anger at having Rick on its neck brought it out of its daze. With amazing speed for such a monstrosity, it rolled onto its feet, crouched, and gave a flap of its enormous wings and leapt.

Rick could not help but give a shout of fear and surprise as the creature rose swiftly into the air, carrying him with it. He clung to the twisting neck for dear life. Within seconds, the red earth was far below him. The moat became a silver strip in the downward distance. Even the pinnacles of the fortress towers fell away beneath him as the furious dragon flapped its wings again and then again, and pulsed up into the yellow sky.

At first, Rick was just too scared of falling to think at all. He hugged the beast's rough neck with all his might as the chill orange mist of the upper atmosphere began to swirl around him. He just barely dared to glance down and see the fortress growing smaller and smaller as the dragon rose and rose.

Then—*fritz!* Another nauseating dissolution of the world.

And at the same moment, the creature let out its ear-splitting, high-pitched scream and thrashed its head back and forth, trying to dislodge the unwanted rider.

Sheer terror snapped Rick back to alertness. He shouted again as his feet flew out to the side. His cries became increasingly high-pitched with panic as he nearly lost his grip on the dragon's neck, nearly went plummeting to his death. He only barely managed to hang on until the beast grew tired of fighting him. Then he scrambled over the thing's neck again and got a better grip on it with both arms and legs.

He lay there panting, his cheek pressed hard against the creature's scaly skin. He could hardly bear to look through the orange mist at the fortress and moat and ground so far below. He was almost too afraid to move at all.

But he had to. He dared to let go of the creature's neck with one hand just long enough to check the time: 2:47 left. He had to do this fast. He had to try to direct the dragon across the moat, try to get it to land near the fortress. He had to get out of here before his mind dissolved.

Rick gritted his teeth. He gave a grunt and, using all the strength of his arms, wrenched the dragon's head to the side, trying to direct him across the water far below.

To his surprise, the dragon responded instantly. Its whole body turned to follow its head. It banked, tilted—and dove, sending Rick's stomach up into his throat as man and beast circled down and down together toward the earth.

Rick dared to peek out around the dragon's neck. His mouth opened, his eyes widened in amazement.

It's working! he thought.

It was! The fortress was growing bigger and bigger as the dragon, following its head, circled down and down. And yes, as Rick adjusted his grip, as he adjusted the angle of the dragon's neck, they began to cross the moat. The silver water was now rippling directly below them, throwing their huge reflection back up toward them.

Another fizzle of static—another frightening interruption

of the reality of the Realm—told Rick he had to hurry. But all he could do was keep the pressure upon the dragon's neck, keep it turning in slow, tight, descending circles. Now he could make out the purple light of the portal point beneath the fortress. He could see the floating diamond gleaming brighter and brighter as it regained the energy Favian had taken from it. As much as his stomach felt hollowed with nausea, his heart began to rise and pound with excitement as he thought he just might be able to pull this off.

Then, suddenly, something flashed by him—so close he heard the whisper of its passing, felt the wind of it on his cheek.

What was that?

Had it been another burst of static? Another sign that his time was running out?

No. It was a projectile of some sort. Another went by him, and then another.

Arrows!

Someone was firing arrows at him! One, then more, then half a dozen of them went spitting past.

Rick shifted to peek around the dragon's neck again, the wind of descent rushing over his face. The beast had circled even lower now. The fortress was right below him.

And he saw that there were men—what looked like men—some sort of guards—rushing onto the fortress ramparts. As the dragon took another descending turn, Rick saw the legions spreading out to line the walls. Every moment, there were more and more of them. And all of them held longbows in their hands. One or two of them stopped to let off a wild shot, the arrows rocketing into the sky, flying wide of Rick where he sat.

But now, another guard—or something—some red and hellish creature with wings—rose off the surface of the walls to hover over the others, calling them to order. The guards immediately became more disciplined. Lined up along the walls, they raised their bows in a unified motion, ready to let fly a single concentrated volley of death.

They released their bowstrings in unison. Rick saw a dense black cloud of arrows soaring up toward him. He ducked behind the dragon's neck as a few arrows flashed by harmlessly on either side.

Then the beast let out a tremendous and hideous cry of agony as the bulk of the arrows struck. Rick felt the jolts as the projectiles' points thudded into the creature's belly. He held on desperately as the wounded beast bucked and thrashed in his arms.

The dragon's gliding descent faltered. It fizzed with lines of purple lightning. Rick knew what that meant: it was dying. Sure enough, it could thrash its wings only weakly now, fighting to stay aloft.

Below, obeying the shouts of their winged and terrible leader—shouts audible even to Rick—the guards had reloaded their bows. They fired again. More arrows struck the beast, burying their deadly points into its neck and body.

The dragon let out another woeful cry. In its death agony, its body snapped like a whip, nearly throwing Rick away. More electric lines of purple energy bolted through it so that Rick felt the thing becoming insubstantial in his grasp. Its wings sagged weakly.

And giving one more dying groan, the dragon plunged toward the earth, carrying Rick down with it.

23. DARK FALL

RICK AND THE dragon fell and fell. The dark walls and towers of the fortress swept up at Rick's side as he sped down past them. The silver moat-water flashed and the red earth screamed up to meet him. Rick held on desperately to the dragon's neck, waiting for the impact he felt certain would kill him.

It was a bad way to die—and even worse than death was his failure. His heart was black with failure as he fell. What had he ever done but fail? He had failed to fulfill his athletic promise. Failed to become the man of the house when his father had disappeared. And now he had failed in his mission into the Realm . . . failed to rescue Favian and Mariel . . . failed utterly.

The long fall went on and on. The backwash of wind grew stronger as the dragon tumbled faster. Rick felt the creature's neck grow flaccid and insubstantial in his grasp as the beast's lifeblood drained out through its arrow wounds. Only at the last moment did the dragon seem to understand that this was the end for it. Only then did it make one last attempt to save itself. Letting out a groan, it flapped its wings a final time. It was a weak effort, but it did seem to slow the downward plunge a little.

Then the earth rushed up and the crash came with a noise like thunder. The next thing Rick knew, he was flying helplessly through the air.

He could not believe what happened next. He hit the ground flat on his back. He hit hard—it made his bones ache. But—and this was what shocked him—he was still alive! Not just alive, but fully conscious. The dragon's great body underneath him had absorbed most of the impact. Rick was hurled off the beast—and he smacked into the ground at speed—but he'd fallen harder on the football field. He was jarred by the impact, but unharmed.

Fresh hope flooded through him and brought him leaping to his feet. There was chaos on every side of him. He saw his dragon, the creature of the air—dead on impact—dissolving into sparking purple energy before it vanished with a flash. He saw the swarm of other dragons circling and screaming in the sky above him. Saw the archers on the fortress walls high overhead, leaning over to direct their bows down at him. He saw, too, that the front gate of the fortress was rattling open and more soldiers were pouring out of the building onto the red field, charging after him.

And he saw the floating purple diamond of the portal point glowing in the air about twenty yards away.

Then it was all gone—all digitalized, dissolving into static. The fizzing nothingness went on for a long second, frighteningly long. Rick knew he was out of time. His mind was disintegrating and taking the Realm with it. For an instant, he felt he was on the very edge of existence.

But in the next moment, the Realm snapped back into clarity. The static vanished. Rick wasn't gone quite yet.

He glanced reflexively at his palm. Forty-nine seconds left. No time to think. No time to do anything but run—run toward the purple glow of the portal point.

He took off. Stretching his legs as if heading for a touchdown, he dashed across the front yard of the fortress. Quick deadly whispers filled his ears as a fresh volley of arrows rained down on him from the ramparts, the projectiles jabbing into the earth to his left and right. Somewhere in the sky above him, the dragons screamed as they spotted him. One sharp cry grew quickly louder as a creature of the air launched itself into a diving attack.

But the diamond of the portal point was right in front of him. He was almost there.

I'm going to make it!

Then one of the guards—the first to have raced out through the fortress gate—reached him. It stepped into his path, blocking his way.

What a monster it was! It stood on two legs, as tall as Rick. It was clothed in red and silver armor like a man, but it was not a man, not at all. It had an extended face something like the face of a crocodile. It had a long lizardly tail like a croc's tail. It had sharp teeth and bloodshot yellow eyes. And it held a long, gleaming sword in its wickedly clawed hands.

Rick grabbed the hilt of his own sword and drew it from its scabbard quickly. The crocodile guard raised its weapon and swung. Its blade and Rick's clashed together with a singing sound. Rick drew his weapon back to strike again.

Then the static—and nothingness. Rick froze, blinked, dazed. Clarity returned—but it was too late.

The guard had already unleashed another strike. Rick tried to dodge it, but the blade hit his armor on the shoulder—and struck through to bite into his flesh. Rick screamed in pain. In an instinctive spasm of self-defense, he reeled away, jabbing his sword point in the direction of the guard. The point struck the lizard-man on his breastplate, driving him back a step. There was red pain again as the guard's blade was torn out of Rick's shoulder.

Rick's head swam with agony. He felt his blood pumping out of him. He felt himself fading into unconsciousness. The whole world was crisscrossed with lines of purple energy. It was dissolving into nothingness. *He* was dissolving . . .

But he turned and saw the portal point again, looming large, right beside him. He plunged into it headfirst. He willed his wounded spirit down a snaking cylinder of white light.

There was a liquid moment of un-being.

Then Rick woke up shrieking in mindless terror! He was trapped in a glass box the size of a coffin! Wrapped in some sort of metallic foil that gripped him tightly, that wouldn't let him go!

He didn't know where he was. There was nothing inside him but pain and confusion and fear. He went on screaming even as the lid of the box opened with an electric buzz.

Hands were grabbing at him. He fought them off wildly, screaming and screaming. Voices were shouting above him.

"Get him out of there!"

"Get a gurney!"

"Alert the infirmary!"

Rick's eyes were wide and white with horror. He kept screaming, "Get off me! Get off me!"

Strong hands pushed his hands away and got a grip on his arms. He was dragged out of the box.

"My legs!" he shouted as he was dragged to his feet and a jolt of pain went through the lower half of him.

"It's all right, you're all right, Rick!" said a voice—a woman.

He turned and saw her. A smallish person in a dark suit. A serious face with short black hair. Who was she? A stranger. He didn't recognize her.

Rick recoiled in fear from her even as the large block-headed man beside him tried to keep hold of him, even as the pain in his legs threatened to overwhelm him.

"Who are you?" Rick shouted at the woman. "Where am I?"

"It's me. Miss Ferris! You're at the MindWar Project HQ!" The woman spoke loudly but with determination. "You're back! You're fine!"

Miss Ferris? The MindWar Project? Trying to take in the meaning of her words, Rick looked wildly around him. He saw monitors on the walls. Staring faces. His arm was covered in blood. There was a gash in his shoulder and the blood was coursing out of it.

"You're all right! You'll be all right!" the woman said. Then she shouted, "Where's that gurney?"

Rick stared at her. Stared at the man holding him.

"Who am I?" he asked them. He could not remember. He could not remember anything.

The woman's head whipped back toward him. He saw a flash of something in her eyes—something like fear. "Rick?" she said. "You're Rick! You're Rick Dial! You remember. Say you remember!"

He heard someone nearby mutter: "We've lost him. His mind is gone."

Then Rick's eyes rolled up in his head, and the room went dark. His agonized legs folded under him. He sank down toward the floor.

Darkness everywhere.

LEVEL FIVE:
THE MISSING MAN

24. AUTO ASSAULT

THEY CAME FOR the Traveler just before dawn.

Victor One was sitting with him inside the cabin. The big, rangy bodyguard was squeezed into a chair built, he thought, for a delicate old grandma about one-third his size. He was sipping coffee out of a cup that looked like it was meant for a dollhouse. Plus it was lousy coffee, black as sin and almost as sour.

Still, it had been kind of the Traveler to let him come in and warm himself. It was cold on the hilltop at this hour.

"Any idea when they'll be here?" the Traveler asked him. The small, bald scientist was seated at his desk, his laptop and his packed bag on the floor by his feet. He had his own coffee cup lifted to his lips. The steam fogged the lenses of his glasses so that his thoughtful, dreamy eyes disappeared behind them. It looked pretty silly to Victor One, but the Traveler didn't seem to mind being blinded like that.

Victor One shook his head. "No way to know. No phones. No Wi-Fi. No commo at all. That was the whole point of this place, I guess. But it does make it hard to find out what's going on, doesn't it? Shouldn't be too long now—that's my guess."

The Traveler set his cup in the saucer, set cup and saucer

down on the desk beside the photo of his family and the cross that until last night had decorated the wall. Victor One found it touching that the Traveler had left these—the picture and the cross—out of his bag until the last minute. It was as if the scientist couldn't bear to be without them even for a few hours.

"Guess you're pretty eager to see your people again, huh, Doc," said the bodyguard.

The Traveler nodded absentmindedly, his eyes meditative and far away. "There's a verse in the Bible I particularly like," he said. "'Do not worry about tomorrow, for tomorrow will worry about itself. Sufficient unto the day is the evil thereof.'"

Victor One nodded. He remembered the passage, part of a hymn he'd always liked. "'Seek ye first the kingdom of God and His righteousness; and all these things shall be added to you . . .'"

"What I find fascinating about that advice—the advice not to worry about tomorrow"—the Traveler spoke in a mild, speculative tone, as if he were talking about a mathematical problem or a dissected frog—"is how clearly wise it is and yet how nearly impossible it is to follow!"

Victor One laughed, nodding into his lousy coffee. "It is a tough one, isn't it? You think God is just messing with us?"

The Traveler laughed back. "Somehow I doubt it." He pulled his misted glasses off and wiped them clean on his sweater. His laughter subsided, and the weariness was plain on his face. "I wanted to keep them safe—my family," he said. "That was the whole point of all this." He gestured at the cabin.

"To be where no one could find me. Where no one could give me away. I thought it was the best way to protect them. But I seem to have done just the opposite."

Victor One tried to think of something to say to that. "It's just not a safe world, Doc," he said finally. "We do the best we can . . ."

But the Traveler shook his head, gazing sadly into the middle distance. "I trusted Leila . . ."

Victor One didn't want to get into *that* at all. He had overheard part of the argument between the Traveler and Leila Kent, but he wasn't sure how much he was supposed to know. Officially, Leila was Victor One's boss on this mission, and he didn't want to say anything that would get him in trouble with her. To give himself time to figure out how to respond, he drained his cup. *Man,* he thought, *that is one bad cup of coffee.* Then, when he lowered the cup, he said, "I'm sure Miss Kent wouldn't do anything to hurt you, Doc. Not on purpose, anyway."

"Are you?" said the Traveler. "Are you really sure?"

"Oh yeah. Oh yeah, definitely. I mean, anyone can see how she feels about you . . ." The minute the words came out of his mouth, Victor One regretted them. He thought it was so obvious that Leila Kent was in love with the Traveler that for a moment, he hadn't considered the idea that a smart guy like the Traveler wouldn't have noticed. But, of course, the Traveler was so absentminded, his mind so occupied with his work and his God and his family, that he hadn't noticed Leila Kent's feelings at all. Until the moment Victor One opened his big mouth, he had had no idea.

He stared at the bodyguard. "Leila? How she feels about me? What do you mean?"

Wishing he could stuff the words right back into his stupid piehole, Victor One stammered, "Well, you know, I'm just . . . just looking at her you can see . . . I'm just saying it's kind of obvious . . ."

"Are you talking about romantic feelings?" said the incredulous Traveler. "But all that's been over between us for a long time!"

"Uh . . . ," responded Victor One.

He was rescued by the sound of footsteps on the leaves outside. Quickly, he set his grandma cup aside and jumped to his feet.

"Sounds like they're on their way," he said.

Just to be on the safe side, he put his hand on the holster of his gun as he moved to the dark window. But there was no reason to expect trouble in this isolated place.

Sure enough, he looked outside and saw the flashlights coming—and then there they were: Alpha Twelve and Bravo Niner escorting Leila Kent up over the hill.

Victor One opened the door for them. The Traveler got clumsily to his feet as Leila Kent stepped over the threshold. Victor One was amused to see that the Traveler's cheeks turned bright red as he faced the elegant woman with her sleek clothes and golden hair. Now that the Traveler knew the truth, he could barely meet Leila Kent's eyes. If Victor One could have slapped himself in the face, he would've.

"We have to move," said Leila briskly. "Quickly. Now."

A moment later, as the sky began to lighten with sunrise, they were on their way, Leila Kent and the Traveler hurrying down the hillside together, while the three bodyguards surrounded them, their hands on their weapons, their eyes scanning the trees in the new gray dawn.

A large black Mercedes was waiting for them on the dirt road at the bottom of the slope. The bodyguards escorted their two charges into the backseat. Then Bravo Niner slid in behind the wheel and Victor One got in the passenger seat beside him.

Alpha Twelve shut the rear door on Leila and the Traveler. He would stay behind on the mountaintop, waiting for the team that would come up to disassemble the cabin and remove every trace that the Traveler had ever been there.

A moment more, and they were rolling, the leaves and gravel crunching under the tires as they accelerated quickly over the forest path, heading for the road.

In a few minutes, they were clear of the trees and winding down the mountain. The road was perilously narrow; the drop over the side was perilously steep. Though the sky was growing lighter by the minute, it was still dark down here in the shadows of the towering pines. Victor One looked out the windshield. Saw the Mercedes' headlights picking out a few yards of twining pavement as it rolled ahead. He glanced out his window and saw the frail, wooden railing flashing by him, the cliff beyond.

"You're going awfully fast for this road," he said to the driver.

Bravo Niner was dark and stringy, like a piece of beef jerky.

He had hard eyes, and a permanent sneer on his mouth. He was a tough guy, Victor One knew, and had driven Humvees through some of the most battle-hot cities in the world.

"We'll be okay," he said, with a small smile at the corner of his mouth.

But now Victor One heard the Traveler in the backseat. "Are we expecting trouble?" he asked Leila Kent.

"We're just being careful," she told him. "The faster we move, the less chance anyone will catch up to us. We're eager to get you to the new compound and out of harm's way."

After that, they raced on in silence. Victor One could practically feel the tension between the two passengers in back of him. Maybe he was just imagining it, but he didn't think so. He pretended to check the rear window for following cars—and looked them over. He saw Leila Kent staring straight ahead, and the Traveler stealing sidelong glances at her. He was probably curious to see these signs of romantic attachment Victor One had stupidly told him about.

After a while, he heard Leila Kent say quietly behind him, "This is almost over, Traveler. You'll be with your family very soon." To Victor One, she sounded sad about it, but again, that might have been his imagination.

Just then, headlights appeared on the road ahead of them.

"Someone coming," murmured Bravo Niner, working the wheel.

Victor One drew a breath, growing tense.

Behind him, Leila Kent said, "It's a public road. There's going to be some traffic. Just keep driving."

Bravo Niner obeyed, but Victor One discreetly drew the pistol from underneath his arm. He kept his eye on the windshield, sitting very still as the headlights of the oncoming car grew bigger and bigger, brighter and brighter. There was enough daylight now to see that it was a red BMW. It came toward them on the far side of the narrow two-lane. It was about to pass by.

But it didn't pass.

Suddenly, the Beamer swerved in front of them. Its tires screeched as it braked to a halt before it could crash through the railing and go flying off the side of the mountain. It lay across the road now, cutting off the way.

The tires of the Mercedes let out an answering screech as Bravo Niner reacted. He hit the brakes hard and spun the wheel to the left. The Mercedes turned to the side and stopped, just before it struck the other car broadside. For a moment, it sat parallel to the Beamer. Victor One looked out and saw men—four men—pouring out of the Beamer's doors. All of them were carrying machine guns.

Bravo Niner threw the Mercedes into reverse. Victor One swung around to scream into the backseat. "Get your heads down, both of you!"

But the Traveler didn't duck. Instead, he reached out and grabbed Leila by the back of the neck. He pulled her down and toward him so that her head went beneath the level of the windshield. Then he bent his body protectively over hers.

Right, thought Victor One. *He would.*

At the same time, the Mercedes straightened out and

started to back up fast—and the men with machine guns opened fire.

Leila let out a scream, muffled by the Traveler's body. Starbursts appeared on the Mercedes' windshield as the bullets struck the reinforced glass. As the Mercedes kept careening backward, Victor One ducked his head, buzzed down the window, then popped up and leaned out, firing off several rounds in answer to the barrage.

"Stay down, stay down!" Bravo Niner shouted. He stopped the car short, smacked it into gear, and hit the gas.

The Mercedes shot forward, straight into the hail of bullets from the machine guns. Victor One heard Leila scream again. Then a starburst appeared on the windshield and his arm flared with searing pain.

"I'm hit!" he shouted, falling back against the seat.

He felt the Mercedes swerve to avoid the Beamer in its path.

Then they were past the ambush. They were speeding down the winding road again. There were a few final shots as the gunmen tried to stop them. Then the sound of gunfire fell away completely.

Victor One held his arm, grimacing with pain. He turned to look at the passengers.

"You all right back there?"

Slowly, carefully, the Traveler sat up. Leila sat up beside him. They looked over their shoulders out the rear window to see if they were being chased, and Victor One looked, too. The attackers and their car were already out of sight around a bend.

Victor One faced front. He saw dawn lighting the sky ahead. Good thing, too: both the Mercedes' headlights had been shot out.

"Will they come after us?" asked Leila Kent, her voice trembling.

"They can try," said Bravo Niner. "But it won't do them much good. I can outrace them in this baby easy."

As if to prove it, he kept his foot down hard on the gas pedal, twisting the wheel this way and that as the Mercedes rocketed around one narrow curve after another.

The Traveler spoke now—and Victor One was impressed by his calm, steady voice. He sounded like a man who got shot at every day.

"You said you were hit," he said to Victor One. "Is it bad? We have to get you medical attention."

Victor One was already examining the tear in his windbreaker and his sleeve, and the hole in the seat behind him. "No, I'm good," he said. "It just burned me as it went past. There's nothing in me. I'll be fine."

"Soon as we're down within cell range, we've got to let MindWar know we're heading for B Site," said Leila Kent.

"Better be careful who you tell," said Victor One.

"What do you mean? That's ridiculous . . . ," Leila Kent began to say, but her voice faltered as the Mercedes' tires let out another screech and the car took yet another curve at high speed. When it steadied, she continued, "We haven't sent out a single electronic communication in months. There's no way Kurodar could have used the Realm to intercept any intel."

Victor One nodded. "That's right," he said. "Which means someone must have told him."

"What are you saying?" said Leila Kent.

Victor One was about to answer her, but the Traveler had already figured it out.

"It means someone in the MindWar Project is working for the enemy," he said. "Someone very high up. Mars. Miss Ferris. One of us."

Leila Kent could only turn and stare at him as the car continued racing through the day's first light.

"Someone can't be trusted," said the Traveler.

25. MARS

IMAGES FLASHED THROUGH Rick's mind as he swam in and out of consciousness. The ceiling tiles passing overhead as he lay on a gurney rolling through white halls . . . Doors, endless doors . . . Faces leaning over him. Voices shouting . . .

Have we lost him?

Stop the bleeding!

We've got to download his memory before it fades!

The bleeding first!

Tell me we haven't lost him!

He's still with us . . .

Thank God, thank God.

He was still with them, yes. He remembered who he was now, too. It came back to him in stages.

I'm Rick. Rick Dial . . .

That was his name, anyway. But who was Rick Dial?

Ceiling tiles . . . Frantic faces . . . He swam in and out of consciousness.

Number 12. Rick Dial was Number 12. He was a quarterback. No. He was a cripple with ruined legs. No. He was a MindWarrior of the Realm . . . His dragon was falling and falling out of the sky . . . He had failed . . . failed at everything . . .

What are you doing?

The gurney had stopped. A closed door. Miss Ferris was barking in that hard, weirdly emotionless voice.

Not through there . . .

I thought they said he was . . .

That door is never to be opened without my express permission! Ever! Do you understand?

On they went. Into a room. Monitors. Faces. Someone attaching electrodes to his temples. Someone cutting off his T-shirt with a knife. Hands gently bathing the wound in his shoulder. Hurt . . . it hurt. Miss Ferris's face was hovering over him. Strange . . . her blue eyes looked almost gentle . . . Not like her. Rick thought he must be dreaming.

He swam in and out of consciousness.

He thought he saw Miss Ferris standing at the foot of his bed. Was he awake? Was he dreaming? He wasn't sure. There was Commander Jonathan Mars—or was it the hologram of Commander Mars? It was the hologram, yes: a weirdly illuminated figure in the darkness. He was talking quietly and Miss Ferris . . . had to be a hallucination because Miss Ferris was weeping. She had her head bowed. Her fingers were pinching the bridge of her nose. Her shoulders shook and tears poured from her eyes, ran over her hands, and dripped to the floor.

Mars watched her with the crags of his face pulled down in that fixed frown of his, his bushy silver eyebrows knitted together.

"You can't let yourself care this much, Barbara," he told her.

She looked up at him, her damp eyes flashing and furious. "Don't you dare tell me that!" she said.

"You know what's at stake. Everything. The country could go up in smoke in an instant."

"You can't send him back in there so soon. It's inhuman."

"He knew the dangers—"

"He's eighteen years old! He's hardly more than a boy! He's too young to understand what will happen to him, what it would be like if . . ." Her voice broke. She looked down again, the tears spilling off her cheeks. Rick knew he had to be dreaming. It was impossible that Miss Ferris could have so much emotion in her. "I couldn't stand it if we lost another one," she said.

The scene—dream—hallucination—whatever it was—faded away. The next time Rick was aware of anything, he was alone, staring up through the darkness at the ceiling.

He remembered now. The Realm. The fortress. Mariel. Favian. Falling from the sky on the back of the dragon.

I've failed at everything . . .

He lay there for a long time, thinking about that. His family—broken. His body—crushed. His football career—over. And he had nearly died in the Realm . . .

He felt something changing inside him. Something growing harder. Tougher. A fever of impatience rising into a fire of anger . . .

As full consciousness came to him, he sat up in bed. He sucked in a sharp breath through his teeth as the pain struck him. There was pain everywhere. His head was pounding. His shoulder throbbed. His legs felt as if they were being stuck full of pins.

Where was he?

He looked down at himself, touching himself to make sure this was real now, not a dream. He was wearing nothing but sweatpants, no shirt. There was a bandage wrapped around his left shoulder.

Mariel! Favian! They're going to die in there. I've got to get them out!

He looked around the room. A bare, windowless cell. No lamps. No furniture. Just the bed. It would have been pitch–black in there but for the light seeping in around the edges of the door.

Was the door locked? Was he a prisoner here? Where were his crutches? How was he supposed to get out of bed? Was anyone near enough to hear his voice if he shouted?

He tried it: "Hey! Hey! Is anybody there? Where am I? Hey!"

He listened, hoping to hear footsteps running to find him. Nothing. He stared at the door.

"Hey!" he shouted.

"It's all right, Rick."

Rick was so startled, he nearly jumped right off the mattress. There, out of nowhere, was Commander Mars: his hologram, at least, glowing in the shadowy darkness!

"Mars," Rick snarled. The man who had gotten him into this. The man in charge. "Where am I? What's going on?"

"Just take it easy," said Mars—coming from him, it sounded

like a command. "You were wounded in the Realm. You've been taken to our medical wing to recover. You're going to be fine."

Rick drew a breath, trying to keep his impatience—his anger—under control. There were so many questions he wanted to ask this guy, he didn't know where to begin. He touched the bandage on his arm. He remembered the sword fight.

"Wounded," he muttered, trying to get it all straight in his head. "By a crocodile. A man with a crocodile head. With a sword. Crazy."

But Commander Mars didn't seem to think it was crazy. He merely nodded. "We've scanned your memory. We know what happened."

"That makes one of us," said Rick, still fighting off his lingering grogginess. "Who were they? Those alligator guys . . ."

"Security bots. Kurodar has brought in a man—an actual human being—named Reza, to run them. When you climbed on the dragon, Reza felt it was time to send out his army and bring you down."

"Reza," said Rick.

Mars pointed to the wall and another man appeared there suddenly, startling Rick again. But in a moment, he realized this was just a three-dimensional picture of a man, not a living hologram like Mars. The image turned this way and that so that Rick could see the long, slender figure and the sharp, dark, Middle Eastern features.

"That's Reza," Mars told him. "Former terrorist and professional assassin—now chief of security in the Realm."

Rick stared at the man. He seemed familiar to him. "I know him. I've seen him."

"I doubt it," said Mars. "He's not the sort of person who—"

"He was there!" Rick broke in. "In the Realm. On the ramparts. I saw him."

Mars's craggy features gathered like storm clouds. "Are you sure?"

"It was him. Except he was . . ." Rick hardly knew what word would describe him. "He was like a demon there. He had this kind of pink-purple skin. Wings and claws. He was giving orders to the archers who shot down the dragon I was riding. It was the same guy. I recognize his face." Rick could hardly believe the words coming out of his own mouth: demons, crocodile men, dragons. It sounded like some kind of nutty joke.

But Mars didn't crack even the hint of a smile. He nodded slowly. "If you're right—if that was him—you're lucky to be here. The man is deadly."

Rick looked at Mars a long moment—looked with that new toughness, that new impatience inside him.

"I'm risking my life in there for you, and you haven't told me anything," he said.

"You're risking your life for your country, and there's not very much I can tell you."

"What does the MindWar have to do with my father? What does it have to do with the truck that ran into me, that busted my legs?"

Mars's expression remained thunderous and unmovable. "If I could tell you, I would. I can't."

A frizz of static went through his holographic image. It brought back another memory to Rick: a sickening memory of how the Realm had started to dissolve as his time ran out, as his mind began to disintegrate. He gingerly touched the side of his head.

"I nearly lost my mind in there, didn't I?" he said.

"Yes," said Mars. "You stayed too long. Another minute or so, we wouldn't have been able to bring you back."

"And then I would become . . . ," murmured Rick. "Like that creature I saw . . . a person . . . dead . . . only not dead . . . stuck in a web in the spider-snake's tunnel. That's what happens to you when you get stuck in the Realm, isn't it? Your body goes into a coma here, and your spirit is trapped over there."

Commander Mars's frown grew deeper. "Don't," he said.

"Don't what?"

"Don't get stuck in there, Rick."

"There are two other people in there already," Rick said. "Are they yours? Did you send them in?"

"Get some rest," said Mars. "We need you to go back in. Soon. Very soon."

"Wait," said Rick. "Those people—Favian and Mariel—are my friends. They've saved my life twice. They're going to die in there if we don't help them. They're going to become like that other guy. If you want me to go back in, you have to help me get them out."

"I don't make deals," said Mars. "We're doing what we can. We're developing a technology that might help them, but . . . I'm not making any promises. Go back in or not. That's your choice. For now, get some rest."

"No, wait!" Rick shouted. "Don't go! I have more questions! I want to know . . ."

But Mars had already vanished.

26. PAST MEMORIES

IT WAS 6 p.m., the first blue-dark of an autumn evening. The unmarked green van pulled up at the front entrance to the university. Juliet Seven twisted around in the driver's seat to look at Rick in the back. He nodded at the crutches lying on the van floor at Rick's feet.

"You want me to hang around and give you a lift home?" he asked.

Unstrapping himself from the rear seat, Rick gathered the crutches up. "I'll be fine," he said brusquely.

"Suit yourself," said Juliet Seven.

He hit a button and the van's back door lifted electronically. Rick slid out into the dusk.

The van drove away. Rick stood alone on the sidewalk, looking through the filigreed iron gate that led into the campus. He could see students moving in small groups along the campus pathways under the streetlamps. They had books under their arms and backpacks on their backs. Their voices and laughter trailed to him where he leaned on his crutches. Normal life—the life he should have been living. He watched the students passing by, and his solitude weighed heavily on him.

He was going back into the Realm at midnight—just a

little over twelve hours since they'd brought him out—as early as possible. The MindWar scans showed that Kurodar's fortress was nearly complete. Whatever Kurodar was planning to do, he would do it soon. It could be anything. He might destroy a nuclear plant or set off a missile. They didn't know, but they had to find out.

"You don't have to go back," Miss Ferris had told him. "Mars will use you and use you. He doesn't care what happens to you, as long as he stops Kurodar." She spoke in her usual unemotional way, with the usual blank expression on her face. Rick could not quite bring himself to believe that he had really seen her sobbing. It must've been a dream or something. "You nearly lost your mind in there," she said. "And if you go back so soon, it could happen again. It could be permanent this time."

"I'll go," said Rick quietly. "I want to go." He was still lying in the hospital bed, though he was wearing a fresh black T-shirt one of the nurses had brought him. He felt much stronger than he had when he first woke up. In fact, he felt much stronger than he had in months. He said to Miss Ferris, "But you have to help me. You have to help me get Mariel and Favian out of there. I can't just leave them there to die—or worse than die. I won't."

"We're working on it," said Miss Ferris. "We'll do what we can."

Rick had heard this before. He didn't know whether to believe it or not. But he didn't have much choice. "I need to get out of here for a while," he told her. "If I'm going to . . . well, if there's a chance I won't come back this time, there are some people I want to see . . . say good-bye to."

"I'll get Juliet Seven to drive you home," Miss Ferris said.

But Rick had told the blockheaded bodyguard to bring him here, to the campus, instead.

Now, gritting his teeth, Rick braced himself on his crutches and hobbled through the gate, onto the university grounds. With every step, he flinched as fresh pain shot through him. Because he was going back into the Realm so quickly, the MindWar Project doctors had refused to give him any pain medication that might mess up his mind. His headache had subsided, but his shoulder still throbbed and his legs felt as if they were on fire.

Good, he thought grimly as he hobbled along. *Let it burn.*

He wanted the pain. He wanted to hurt. He wanted to remind himself that he had changed. That he was a new, tougher Rick. Or, that is, he was the old Rick again, the unbeatable Number 12. He had changed in that moment when the dragon fell out of the sky. That moment when he thought he had failed at everything. Now he was going back into the Realm, and if he failed again—if Kurodar pulled off his mission, whatever it was—he would have nothing but failure to show for his time on earth. And that was unacceptable. That did not happen to Rick Dial. It could not happen to Number 12.

He had let himself go. He knew that now. He had let himself become weak. Ever since his father had gone, he had nursed his hurt and anger. Ever since the accident, he had hidden away in his room playing video games. He had whined and sulked about the end of his football career without even trying to get back into shape. He had wasted four months of his life, and now it turned out they might have been the last four months he ever had.

So let the pain come, if it made him angry, if it made him strong, if it made him mean enough to win.

He hobbled farther into the campus. The university buildings loomed around him, large and impressive: majestic stone edifices with massive columns and carved pediments. Lights had come on in their windows, and as Rick labored past, he could see night students in their classes and lecture halls. He saw them leaning on their desks, listening to professors, sometimes raising their hands. He felt an ache at the sight, a yearning to be among them, living the life he had thought he was going to live.

Too bad, he told himself. His new-old toughness. *Live this life.*

He hobbled on.

He knew Professor Michael Jameson would still be in his office at this hour. Jameson was the chairman of the Physics Department. He always worked late—Rick's father had often talked about it.

Sure enough, when Rick reached the Physics Building—a five-story white structure in a more modern style than most of the others on campus—he saw the light still burning in the professor's window. Gripping his crutches in one hand and the banister with the other, he hopped his way up the front steps, flinching with the pain and thinking angrily, *Good, good, good! Let it hurt! You deserve it!*

All the same, he was glad there was an elevator inside. He rode it up to the third floor.

Jameson's outer office was empty. His secretary had gone home. The door to the inner office stood open, and Rick could see the professor in there, assembling some papers, stuffing them into a briefcase, preparing to leave for the night.

He heard Rick's thumping steps and looked up. Startled, he let his mouth drop open a moment before he spoke.

Then he said, "Rick?"

Rick flashed a tense smile and limped into the small, book-lined room. Professor Jameson watched him, motionless with surprise, his hands still on the briefcase that sat atop his massive wooden desk.

Jameson was a tall man, stooped and paunchy. Sloppy, with wrinkled slacks and a shirt that was always coming untucked in back. He had thin reddish hair, strands of it combed over the top of his head in a useless effort to hide his increasing baldness. He had light, kindly, intelligent eyes behind large glasses. A soft, thoughtful face. Rick's father and he had been friends a long time. Jameson was the man who'd convinced Rick's dad to bring his work here to Shadbrook U. But Rick couldn't help but notice the professor was not glad to see him. In fact, he looked nervous, worried.

Rick came to rest in front of the desk, breathing hard from the effort.

"Good to see you, Professor," he said.

Jameson nodded. "You, too, Rick. It's been awhile. You . . . you're looking good."

It didn't sound convincing and Rick wasn't convinced.

Rick noticed that Jameson's glance flashed past him toward the door—as if he were waiting for someone, nervous that someone would walk in and find Rick there. "Do you . . . do you want to sit down?" the professor said. He tried to sound casual, but he didn't.

Rick shook his head. "I won't stay long," he said. "Really, I just want to ask you one question."

Jameson took a deep breath. He nodded. "All right."

"Did my father say anything to you before he left town? Did he give you any idea of where he was going? Or why?"

The professor wasn't much good at masking his emotions. Rick could see how uncomfortable the question made him. He did that thing people do with their mouths where they open and close them and make noises but don't actually say anything: *bff, bluff, boof* . . . Gesturing with his hand all the while. Finally, he got some words out: "I understood he . . . he left a . . . a . . ."

"A note," Rick said. "He did leave a note. It said he was running off with a woman he used to date in college."

"Well, uh . . ." More *bff*ing and *bloff*ing. The professor's cheeks actually turned pink. Then, not unkindly, he said, "Look, I know this has been a hard time for you, Rick. You've been through a lot. Your father. The accident . . ."

Yeah, and you don't even know about the dragons and spider-snakes and crocodile men, Rick thought with a small smile. But out loud he said, "I'm not looking for false comfort, Professor. I've been sitting around with my thumb stuck in my mouth too long. I just want the truth, that's all. When I saw that note, I guess I was so angry, so hurt . . . I didn't really think about it. But now . . . Well, look, you knew my father as well as anyone. Does he strike you as the sort of guy who walks out on his family without a word?"

The stooped, sloppy professor made another series of uncomfortable gestures and shrugs. "Well . . . sometimes . . . sometimes when a man reaches middle age, he goes through an emotional crisis . . . he starts to reexamine his life . . ."

"Sure. But did you ever know my dad to do anything—anything at all—without being straight and honest about it?"

Professor Jameson finally stopped spluttering. He looked Rick straight in the eye and spoke as if the answer had just occurred to him. "Actually . . . no," he said. "No, I never did. His just running off like that . . . It stunned me as much as it stunned anyone. It didn't make sense."

"That's right. I've been so ticked off about it . . . so depressed . . . it didn't even occur to me until now. But it *doesn't* make any sense. That's why I'm asking: Did he say anything? Anything at all that might have given you a clue about his state of mind?"

Professor Jameson began to shake his head no—but then he hesitated. He went on gazing at Rick. And Rick could see the thoughts unspooling behind his eyes.

"There was this one conversation we had," he said at last. "About—I don't know—maybe a week before he left, a little more. I walked in on him in his office. The door was open. He was sitting there in his chair. He was playing with a rubber band in his hands and he was looking, you know, at that cross he always had on the wall. And when he heard me come in, he turned to me . . . He looked like his thoughts were a million miles away. And he said, 'What if you had to sacrifice everything you love in order to save everything you love?' I had no idea what he was talking about. He was looking at the cross, so I naturally thought . . . Well, I thought I had interrupted him while he was thinking about some sort of Bible stuff . . . Jesus . . . sacrifice . . . Not my kind of thing. And before I could say anything, he snapped out of it. We started talking about other things . . . school things. I didn't give it much thought after that, but . . . well, that was only a week or so before he disappeared."

As the professor spoke, Rick found himself slowly raising his head, lifting his chin.

What if you had to sacrifice everything you love in order to save everything you love?

Rick didn't know exactly what that meant, but he knew it meant something, something important.

"Listen," he began, "do you have any idea what my dad was working on when—"

But before he could finish, another voice sounded behind him:

"All right, Daddy, I'm ready to drive you . . . Oh!"

Startled, Rick turned—and there in the doorway was the professor's daughter: Molly.

27. THE LOST

HE HAD FORGOTTEN how pretty she was—or maybe he just hadn't let himself think about it too much. She was wearing jeans and a sleek yellow coat belted at the waist. Her round freckled face was pink with the cool evening weather. She looked good, Rick thought. He had forgotten how good.

Now Rick knew why the professor had seemed so nervous. He had been expecting his daughter to arrive and was worried about what would happen when she and Rick met after Rick had avoided her for so long. The three of them—the professor, Rick, and Molly, frozen with surprise in the doorway—all stood in startled silence a moment. Then they all started talking at once.

"Oh, I didn't know you were . . . ," Molly started.

"Molly, I didn't . . . I wasn't . . . ," the professor said.

"Oh, hey, I didn't know you were going to . . . ," said Rick.

And then they all fell silent again.

Molly broke the silence with a laugh. "Okay, that was awkward!"

Rick gave a rueful smile. "Look, I didn't mean to break in on you guys. Actually, I was just gonna head for home . . ."

"No, don't," said Molly firmly. And then she said, "I mean it, Rick. Don't. I'm tired of being avoided. It's bad for my ego."

Professor Jameson quickly snapped up his briefcase. "I'll just . . . I'm going to . . . I'll wait for you in the car," he finally managed to say. And then he rushed out of the room as if the police were after him.

Molly lifted one shoulder and one corner of her mouth. "Daddy doesn't do too well in awkward social situations."

Rick nodded. "Me neither," he said.

"Well, it can't be that bad," said Molly. "I mean, we've known each other a long time. It's kind of silly for us to be all embarrassed like this."

Rick nodded. "I guess."

But then they were silent again, and the awkwardness hung over them.

Finally, Rick said, "Look, I'm really sorry I haven't called you or anything."

"Well, yeah!" said Molly. "You should be. It hurt my feelings. I'd beat you senseless, but you're all on crutches and pitiful and everything, it wouldn't look right."

Rick nearly smiled. "You're all heart."

"You don't even send me an e-mail? You know how bad that made me feel?"

"Yeah. Sorry. I stink."

"You do. Definitely."

"I was feeling sorry for myself basically. I was afraid you were gonna feel sorry for me, too."

"That's what you say," said Molly. "But I think you were

really afraid I'd drag you to the gym and make you work out and get you back in shape."

Rick snorted. It actually was kind of funny. He had been so afraid of this moment. The two of them meeting. Her seeing him on crutches. He'd been so afraid she'd pity him, and force herself to hang around in his room with him when all the time she was dying to be outdoors, at the track, on the bike paths or something. He hadn't considered the fact that Molly wanted to be a school athletic coach. Dragging him to the gym—that's probably exactly what she would have done.

"Just answer one question," Molly said. "And don't lie."

"I won't lie," said Rick. "Or if I do, I'll try to make it sound really believable."

She ignored the joke. She said, "Is there some other girl? Is that why you didn't want to see me?"

Rick was about to protest that there was no one else, but the words went silent in his mouth. He thought of Mariel. Did she count? Was she even real? How could he begin to explain his feelings about a silver spirit who only lived in a computerized universe?

"Okay," said Molly when he didn't answer. "I take the question back. You figure it out, and then explain it to me. But whatever you do, don't just go dark on me again, okay? I'm insecure enough as it is."

"Yeah," Rick said with a laugh. "Right."

There was more awkward silence between them. They seemed to have an endless supply of it.

Then Molly said, "Well, look, I'd like to stay around and

torture you about what a jerk you've been, but my dad's waiting out in the car and you know these absentminded professors: he can't find his way home by himself. So I'm gonna give you one more chance. But I'm warning you: if you do call me, I'm gonna put you through a rehab so painful, you're gonna *wish* I pitied you."

Rick smiled at her. "It's good to see you, Molly."

When she smiled back, her round cheeks glowed. She stepped forward and kissed him lightly.

"It's good to see you, too, Crutch-Boy," she said. "Don't be a stranger. Okay?"

"You got it," said Rick.

He saw her start to blink back tears—then she quickly said: "Seeya."

She turned and hurried out, and Rick thought: *If I live.*

28. RECKONING

HE COULD FEEL the minutes passing—what might be the last minutes of his life. All through dinner, he felt them going by, one by one by one.

They ate at the kitchen table, Rick and Raider and their mom. Raider chattered away the whole time. Yammer, yammer, yammer. It seemed his piping voice never ceased. Such-and-such happened at school and his teacher said such-and-such and his best friend Shane did such-and-such and wasn't such-and-such stupid and wasn't such-and-such great and on and on. *When did he find time to breathe?* Rick wondered. *When did he find time to eat?*

On another day, he might've been annoyed by the constant chatter. He might've told the kid to clam it. But today, he listened patiently. He thought: *These may be the last minutes I get to spend with him.* If he didn't make it back tonight, he wanted Raider to remember that his big brother listened to him, cared about him.

Amazingly, Raider somehow managed to clean his plate and eat dessert without ever shutting up. Then he got up from the table and announced he had to finish his homework. Rick stuck out a fist and touched knuckles with him by way of good-bye. He wanted to say something more, some words of wisdom the kid could remember in case he didn't come home. He wished he could think of something profound or important. But all that came into his mind were the words of the famous football coach Vince Lombardi.

"Remember, kid," he said. "It's not about whether you get knocked down, it's about whether you get back up."

Rick thought it sounded dopey, him giving Raider advice like that for no reason. But the eight-year-old's big round freckled face beamed like sunrise. The kid pressed his lips together with determination and gave Rick a second fist bump for good measure. Then he was gone, and Rick sat at the table, feeling hollow.

When he looked around, he saw his mother watching him from the other end of the table. She didn't say anything. Just watched him. It seemed to him she'd been doing that a lot these days—watching him silently. And yet she never asked him anything: where he'd been, what he'd been up to. She just watched.

Rick tried to think of something to say to her. But he couldn't.

"Well . . . ," he said.

He worked his way to his feet. Got his crutches from the wall. Thumped his way out of the kitchen and down the hall, his legs aching under him. But before he got to his room, he paused at the foot of the stairs. He looked up. He could hear Raider making dopey noises in his room: singing the theme song to some cartoon show or something. He was probably blowing up his friends on his computer instead of doing his homework. Whatever.

Rick changed course. He put both his crutches in one hand, grabbed hold of the banister, and started hopping up the stairs. *Good, good, good,* he thought with each new thumping jolt of pain. When he reached the landing, he hobbled down the hallway to the room at the end of the hall. It was a room with a closed door—a door that hadn't been opened in months. He opened it now. He went through.

He was in his father's study. Such as it was. Little more than a closet really. An almost empty cell. There was nothing in the small corner cubicle but his dad's wooden work desk and wooden chair. A few stray papers stacked on the floor in the corner. There wasn't even a rug on the wooden floor.

Rick hobbled across the small space, leaned his crutches against the desk, and plopped down into the chair. He stared at his father's empty desktop. The laptop that had been on the desk was now gone. So was the framed family photograph—the only photograph in the room. So was the cross that had hung on the wall—the only decoration. His father must have taken that stuff with him when he left.

Rick took a deep breath of the musty air, trying to feel his father's presence, trying to touch his dad's mind with his own.

Where did you go? Why did you leave us? What does it have to do with the MindWar?

He was so intent on his own thoughts that he was startled when he looked up and saw his mother standing in the doorway.

Without a word, she came in and closed the door behind her.

It struck him again how bad his mom looked, how worn and weary. No makeup on. Her blond-and-silver hair pulled back sloppily off a face that looked as if it had aged ten years in the last few months. She leaned against the door and looked at Rick—and still, she didn't say a thing.

Rick finally felt compelled to say . . . something. Something to fill up the silence. So he said, "I have to go out tonight."

His mom nodded. Still silent.

It struck Rick full force now how strange this was: her silence. How strange her silence had been these last four months. As strange as his father walking out on them and leaving nothing more than a note.

"How come you're not saying anything?" Rick asked her.

"What do you want me to say?" she said.

"I don't know. You could say, 'You've been acting strangely, Rick.' Or 'How come suddenly you disappear for hours on end and come home all beat up?' Or 'How come gunmen break into our house in the middle of the night?' Ever since Dad left, you hardly ask me anything."

She shrugged. "I trust you. I know you'll tell me if you want to."

Rick tried to meet her tired, steady gaze, but he couldn't. He looked down at the empty desktop. "I can't," he said. "I can't tell you."

"I know that, too," said his mother. "That's why I didn't bother to ask."

He looked up at her again, surprised. She knew? How much

did she know, exactly? Her face was impassive. It gave nothing away. But as he continued to stare at her, her eyes shifted, just a little. She glanced at the desktop. The slightest smile played at the corner of her mouth.

What was she looking at? Rick followed her eyes to the spot. She was looking at the corner of the desk where the photograph had always stood. It had been a framed snapshot of the four of them—Dad, Mom, Rick, Raider. They were standing in front of the gigantic Christmas tree in Rockefeller Center during last year's trip down to New York City. A police officer had been kind enough to take the photo for them. Rick remembered it. In the snapshot, Raider was doing his funny skeleton grin, and Rick was rolling his eyes and laughing in spite of himself. Dad had his arm around Mom. She had put her head on his shoulder and he had turned his face toward her slightly as if to kiss her hair . . .

Rick's lips parted as a thought came suddenly into his head. He stared at his mother.

"He took the picture with him," he said.

His mother went on smiling. She nodded, as if she had been waiting for Rick to notice this very thing. "He did."

"If you're running away with another woman," Rick went on, "you don't take a picture of your family with you—"

She cut him off, putting her finger to her lips. "Raider's still awake," she said softly.

She came across the room then. She sat on the edge of the desk, looking down at Rick. She seemed to take a moment to gather her thoughts, to figure out exactly what she wanted to say.

"Your father is a funny kind of a man," she said. "He has a very complicated mind, but a very simple soul. Do you know what I'm talking about?"

Rick thought it over. "Sort of. I remember how he was always forgetting things . . ."

"He once walked out in the middle of a blizzard without his shoes on."

Rick smiled. "You had to run after him almost every morning. It was like he never left the house without forgetting something. His glasses. His briefcase. His coat. Something."

"For the longest time after we moved here, he used to forget our address and get lost coming home. He'd have to phone me and I'd give him directions. Then, one time, he forgot his phone. A policeman found him wandering around aimlessly and had to bring him back in his patrol car."

Rick laughed—and then he stopped laughing and his voice choked up, his eyes filling with tears. He had forced himself to forget how much he missed his father, but now it hit him hard. "He's really absentminded," he said hoarsely. "I guess he's always thinking about his work and stuff."

His mother looked away to give Rick a chance to discreetly wipe his eyes with his hand. "It isn't always easy living with a man like that. Taking care of him is a lot of work. Throw in a couple of kids, and it's more than a full-time job."

"Yeah, I can see that," said Rick.

"Dad's old girlfriend understood that. The girl he was with in college, I mean: a woman named Leila Kent."

Rick didn't answer. He and his mother both knew, of

course: this was the woman in his father's note, the woman he said he'd run off with.

"Leila was a really nice girl," his mother went on. "Incredibly smart. And very, very ambitious. She had big plans—very big plans—for her career. And she knew that she was going to have to choose between her work and your dad. She understood that both of them were going to need all her time and attention. And in the end? Well, I guess she decided she didn't want to spend her life making sure that Dad was wearing shoes when he walked out into the snow. So they broke up. But they stayed friends. In fact, Leila came to our wedding."

"She did?" said Rick, surprised.

"Sure. After the ceremony—and a couple of glasses of champagne—she told me that she sometimes wished she could've been more like me, the kind of girl Dad needed, but . . . She was who she was. And she went on to have a very important, high-level career in government. As I understand it, she helps coordinate between the State Department and our intelligence agencies, the spy guys. She helps the country defend itself against terrorists. Very secret, high-security stuff."

Rick opened his mouth, but at first he couldn't speak. It was a long moment before he said, "And all this time . . . you trusted him. Dad. He didn't tell you anything. You didn't hear anything. You just . . . You read his note, and you trusted him anyway."

"Him," his mother said. "And you, Rick." And she leaned toward him as if she were about to tell him a secret, and she whispered, "And it's been really, really hard."

She gave a quick, tired smile. She got off the desk. She walked to the door.

The pain in Rick's legs was nothing compared to the pain he felt in his heart just then. As his mother's hand moved to open the door, he cried out to her in a lost small voice, sounding almost as if he were still just a kid. "Ma!" he said. "I've messed up everything! Ever since he left. Ever since the accident. I didn't trust anything! I didn't have faith in anything! I made it so much tougher on you. It was like a test and I failed it!"

He was glad his mother didn't turn around. He was glad she didn't see his face. She kept looking at the door.

"You just got knocked down, Rick," she told him. "And now—you're getting back up."

She pulled the door open. She glanced back at him where he sat with his hand covering his eyes.

"Wherever you go tonight," she said, "be careful."

29. ENDGAME

"THIS IS GOING to be the most dangerous immersion yet," said Miss Ferris.

They were the first words she spoke to him when Juliet Seven escorted him into the Portal Room at ten minutes to midnight. She didn't even say hello.

All around the room, at every workstation, from every monitor and flashing graph, from every keyboard and control panel, the MindWar workers turned to look up at him, the lights from the machinery playing on their faces. The mood in the room was solemn and heavy. The workers offered smiles of encouragement, but their eyes showed anxiety and even pity.

Not Miss Ferris. She was as blank-faced and cold as ever, her voice just as impassive and expressionless.

"It's good to see you, too," Rick said to her.

"We don't have time for joking; just listen," she said. She walked beside him toward the glass box embedded in the far wall. "Our instruments show that almost all the energy in the Realm is being channeled into Kurodar's fortress now. Whatever he's planning, we know it's going to happen soon, probably tonight. Somehow, you've got to get inside that fortress. You've got to see what he's up to and get back in time to tell us. If we know where he's going to strike, then at least we have a chance to defend against it. If not . . ."

"I'll get inside," said Rick. "Don't worry about that. But what am I going to do about Mariel and Favian?"

Miss Ferris took a deep breath. "The truth is, right now, we don't have the technology to extract them," she said.

Rick stopped in his tracks, leaning on his crutches. "That's not good enough. They can't last much longer in there. They're going . . ."

"We're working on it—"

"You keep saying that, but—"

Miss Ferris cut him off. "Until we can get them out, we've come up with a stopgap. When you arrive, you'll find a new program embedded in your left hand, the same way the clock is embedded in your right. Show it to Mariel. She'll know how to use it. It won't save them, but it should buy her and Favian both some time."

Rick took a breath, trying to calm himself. "You promise?" he said.

"No," said Miss Ferris. "But it's the best I can do."

She turned away and continued marching toward the glass coffin. Rick had no choice. He followed her.

Rick looked up at the coffin and drew his breath. He wondered if he'd ever see the real world again. Then he forced himself to stop wondering. What did his dad always tell him? *Don't worry about tomorrow; tomorrow will worry about itself. Sufficient unto the day is the evil thereof.*

He took his crutches out from underneath his arms and

handed them to Miss Ferris. Juliet Seven stepped forward and took his elbow to help him up the stairs. Rick grabbed hold of the edge of the portal and coffin (he really wished it didn't look so much like a coffin!) and lowered himself in.

As always, Miss Ferris climbed up to lean over him and recite her final instructions in her robotic voice.

"We've given you ninety minutes this time . . ."

He blinked up at her. "But I barely lasted seventy-five minutes last time."

For a moment, she didn't answer. Then, brusquely, coldly, she told him, "It was Commander Mars's order. But . . . you're right. We're pushing it. You're going back in after the minimum amount of rest, after a very stressful immersion." She drew a deep breath as if she needed strength. Then—still without any expression—she said, "Stay on the safe side, Rick. Come back as soon as you can."

Rick gave a small snort. "I guess if I were gonna stay on the safe side, Ferris, I wouldn't go in there at all."

Miss Ferris didn't even crack a smile. She just continued: "Be prepared. Kurodar's guards could be watching the portal. Get out of sight quickly, the moment you arrive. We suggest you go into the moat."

The lining of the glass portal box was beginning to wrap itself around Rick now in that almost living way it had before. He began to feel the familiar prickling sensation in his scalp.

"The moat?" he said.

"Yes. Our instruments show it flows into the base of the fortress. That may be your way inside."

"Yeah, but Favian said there are guardian bots in there. Like the spider-snake and the dragons, only for water."

Miss Ferris nodded, completely blank-faced. "That's probably true. Try not to let them kill you."

"Thanks. You're a big help."

She pressed the box's lid and it swung shut over him.

The lining of the portal continued to tighten. The prickling in his scalp grew sharper and more painful. As the lid sealed, Rick peered up into the fogging glass. He peered beyond the fog.

He thought: *Hey. I'm still here. Please be with me. Even in the Realm.*

And one more time, the darkness surrounded him, and the white cylinder opened . . .

BOSS LEVEL:

REZA

30. FORTRESS

THE AIRFIELD LAY silent under a big sky full of stars. *Airfield* was a fancy word for it: It was nothing but a dirt runway in a field of grass in the middle of what looked very much like nowhere. There were no people visible around it in the night darkness. There was no traffic on the country two-lane nearby. Nothing was moving here except for an orange wind cone, which lifted off its pole a little whenever a breeze whispered over it.

Across the runway from the cone, there was a small, low building, a one-story clapboard structure with plate-glass windows on three sides. Inside that small shack, Victor One was waiting. He stood by the window on the eastern wall, watching the starry sky through the glass.

Behind him, Leila Kent paced nervously, her low heels rapping the floor tiles. The Traveler sat in a small metal chair against one wall, staring off into nothingness, lost in his own thoughts. Bravo Niner sat behind the counter opposite. The leathery tough guy was very still, but Victor One could sense his tension and alertness.

Victor One rubbed his arm absently. He'd used the first-aid

kit in the car to clean out his bullet wound and bandage it, but it still hurt like the devil. Plus his mind was troubled. He was no deep thinker, he never pretended to be, but the old brain was working overtime now. How had those gunmen in the red Beamer found them? Who had told them the Traveler was on the move? Was it someone in the project? Leila? Mars? Ferris? Or even one of the other bodyguards, Alpha Twelve or Bravo Niner himself. And had they been trying to kill the Traveler? Why? What good was the scientist to anyone if he was dead? Had they been trying to capture him? Or something else . . .

The whole thing didn't quite fit together somehow.

But before Victor One could unpack the problem any further, the landing lights outside suddenly went on. Two lines of white bulbs appeared along the edges of the strip, a line of green bulbs along the bottom, and a line of red bulbs shone where the runway ended. They had been turned on by a signal from the oncoming plane. Victor One scanned the sky for it.

"Here she comes," he murmured.

At that, the others quickly joined him at the window. Leila Kent reached him first. The *clop-clop* of her pacing heels stopped, and she was at his right shoulder in a moment. Then the Traveler's chair scraped, and he was at Victor One's left shoulder. Finally, Bravo Niner strolled over to join them, a little bit apart.

The four stood at the window, staring up into the night sky. A silent moment passed. Then, sure enough, they all saw it. What at first seemed just another star began to grow brighter, larger. The plane detached from the constellations and descended through the faint night mist.

Victor One took a deep breath. He heard the Traveler do the same behind him. He glanced at Leila Kent and saw her hugging herself anxiously. He lifted his eyes to Bravo Niner, and B-9 looked back.

"All right," said Victor One tensely. "Let's do this."

In the Realm, in the Sky Room, Reza waited for the moment. His demonic figure hovered a few inches off the stone floor, his bat-like wings waving intermittently to keep him aloft. His great claws curled and uncurled nervously. His oversized eyes watched his master floating in the air above him.

This is Kurodar's hour, Reza thought, excited. The second Real Life test of the Realm was under way. It would be a relatively small operation—though still much bigger than the Canadian train crash. And far more important. Assuming it was successful, it would guarantee their funding from the Axis Assembly and secure the technology that would put the Realm beyond the reach of the Americans forever.

In the last moments of suspense, Kurodar's misty presence drifted silently beneath the starry dome. Reza could see a blinking beacon of white light moving slowly above him, crossing the night-like blackness. This represented the Traveler's transport plane. It was coming in for a landing, ready to bring the Traveler on board.

Reza held his breath as the beacon moved. Even the beetle-like bots swarming the dome's edges seemed to pause in anticipation.

Then came the signal. It appeared on the dome as a flash of blue lightning: there and gone in an instant. This was the radio wave that was sent from the plane to the computer in the landing field in order to automatically switch on the runway lights.

Now! Reza thought eagerly.

And even as he thought the word, Kurodar moved. The master's misty presence darted forward like a striking snake. It seemed to seize the blue signal. And as the signal flashed back into the plane, a tendril of Kurodar's misty pink went with it.

Reza let out his breath in relief. Kurodar had done it. Of course he had.

His mind had entered the controls of the Traveler's aircraft.

At that same moment, Rick slipped out of the portal point and entered the Realm.

But what was going on? He couldn't see! Everything was dark. For a moment, he stood where he was, completely disoriented.

Then he understood. It was night in the Realm now. The once yellow sky had gone black. There were enormous stars burning in it—red, purple, blue, green bursts of light the size of saucers. On the horizon, there was a sliver of a golden crescent moon.

None of which makes any sense, Rick thought. There wasn't even a sun in the Realm. Why should there be night? Kurodar could have just created a world that was in daylight always. *But maybe things here don't have to make sense.* The Realm emanated from Kurodar's mind, after all. It was a product of his twisted imagination. He remembered how Mariel had told him that Kurodar thought he was God. Well, maybe he made a world with day and night—a world like the real one—just so he could go on pretending.

Rick peered around him as his eyes adjusted. He saw he had come out right where he had left, right beside the purple diamond that floated between the moat and the looming fortress wall.

And then he saw the guards.

That is, he saw the twin red beams shooting from their eyes first. The beams were moving all along the verge of the moat, sweeping the area. A second or two later, he made out the shapes of the alligator guards themselves. There must have been at least a dozen of them, walking here and there, looking left and right, searching the area.

Searching, Rick realized with a jolt of fear, for him!

Of course. They were keeping an eye on the portal point and the moat and the spider-snake's tunnel.

And one of the guards was coming right toward him.

The two red beams that shone out of the alligator's eyes swept back and forth across the dark grass, coming closer and closer to Rick as the big two-legged lizard patrolled the strip of land between fortress and moat, moving his way. Another few seconds and the beams would touch Rick's leg. The alligator would send up the alarm, and the others would converge on him, their huge swords drawn and ready.

Rick dropped onto his belly, fast. He crawled quickly through the grass toward the edge of the moat, trying to get out of the guard's path. The alligator kept coming, the beams cutting through the air just above Rick's body.

The alligator guard stopped, his massive clawed hand curling around the hilt of his sword. He had spotted something. In the grass, right by the portal point: Rick's footprints.

His voice—a cross between an animal's growl and an electronic hum—uttered one guttural word:

"Intruder!"

All around the strip of grass, the red beams turned his way. The alligators began tromping over the grass toward the portal point. They scanned the area where Rick had been crawling on his stomach.

But Rick was gone. He had dropped over the edge of the moat and sunk himself in the water.

The shock of the plunge nearly knocked the breath out of him. The water was not like the water of the real world. It was thick and viscous like melted metal. And cold! If real-world water had been that cold, it would have been solid ice. The freezing liquid seemed to bite into Rick's flesh with a million tiny teeth. He wanted to let his breath out in a shout of pain. But when he glanced up toward the surface, he could just see, through the metallic waves, the red beams of the patrolling alligators, searching for him. He forced himself to push downward off the moat wall, until he was fully submerged. Then he turned his body and swam for the bottom.

He swam hard, frogging with his arms and legs. The metal resisted him and the effort tired him quickly. Maybe—he thought hopefully—maybe he wouldn't have to hold his breath here. It was like that in some video games he'd played: the character could stay submerged underwater as long as he needed to. The Realm, unfortunately, was more realistic. A few more strokes, and he could feel the pressure on his chest as his lungs called for fresh air.

But there was no going back to the surface, not with the alligator guards swarming up there. He went on swimming, down and down. It was hard to see through the water's metallic thickness. Only a few feet ahead of him were visible, and even those were unfocused and shifting. Miss Ferris had said the moat might drain into the fortress—but how in the world was he supposed to find his way to the drain before he drowned? Maybe he'd better try to sneak up to the surface for a breath so he could . . .

But before he could finish the thought, something swam past above him. Something huge.

Oh no! Rick thought.

He twisted his body around and looked up. There was a creature circling in the water up there. He could only guess what sort of enormous, vicious, sharp-toothed beast Kurodar had created to patrol the moat. He didn't want to get any closer and find out. He just wanted to get out of there.

He turned and headed down again. If there was a drain or

a culvert of some sort, it would be at the bottom. But though he kicked and stroked even harder than before, he seemed to make no progress. The moat seemed bottomless. His lungs were starting to pump desperately in his chest. He was out of breath. He had no choice. He had to get to the surface, now.

He reversed himself. Pointed himself upward. He gave a great kick with his legs. He rose through the freezing mercury-like fluid. His lungs screaming in his chest, he peered upward eagerly, hoping to see the surface. But it was still too far away, out of his limited field of vision. He kept rising.

What happened next happened so quickly, he could hardly take it in.

He felt the water quake. He felt a wave of pressure push against his body. A second before he saw it, he understood with a feeling of despair that something was coming for him out of the deep.

Then, suddenly, the black mouth of the monster was speeding toward him out of the water. Its jaws were spread wide. Its teeth were gleaming. It was about to swallow him, devour him whole.

But before it could, a rushing tide seemed to sweep Rick away and carry him down out of the creature's path.

Everything was confusion. The cold of the water was gone and he was bathed in warmth. The monster—whatever it was—was passing overhead without following him, as if Rick had simply vanished from its sight. Rick, meanwhile, was being dragged downward relentlessly by the tide—and yet his urgent need to reach the surface was gone. Somehow—amazingly—he could breathe again! He was breathing underwater! What was happening? How was it possible?

As he began to gather his wits about him, he realized: *Mariel.*

She had him in her arms. She had somehow surrounded him with her presence. The warmth was her warmth. The air was her breath. He could even feel the softness of her imprinted on the liquid around him. If he squinted and peered, he could almost make out her face just above him. Once again, she had come to his rescue, fashioning a shape for her spirit out of the metal liquid and using it to protect him.

He looked below him—and now he saw the drain he had been searching for. She was carrying him right to it. It was a round opening in the base of the moat with a large valve built into the wall beside it. The cold washed up over his feet again—then over his knees. He understood: Mariel was releasing him so he could open the drain.

He drew a last deep breath from her and held it. As Mariel let him go, as the bone-chilling cold surrounded him, he swam down the last few feet until he could get his hands on the valve. He had to brace his feet against the wall for leverage. He had to strain his muscles—so hard that the metal water bubbled around his mouth as breath squeezed out through his teeth. But now the valve began to turn. Hand over hand, he moved it a half circle. It went slowly. Rick looked toward the drain. It was still closed. He turned the valve another half circle, then another.

The drain sprang open and Rick was swept away. As the

moat water was sucked down into the opening, it sucked him with it. His hands were torn from the valve. He was carried toward the drain in a swirling flood of liquid metal. His heel scraped against the drain's edge, and then his feet went into the hole and he was dragged through in an instant. In an instant, he was falling helplessly through a narrow pipe, banging painfully into the sides with the freezing water splashing all around him.

He expected to slam into the bottom of the pipe or smack into the wall, but in the next moment, the water was warm again, and he landed softly, somehow held still while the freezing metal went on rushing past him and pouring over him.

Now, from where he stood, he saw another valve in the wall. He grabbed it as the flow of water hammered harmlessly past him. Gritting his teeth, he turned the valve once . . . twice . . . then the drain snapped shut above him and the flood of water ceased.

Breathless and shivering, he looked around. A glow that came to him from the far reaches of the pipe gave him just enough light to see by. He saw that he was standing at the elbow of the pipe, right at the spot where the drop ended and the pipe turned off to travel underground toward the fortress. The water had stopped pouring in, and what was there had spread out so that it only covered his feet to his ankles. It was like standing in a freezing puddle.

He tried to catch his breath, gather his thoughts. And as his mind cleared, he understood that she was there with him.

Mariel had flowed out of the moat with the water. It was

she who had caught him and softened his fall and kept him from being swept past the bend in the pipe.

He spoke her name softly: "Mariel."

On the instant, she rose up before him out of the water around his feet. Silver and lush and beautiful, she was standing very close to him in the narrow space of the pipe. He could feel the warmth of her even as he shivered with his feet submerged in the freezing water. Her face—or the mercurial impression of her face—was inches below his, turned up toward him. Before this, she had always loomed above him like some sort of goddess. He was surprised to see how small she was up close. She was just a girl—no older than he was: he could see that now with her gentle eyes so near to his and her lips too close even to think about.

"Are you hurt?" she asked him softly.

"No," he said. "No. Are you?"

She didn't answer. She only smiled. But it was a weary smile and her eyes looked weary, too. He could see that the effort to help him had drained her.

Which reminded him. He looked at his left hand. He could see a red light pulsing in his palm.

"They gave me something—for you," he told her. "It's supposed to help. They said you'd know how to use it."

Mariel glanced at the pulsing light. "I do," she said. "But there isn't time now."

"But . . . you have to," said Rick. "You have to restore yourself . . . You've come to my rescue three times. You've used up so much energy helping me . . ."

"That's what my energy is for," she said. "And that's why you have to listen to what I tell you now. It's important."

"But . . ." Instinctively, Rick reached out to touch her—but, like water, she was barely there. Her substance surrounded and warmed his hand, but there was no presence to it, no flesh. "*Who are you?*" he said. The words broke out of him. "*What* are you? Where did you come from?"

She shook her head. "There's no time for that either, Rick. Listen to me. Please! I'll be with you as much as I can, but there are things you have to know . . ."

"I might not make it back," he said. "Then I wouldn't be able to help you."

"You have to make it back. You will make it back. If you listen."

He began to speak again, but forced himself to stop. "All right," he said. "What. Tell me."

"I'm going to give you your armor again . . ."

"No! It takes too much energy out of you. You'll kill yourself . . ."

She held up a glistening finger. "Listen!" Her echoing voice was soft but forceful.

Rick clamped his mouth shut, swallowing his protests.

"Remember what I told you before. Your spirit has power here. A lot of power. If you focus it, use it, it can transform the substance of the Realm itself. You need to learn how to do this."

"But I—"

"Shh. Listen. I will give you armor, but they have armor, too. I'll give you a sword, but they have swords as well. Your spirit is the only weapon you have that can make you more powerful than they are. You can't let it go weak, no matter what your emotions are. Do you understand what I'm telling you?"

Rick began to say yes, but then only shook his head: in fact, he wasn't sure what she was telling him at all.

"There are so many of them in there," Mariel told him. "And their leader is like a demon."

"Reza, yes, I saw him," said Rick.

"You're going to be afraid, but if you surrender to your fear, you're lost. You might despair, but if you give in to your despair, they'll destroy you. Remember, your emotions are only emotions. Live in your spirit, Rick, however you feel. Live in your spirit and you can defeat them." She lifted her hand—a small hand, he could see now—a girl's hand. She held it so close to him he could feel the heat of it on his cheek. "Now, take this."

He reached his hand up to hers, trying to stop her. "No, don't waste any more of your strength on me, don't . . ."

But before he could finish, she made a sweeping gesture toward him. Once more, her silver substance spilled over him, covering him head to foot.

"Mariel!" he said.

But she was gone.

Rick looked down. He was clothed in armor again—fuller, stronger armor than before and yet as flexible and free-moving as the mercurial liquid out of which it had been formed. The sword that was suddenly gripped in his hand was a mighty weapon, nothing like the rude blade of pitted iron Mariel had given him at first—stronger even than the one she had coated over with steel. This was some rare and gleaming metal clear through, a dangerous battle-tool, long, thin, light as air. The blade flared at the bottom to form a solid defensive bar, then tapered to a vanishing point that looked sharp enough to pierce stone. The handguard was fashioned into the shape of wings, and the hilt—like the hilt of the other swords—was braided to fit perfectly into his hand and topped off by the image of a woman's face, now shaped so expertly and in such detail that Rick could see clearly it was Mariel.

The sight of the armor and the blade made him ache. He knew he was going to need them—but he wished Mariel had not expended her dwindling life force to give them to him. But here they were and she was gone, and if he did not use the weapons well, it would be a waste of her sacrifice. With a sigh, he slipped the sword into the scabbard built into the side of his armor.

He looked down at his right hand. The timer in the palm there was just ticking down to the seventy-five-minute mark. He could almost hear Miss Ferris speaking in his ear:

We've given you ninety minutes this time . . . We're pushing it . . . Stay on the safe side, Rick. Come back as soon as you can.

The safe side! The safe side was back in his stupid room!

He bowed his head and ducked into the pipe that led toward the fortress.

"Now!" said Victor One.

Gun drawn, eyes moving, he led the others across the dark

airfield. Leila Kent and the Traveler were just behind him. The leathery hard man, Bravo Niner, was bringing up the rear. They moved quickly over the grass to the runway.

There the plane sat like a throbbing shadow, its lights off, its propeller beating the night air. The plane was a U-28A, Victor One saw, a single-engine turboprop the military often used. This one had been repainted in civilian colors, the fuselage white and gold; the nose, wings, and tail deep blue. It had landed on the dirt strip gently and expertly. It had slowed quickly and turned around at the end. Now it was just waiting for its passengers before leaping into the sky again.

As the four people came near, a door opened up in the plane just behind the cockpit. A short stairway unfolded from the fuselage to the ground. A man leaned out and beckoned to them. Victor One recognized his old pal Echo Eight, a large black man with a voice like a roll of thunder. Ex-Army, like Victor One. Good soldier; good man. Victor One was glad he'd be on board.

Victor One stepped up his pace, and the others hurried along behind him.

At the base of the stairs, Victor One stepped aside. Leila went up the steps, helped into the plain by Echo Eight. The Traveler followed her, then Bravo Niner. Victor One went up last, checking the shadows over his shoulder before he ducked through the door.

Inside, the U-28A was fitted out like a military cargo plane, stripped of all decoration and with serviceable canvas seats lining the sides.

"No in-flight movie?" Victor One asked Echo Eight.

"No, but I'm gonna sing a medley of my greatest hits," the Echo rumbled, deadpan.

The Traveler and Leila Kent strapped themselves into seats against the right wall. Bravo Niner strapped himself in on one side of them, Victor One on the other. Echo Eight took a seat across from them, next to another man: an older man with silver hair and a craggy face that seemed to be pulled downward into a permanent frown. The silver-haired man was dressed in khaki military pants but wore a civilian's button-down white shirt. He said nothing, merely nodded once at Leila, who nodded back.

Victor One had never seen the silver-haired man before, but he recognized him from his dossier. This was Jonathan Mars, the commander of the mission.

The moment they were all seated, the plane began to roll.

Above Reza's head, Kurodar's shifting essence was spreading out across the Sky Room's dome. He already had the transport plane in his power, but he wanted more than that. The Great Assembly had agreed to fund the Realm in the hopes of destroying America once and for all, but there were plenty who doubted the worth of the project, and some who outright opposed it. The Realm was not ready for full use yet, but with this mission, Kurodar wanted to demonstrate its capabilities.

As the pink mist that was Kurodar's mind spread across the painted sky, Reza was filled with a warmth of admiration—more than that, even a kind of worship. He wanted to stay and watch this first trial of his master's genius from beginning to end.

But just then, there was a soft fizzing in his ear. A mechanical growl said: "Intruder!"

Reza cursed silently. The guards had spotted something. He'd better go see what was going on.

He flapped his leathery wings and flitted swiftly to the room's big double doors. The alligator guards stationed there swung the doors open, and Reza flew out into the Great Hall. He needed to find out what was going on by the moat, but first, just to be sure, he traveled along the wall to the door of the Generator Room. The alligator there pulled the bolt, opened the iron door, and let him in.

All was well. The three-story-high Disperser Wheel was turning smoothly. Down below, Reza could see the intermittent blasts of energy feeding into it from the portal points outside. The power station of the fortress was working perfectly.

Reza flew out through the iron door. He crossed the Great Hall to the stairs as the alligator shut and locked the door behind him.

He flew up the winding stone stairs quickly. Came out on the battlements among his alligator bowmen. They stood arrayed along the castellated stones, their weapons at the ready. They scanned the darkness below, the red beams from their eyes trying to pick out any signs of trouble.

Slin—the chief bot of the archers—saw Reza emerge from the stairs and hurried toward him, his heavy alligator feet tromping loudly on the stones.

"An intruder?" said Reza.

Slin spoke in the inhuman burr of the alligators: part growl, part static. "Kaaf saw signs of disturbance in the grass. They are searching."

Reza nodded, stepped to the edge of the wall, and looked over. Hard to see in the darkness. Reza didn't know why there had to be night here. It only made his job more difficult. But Kurodar had decreed it so, and Kurodar was his master, so he asked no questions and merely peered down into the shadows.

As his eyes adjusted, he could make out the shadows of the alligators searching the grass beside the floating purple diamond of the portal point. He saw the red beams from their eyes crisscrossing in the shadows.

"Kaaf," he said. The communicator was built into his avatar as it was built into the bots. They could hear him when he spoke to them, even at a distance. "Is there an intruder?"

With another *fizz* of static, Kaaf replied, "We do not see him. There is a disturbance in the grass, but the intruder is not here."

Reza was not reassured. Obviously the intruder, whoever he was, was coming and going through the portal points that supplied the Realm with power from RL. These points had to be spread out around the Realm in order to keep the whole world operational, and they had to be left open to keep the power flowing, but it made the Realm vulnerable to invasion. If the grass around the moat was disturbed, it might well mean the intruder had returned.

Reza continued to stare down at his searching soldiers. They were checking the intruder's trail, moving between the portal point and the moat. Reza lifted his gaze a little to scan the silver moat.

He thought, *The drain.*

Aloud he said through his communicator, "Send guards below. He's heading through the pipes for the cellar."

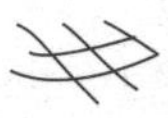

Rick traveled through the network of pipes as quickly as he could, but he felt the digital timekeeper in his palm ticking away relentlessly. He had to keep himself bent over as he worked his way down one narrow cylinder, then down another. The posture made his back ache. A low-running stream of water bathed his feet in freezing cold. After a while, his teeth began to chatter. He felt his will weakening. He had to force himself to keep moving at top speed.

A small glow continually appeared ahead of him like the glow from a fireplace. He kept hoping he would turn a corner or come around a bend and see the source of the light: an exit. But with each new turning, the glow seemed to recede from in front of him. He began to suspect that the light was simply a design flaw in the Realm. Maybe Kurodar had been unable to imagine utter darkness and had put the light here without a source—sort of like the light that shone down from the yellow sky. It was a weird world, after all.

Rick traveled on. He kept his hand on the hilt of his sword. Some kind of strength seemed to come to him through the steel, as if a piece of Mariel herself was fashioned into the weapon.

Remember, your emotions are only emotions. Live in your spirit, Rick, however you feel. Live in your spirit and you can defeat them.

He came to a junction of pipes, and the space opened up above him. He stood erect gratefully, groaning as he stretched his back to work out the aching pain.

He stood still. He listened. At first, all he could hear was the murmuring breath of the running water. But as his ears got used to the sound and set it aside, he heard something more: footsteps. Splashing footsteps.

Guards! he thought.

More footsteps arrived—then more. It sounded like the guards were rushing en masse into the fortress cellar to search for him. Had they somehow guessed he was traveling through the pipes?

Hand on his sword, he bent forward again. He entered another pipe and crept along slowly, moving toward the noise. He slid his feet carefully so as not to splash through the metallic water and give himself away. Meanwhile, the tromping, splashing footsteps ahead of him grew louder.

Then he saw them: beams of red light crisscrossing the circle of darkness where the pipe ended up ahead. He heard the sound of water as the guards kicked through the puddles to search the fortress underbelly.

Quickly, he pulled up short. He pressed close to the iron wall of the pipe. At almost the same time, an alligator—dressed in armor and walking upright—came into view at the exit point. Rick saw the leathery snout of the thing as it bent forward to peer into his pipe. He could make out the teeth overbiting the long jaws as the creature scanned the darkness with its red beams.

Rick had truly stopped himself just in the nick of time. He was just far enough into the pipe so that the angle prevented the guard's beams from reaching him. The red laser-like lights scoured one wall of the pipe then began to cross to the other—coming toward Rick where he pressed himself against the curved side of the iron cylinder. The red beams shot down the center of the tube, right past Rick, not two feet away. He held his breath, his heart hammering in his chest.

But when the beams reached his wall, they fell short. They hit the iron about two inches away from Rick's elbow. The alligator guard could not see him from where he was. Satisfied the pipe was empty, the guard moved on.

Cautiously—very cautiously—Rick edged forward, still pressed tight against the side of the pipe, still bent over in the low space. Inch by inch, he moved to the pipe opening and peeked out.

What he saw made his heart sink.

He had come to the end of the pipe. He had reached the cellars of the fortress. Spreading out on every side of him were dank, dripping walls of heavy stone, dripping archways and moss-covered vaults, running streams of metallic water, corridors vanishing into darkness, and stairways rising out of sight.

And everywhere there were guards. The two-legged alligators in their suits of armor patrolled the cellars with red lights beaming out of their lizard eyes. Their right hands—green, horned, and clawed—rested on the hilts of their swords, each ready to grip the weapon, draw, and fight—and kill—the moment they spotted the enemy.

The enemy—that meant Rick. He just managed to pull back into his pipe as one of the alligators turned its snout and the red lines of light from its eyes swept over the space where he had been. Rick pressed against the pipe's curved iron wall, breathing hard as the lights swept past him. He snuck a glance down at his palm. He nearly groaned aloud to see how much time had been lost as he wandered through the maze.

46:08 . . . 07 . . . 06 . . .

That was all the time he had left—assuming his mind didn't disintegrate early this time.

He had to move. He couldn't just hide here—and yet he knew if he stuck his head out of the pipe again, he would be spotted in seconds. He had to get past this army of guards. But how?

He gripped his sword more tightly, felt Mariel's power flowing up through him.

Live in your spirit, Rick, . . . and you can defeat them.

Yes—but how?

About an hour after takeoff, the plane carrying the Traveler came within radar range of the GTD Terminal Radar Approach Control Facility (TRACON). Three controllers were working the sectional screens in the glassed-in top floor of an air traffic control tower rising about 150 feet above the airport below. Overlapping long-range and short-range radar feeds gave the controllers a view of traffic in airspace that included more than thirty other airports. But the controllers were responsible for guiding and separating only nearby traffic flying below 17,000 feet.

William Lasenby was one of those controllers. He was a quick-witted, intense man in his thirties with thinning blond hair and wire-rimmed glasses that reflected the colored lights on his radar screen. At the moment the U-28A appeared in his section, he was vectoring two commercial flights into their approach for landing, and guiding two more through the airspace above.

"Air East 2612, fly heading 120, descend and maintain 10,000 feet," he murmured into his microphone to one of his approaching aircraft. "Expect visual approach runway 33R."

"One hundred twenty for 33R, maintain 10,000 feet, Air East 2612," the Air East pilot's voice came back.

"Jet Tomorrow 151, descend and maintain 15,000 feet," Lasenby continued in the same low voice, speaking to the other approaching pilot.

"JT 151, descend and maintain 15,000," came the pilot's reply.

It was at this point that the aircraft carrying the Traveler appeared at the bottom left of Lasenby's black screen. But because it was not his responsibility, he considered it "eye clutter," and he didn't pay it any mind. He went on guiding his planes.

"Air East 2612, descend and maintain 8,000 feet . . ."

Lasenby was responsible only for the planes that appeared on his screen in yellow—data-blocks that showed the plane's type, direction, speed, and altitude. The Traveler's U-28A was just a blue dot, with no information at all, which meant it was a private plane carrying no transponder. He ignored it.

"Air East . . . ," he began when his approaching pilot didn't respond at once.

"Air East 2612," came the pilot's voice—suddenly tense. "Controls are suddenly unresponsive here."

Lasenby sat up quickly in his chair, his heart racing. "Say again."

"Air East 2612, controls unresponsive, unable to descend."

"TRACON Approach, Jet Tomorrow 151," came the other pilot's voice. "My controls are unresponsive suddenly . . ."

A cold sweat broke out on Lasenby's forehead. He raised his hand to wave his supervisor over. "Stand by, Jet Tomorrow; Air East 2612, are you declaring an emergency?"

There was a pause. Then the Air East pilot said, "Uh . . . negative emergency, Approach. Air East 2612 is entering a steady holding pattern at 10,000 feet, but . . . well, it's not in my control."

"Approach," came the Jet Tomorrow pilot, "JT entering a holding pattern at 16,000 feet, uh, but, uh, I'm not doing it."

Lasenby blinked, trying to understand what was happening. He looked around for his supervisor, a fat little man named Mark Stanley. Stanley, framed against the night sky seen through the tower's glass walls, was hurrying across the room—but not to him. He was moving to the radar screen two stations down—Julie Winner's station. Julie Winner also had her hand up to signal him, and Lasenby heard her say, "I've got two on approach with unresponsive controls . . ."

Before he could even take this in, Lasenby heard yet another voice coming over his headset, saying, "TRACON Approach, TransNational 3630, controls unresponsive, entering a holding pattern . . ."

"I've got three incoming with unresponsive controls," Lasenby called out. His mind was racing as quickly as his heart, but he couldn't make any sense of it.

And in all the excitement, he failed to notice—everyone failed to notice—that the little blue dot representing the Traveler's U-28A prop plane had disappeared from his screen altogether.

Trapped inside the pipe, with the alligator guards marching back and forth in the cellars beyond, Rick leaned against the wall and tried to think what to do. Again, as he clasped the hilt of the sword in his scabbard, he could almost hear Mariel's voice whispering to him:

Your spirit has power here. A lot of power. If you focus it, use it, it can transform the substance of the Realm itself.

It was not the first time she had told him something like that. He remembered back when he had killed the spider-snake. His sword had been a ruined, rusty relic then. Mariel had said to him:

Your spirit has power here—power over material things, once you learn to use it. Strike with your spirit and the sword will be strong enough.

She'd been right, too. When he attacked the spider-snake, he had focused some power inside himself—some power that was not his brain, not his feelings, not his wishes or hopes—something that was essentially himself—he had focused it, and the rusty blade had been transformed in his hand into a weapon strong enough to do what it needed to do.

Now he had been given a much stronger sword, but so what? What good was a single blade against all those alligator guards marching around out there? There were twenty of them at least, each one a bot programmed to hunt and fight and kill. No matter how powerful his sword was, he stood no chance against them. The moment one of the guards spotted him, they would all . . .

But the thought dissolved in Rick's head as a new idea came to him. He saw at once that it was a great idea. Unfortunately, it was also nuts. There was no possible way it could work, but . . .

Well, but maybe it could. After all, this wasn't what gamers call RL—real life. This whole world was the construction of one madman's imagination. Rick himself had entered the imaginary country by willing his spirit into it, willing it to slip through a portal like liquid through a straw. What he was here—his body—was just an avatar, a digital representation of that spirit inside him. It wasn't flesh and bone like his body back home. If he could will it to become like liquid, then maybe . . .

His fingers tightened on the hilt of his sword, and Mariel whispered into his mind:

If you focus it, use it, your spirit can transform the substance of the Realm itself.

He glanced up. The red lights beaming from the alligator guards' eyes darted here and there across the dungeon darkness beyond the mouth of the water pipe. He drew his gaze away from that and looked down instead at his own hand.

If you focus, he thought.

Rick knew all about focus. Focus was when you were fading back to pass and you had to keep your mind pinned on the receiver downfield, even as two ginormous tacklers were charging toward you like crazy bulls. Focus was when you had to throw with the full motion of your arm, smooth and crisp and accurate, even though you knew some 250-pound guy was about to hurl himself headfirst and full speed into your midsection.

He could do that. He could do this.

Forget the alligator guards, he told himself. Forget the footsteps splashing only a few yards away. Forget the red beams searching for him in the shadows. Think about the hand. There was nothing in the world but his own hand. Nothing . . .

Despite the danger all around him, Rick slipped into a

zone of concentration. His hand. Nothing but his hand. The shape of his hand, the feel of his hand, the substance of his hand . . .

Suddenly, something shifted deep inside him.

The shape of his hand began to change.

Hiding there inside the water pipe, he drew a deep breath. Using the strength of his focus, the strength of his spirit, he forced his hand to grow and metamorphose. He transformed the pink, soft skin into green-brown living leather. He forced the change to ooze up his arm, into his torso, through his whole body. His face elongated into a snout. His teeth grew sharp and overlapped his jaws. His spine extended into a great, heavy tail.

It was a huge effort of will, an enormous expense of energy. It felt like he was bench-pressing the earth and he knew he couldn't keep it up for long. Any minute now, any second, his focus would falter and his body would snap back into the only shape it had ever known.

But for now—for this second—these next few minutes—he had transformed himself into the living image of one of the alligator guards!

Just before the plane started falling out of the sky, Victor One sensed they were in trouble. He didn't know what it was that made him think so. Just something in the motion of the aircraft made him sit up straight in his canvas seat and glance across the heads of the Traveler and Leila Kent into the questioning eyes of Bravo Niner.

B-9 lifted his chin in a question: *What's wrong?*

But it was Jonathan Mars who noticed the look of alarm on the bodyguard's face and spoke aloud: "Victor One, is something the matter?"

Victor One wasn't sure. He just had this weird sense that something had seized hold of the plane from outside, as if a giant hand had wrapped itself around the fuselage. He was about to shrug this off as some kind of superstitious notion brought on by anxiety.

Then the plane went nose down and started plunging toward the earth.

Leila Kent screamed.

"What's happening?" the Traveler shouted.

"We're going down!" shouted Echo Eight.

They were. There was nothing but night at the windows. They couldn't see what was happening, but they could feel the fall accelerating every second, the g-force pulling at their faces, throwing their bodies hard into their shoulder straps. Victor One knew they didn't have much time. The U-28A had already been flying low, trying to stay in uncontrolled airspace and avoid the attention of local air control. Dropping at this rate, they would pancake into the earth in under a minute. They'd all be dead before they ever felt the crash.

"Did someone fire on us?" shouted Jonathan Mars as the plane screamed toward destruction.

"We're going to crash!" Leila Kent screamed.

"I don't think this is damage," said the Traveler—his voice, Victor One noticed even now, was remarkably quiet, remarkably calm.

Then none of them said anything. There was nothing to say. The plane drove downward through the night, its engines letting out a shrieking whine that filled the air around them. Her mouth wide with fear, Leila Kent reached out a hand for the Traveler and he gripped her hand in his own. There was no time for anything else but last prayers and last thoughts . . . pictures in their minds of the people they loved or should have loved . . . spirits reaching out to God . . .

Then, with a stomach-dropping swoop, the plane leveled out. Victor One jolted straight in his seat as the g-force released him. They all did. They all looked out the windows.

Victor One wasn't sure where they were—somewhere over forest near the East Coast, he believed—but he could make out the lights of a house or two in the near distance and he could see how far they'd fallen, how low they were, how close to the earth: close; they were very close! Another three seconds of dropping as they had and they would have been smashed and fried.

The others were staring questions at one another, their mouths still open in shock: *What just happened?* Each of them felt a sort of mad disorientation, as if they'd been torn from the darkness of death and hurled back into the blinding light of life again. Which, of course, they had.

Leila Kent was the first to speak. "Is it over? Are we going to be all right now?"

As if in answer, the door to the cockpit banged open. The

copilot, a young Air Force man named Danny Roth, stood in the frame, one foot over the threshold. His face was white, and his expression showed he was as dazed as all the rest of them.

"We've lost control of the plane!" he said breathlessly. "It's flying on its own." He looked from frightened face to face as if begging someone for help. Then he said, "Which one of you is the Traveler?"

The professor adjusted his glasses and with a voice still almost supernaturally calm, he said, "I am."

Copilot Danny Roth stared at the Traveler for a long moment before he spoke again. It seemed as if even he did not believe what he was about to say.

"There's someone who wants to talk to you," he blurted out finally. "He says . . ."

But before he finished, a new voice came over the cabin intercom. It was a deep male voice with a thick Russian accent.

"Dr. Lawrence Dial," it said thickly.

The Traveler looked up as if he expected to see the speaker floating near the cabin ceiling. "I'm Dr. Lawrence Dial," he said. "Who are you?"

The answer came back at once: "I am Kurodar. And I am in control of this plane."

There was no time to hesitate, no time to waste. Even as Rick started out of the water pipe, he could already feel his alligator morph beginning to fizzle and fade. He had to keep all his focus on maintaining his shape, even as he moved out into the guard-infested cellar. One slip of his focus, and he would snap back into his ordinary form and they would spot him.

He strode with as much confidence as he could muster through the freezing mercury puddles. He stepped out of the end of the pipe and felt his feet touch the slimy moss of the cellar flagstones. With a huge effort of will, he turned his heavy snout this way and that, shooting red lights out of his eyes as if he were searching for someone—as if he were searching for himself! And all the while, he kept moving. The morph would last only another few seconds. He had to get through the guards and get out of there.

All around him, the other alligators were doing the same as he, their clawed feet kicking through the puddles, their tails lashing back and forth behind them, their snouts turning, their red beams lancing the dark.

And now a pair of those red beams passed over him. Rick felt a surge of fear. For a moment, he lost his concentration. A line of static sizzled through his shape before he could will himself to hold his form.

But too late! The alligator guard had already noticed him. The guard's red beams moved on—then stopped—then moved back and pinned Rick where he stood. Rick held his breath. The large guard-bot was looking right at him, staring at him as if it knew that something about him was not quite right.

Rick fixed his concentration, trying to keep his morph steady. If the alligator shape slipped now, he was done for.

The guard stared at him for what felt like twenty minutes. He was a fierce-looking creature with a huge sword at his side and a strange symbol emblazoned on the breastplate of his armor. Rick held his alligator shape in place and kept moving, pretending he didn't see how the guard was watching him.

Then his pulse skipped as one of the other guards shouted, "Kaaf! I heard something here!"

At that, the alligator with the symbol on his breastplate—Kaaf—turned away.

Rick seized the moment. He had spotted a great stone stairway against the far wall. Three other alligators were patrolling the area between here and there. Focusing all his spirit on remaining in his shape, Rick joined them and wove his way among them, moving as quickly as he could over the damp and slippery cellar floor.

He got past the alligators. He reached the stairs: bulky flagstone steps leading to a heavy wooden door above. He started climbing out of the cellar, away from the other guards—and as he did, he felt his energy give way. His mind was exhausted. His focus slipped altogether, all at once. His alligator morph crackled with purple lines of energy—then it faded away. He slid back helplessly into the shape of himself.

He ran the rest of the way up the stairs. There was nothing else he could do. He took the steps two at a time, stretching his long legs to make the leaps, hoping for all he was worth that none of the alligators in the cellar below happened to look up the flight of stairs and see him. He was at the door in seconds. He seized hold of its iron ring and pulled it open.

He stepped through the door and shoved it shut behind him, praying that none of the alligators below would follow him up.

He had come into a narrow hallway. The walls were of rough uneven stones, and rose high, high above him toward a vaulted ceiling. To his left, the corridor dead-ended against a heavy stone wall. To his right, though, there was an exit. Rick crept cautiously toward the exit. When he reached it, he pressed close to the wall and peeked out.

He caught his breath. He saw at once he was in the heart of the fortress. It was an awesome sight: a vast, soaring Great Hall of stone and stained glass. The walls seemed to rise and rise forever. The rosette windows seemed as big as suns, decorated with richly colored scenes that Rick could not identify. Huge statues of men he likewise didn't recognize stood in niches looking out with dead stares. Enormous antique furniture—throne-like chairs and ornately carved tables and tall display cases holding bizarre weapons—lined the walls at the edge of the elaborately designed carpets. Above it all, there hung chandeliers—enormous wooden wheels, each the size of a flying saucer, each with dozens of candles burning in them, bathing the hall in wavering red-and-yellow light.

Below, along the walls, there were heavy black doors. At each door, there stood an alligator guard, his leathery hand resting on his sword hilt, his eyes moving back and forth to sweep the area around him with red beams.

As Rick surveyed the scene, there was a noise . . . a movement. Rick ducked back—then cautiously peeked around the corner again. He saw a great pair of double doors swinging open in the center of the wall across from him. He saw the alligator guard there stand aside respectfully.

And then he saw Reza.

This was the first close look Rick had had of him. An amazing and frightening sight. The assassin whose hologram portrait Jonathan Mars had shown him had been transformed into a long, tall, purple humanoid with leathery wings. He was almost naked except for the heavy belt that held a dark skirt over his lower torso. He had rippling muscles in his narrow chest and strangely thin yet powerful-looking whip-like arms. Huge yellow eyes beamed out of the purplish skin of his sharply angled face. And as he hovered above the floor, a thin tail lashed the air behind him. He had large hands with even larger claws coming out of them. He looked very much like the devil himself.

As he came out the door, Rick got a glimpse of a magnificent room within: a huge circular space with columns and statues and a starry dome like a planetarium's. Hanging in the middle of the air in there, he saw some sort of moving mist. A living mist, it looked like. And there were images inside it. Images of faces. People.

With a jolt, Rick thought he recognized one of them: Jonathan Mars!

But before he could be sure, the double doors swung shut. The guard took his place before them again. And Reza moved away to float farther along the wall of the Great Hall.

The demon moved to a small black-iron door set in the

stone. Another guard stood there. He unbolted the door for the assassin. With a flap of his wings, Reza went through.

Rick had only a moment to glimpse what was inside: a huge moving engine of some kind, a great wheel throwing off crackling purple energy. Some kind of generator.

Then the demon entered the room and the black door clanged shut behind him. The guard moved back into place in front of it.

Rick drew back into the corridor, breathing hard. What had he just seen? What should he do now? He had to think. He needed a plan. His mission was to find out what was going on here. That meant getting into the domed room—that was obviously the center of the fortress; that was where the action was. He had to figure out a way to get in there.

He wasn't sure he had the energy to morph into an alligator again, but he might have to try. Other options? The walls of the corridor were uneven, with stones jutting out here and there. He might be able to climb up one of them. He might be able to get onto one of those chandeliers . . .

He never got to finish the thought. Suddenly, red light pierced his field of vision. He turned and saw that the door to the stairs behind him had opened. The guard named Kaaf had come looking for him, following him up out of the cellar. The beams from the alligator's eyes touched Rick as he spotted him.

Kaaf's jaws opened wide, baring his dagger-like teeth. He was about to call for help.

Rick drew his sword and rushed at him.

Reza had dispatched his guards to search the cellar for the intruder, then tried to contact the master through his communicator. There was no reply. He hurried back to the Sky Room to make his report to Kurodar in person.

"Master!" he cried as he flew in.

"Quiet!" boomed the presence above him. The mist of Kurodar had now spread out in tendrils across the painted sky. It pooled here and there, and moved in some places in circles of light that turned into misty corkscrews. At the foggy pink core of the great man's presence, images were forming. Reza saw they were the images of the people in the Traveler's plane.

Reza understood that the master's enterprise had reached its crisis point. Still, he had to tell him, "Master, I think the intruder has returned!"

"Then find him!" Kurodar boomed imperiously. "Kill him! That's what you're here for! Go!"

Reza bowed his head and flitted out of the room. *The cellar next,* he thought. And he was about to fly across the Great Hall to the corridor on the other side—the corridor where Rick was hiding right that minute.

But then he thought: *No.* He had to check the Generator Room again. He knew he was being obsessive about it, but it bothered him—haunted him: the idea that someone might sneak in there and bring the whole fortress—and Kurodar's plan—to a standstill.

Quickly, he flew to the small iron door. The guard

unlocked it, and Reza ducked in to check the Disperser Wheel one last time.

Sword drawn, Rick charged down the alley toward Kaaf the alligator guard.

Kaaf let out a hissing snarl. With a sting of metal, he drew his own weapon, a massive broadsword. In one fluid motion, he lifted it above his head and brought it sweeping down at Rick as Rick rushed toward him.

Only Rick's athletic reflexes saved him from being cleaved in two. He threw up Mariel's blade crosswise above him. The steel sang out as it caught Kaaf's descending broadsword on the thick of its blade. Rick felt the jolt of the impact as the two swords crashed together only inches above his skull.

The powerful Kaaf tried to force his sword down through Mariel's blade, but Rick grabbed the guard's arm with his free hand, lifted his own leg, and planted it square in the middle of the alligator's belly. He kicked out. The guard went stumbling backward. In almost the same motion, Rick brought his sword whipping around toward the alligator's enormous head.

The corridor was too narrow for such a swing. Rick's sword point scraped the stone wall, sending up sparks. That slowed his attack and Kaaf, still off-balance, managed to bring his sword around to defend himself. There was another sting of metal on metal as the two swords came together, the guard blocking Rick's blow. The alligator went into an answering attack at once, slashing at Rick with a backhand stroke. Rick stepped back, and the alligator's sword point swept past his face, so close he felt the wind of it as it went by.

The force of that swing turned the alligator half around. That gave Rick the opening he needed. He stepped forward. Grabbed the alligator's forearm, holding his sword at bay. Then, with a cry of fear and fury, he thrust the point of Mariel's blade up into the underside of the reptile's enormous snout.

The blade struck home. The point pierced the alligator's throat and continued up into its head. Kaaf's eyes went wide—then blank with death. His body flashed and flickered with purple bolts of energy. Even as Rick pressed the sword point home, the lizardly security bot winked out and vanished in a hot violet flash of light.

But there was no time to celebrate the victory. Rick heard a hissing roar from the vast hall behind him. He heard thundering footsteps on the flagstones out there and more thunder on the flagstone stairs leading up from the cellar below. *More guards!* Rick realized: Kaaf must have raised an alarm.

The thundering alligator footsteps grew louder on every side of him.

He was surrounded.

Victor One's eyes darted from face to face. He looked at the Traveler, who seemed strangely serene as he waited for the voice of Kurodar to continue over the plane's loudspeaker. He looked at Leila Kent, who seemed amazed and shocked at what was happening. He looked at Bravo Niner and Echo Eight: the faces of the professional fighting men were still and watchful. He looked finally at Jonathan Mars, whose deep-set eyes were alive with ferocious intelligence. Then he looked back at the Traveler, as Kurodar's voice once again filled the U-28A's cabin.

"I have taken control of seven passenger planes," said Kurodar in his thick Russian accent. "Altogether, there are two thousand and six people on board these aircraft. They are flying above a city with a population of over half a million. If you do not do what I tell you to do, I am going to bring every one of those planes crashing into the most densely populated portions of that city. I estimate it will take me between one and a half and two minutes to bring down all seven planes. In 120 seconds, I will snuff out an untold number of lives and cause a level of destruction and terror not seen in your country for over a decade."

The Traveler nodded. "Very impressive," he said quietly.

A touch of pride seemed to enter Kurodar's voice as he answered: "It is only the beginning—only a hint, a taste—of what the Realm can do. If there weren't so many doubters in the Assembly, I would have waited and shown you what it could achieve in all its glory. Then you would have seen something. Your entire nation in flames. But you will see it yet. As I say, this is only the beginning."

The voice fell silent. The U-28A continued to skim swiftly over the trees below.

"Go on," said the Traveler, his tone still calm. "What is it you want?"

"I want you, Dr. Dial," said the Russian's voice.

The Traveler shrugged his thin shoulders, blinking bemusedly behind his glasses. "It seems you already have me."

"I do," Kurodar replied. "And it is very helpful. There are many who fear you in the Assembly, you know."

"Fear me? No one of goodwill needs to fear me."

"Oh, don't be so modest, Doctor. We both know what you're capable of. It is you, I assume, who sent the intruders here."

The Traveler shrugged again. "My work made it possible for them to enter your Realm, that's all."

"Then you have sent them to their death, you know."

For the first time, Victor One saw the Traveler's calm demeanor falter. He grew pale. Victor One remembered Leila Kent saying to him back at the cabin, *We've asked Rick to go into the Realm.* He remembered the Traveler had lost his calm then, too, crying out, *You can't do that!*

Now, the Traveler had to draw a deep breath before he could speak again. Now, Victor One knew, he was only pretending to be calm. He said, "You've killed them—the intruders? They're already dead?"

"All but one," said Kurodar. "We are hunting the last one now. He will be dead momentarily, I promise you."

Victor One saw the Traveler begin to breathe normally again. "I see."

"And now we are going to make it so your presence does

not trouble the minds of the Assembly anymore," Kurodar continued. "I am flying you to an island off the coast of your state of Georgia. I will set your plane down there, after which you and your laptop will be transferred to another plane, one of mine. You and your work will be brought to me, and we will review the work together. You will explain everything to me. You will show me this new program you have been protecting so carefully. You will demonstrate what it is capable of and outline what you are planning and how I can defend the Realm against whatever attack you and your masters had in mind. Then there will be nothing more for the Assembly to fear and the work of the Realm—the destruction of your country—can continue safely. It's all very simple."

"Very." The Traveler nodded. "And if I resist or refuse or try to destroy the work on my laptop before it reaches you . . ."

"The planes in my control will crash into the city. All seven of them. Many thousands will die."

The voice ceased. The plane was silent except for the thrum of the engine. Victor One's eyes flitted from face to face. Leila, the other bodyguards, Jonathan Mars, the Traveler again.

He saw the Traveler give another nod, blinking mildly behind his glasses. "All right," he said calmly. "I have no choice. I'll do what you say."

Then Jonathan Mars reached into his jacket, drew out a gun, and pointed it at the Traveler's chest.

"I'm afraid I can't allow you to do that, Dr. Dial," he said.

Responding to Kaaf's alarm, the alligator guards thundered toward the corridor. They came up from the cellar on the stone stairs. They left their guard posts by the doors and rushed across the Great Hall. They all reached the corridor at about the same time and, in a moment, the hallway was crowded with armored two-legged reptiles, their swords drawn, their fangs bared, their eyes shooting red light through the shadows as they sought the intruder.

But the corridor was empty. Kaaf was gone—and so was Rick.

The alligator guard had vanished as he died. And Rick had scurried up the wall.

Fear had spurred him on. He'd climbed quickly, his fingernails and sneaker-tips gripping every outcropping he could find on the uneven stones. He pulled himself up the face of the wall like a climbing chameleon. He was already halfway toward the far distant ceiling when he looked down over his shoulder and saw the guards flooding the corridor below him.

He knew it was only a matter of time before one of the alligators lifted its snout and pinned him with a pair of red beams. He couldn't just hang around up here. He had to keep moving.

Clamping his mouth shut to keep from grunting with the effort, he sidled along the uneven rocks toward the end of the corridor. He crept around the corner and was now hanging high above the Great Hall. The rosette windows soared above his head. He looked down past the candles in the circular chandeliers and saw the statues and furnishings on the floor below.

He saw something else, too: All the guards had left their posts and rushed over to the corridor at the alarm. The Great Hall was empty.

The strength in his arms was beginning to give out. He couldn't stay up here much longer. Soon, the alligators would decide he was gone and come back to their posts by the doors. This was the moment to make his move. He began to climb down the wall.

As he did, the iron door across the way—the door to the Generator Room—was flung open, and out flew the winged demon, Reza.

Rick froze where he was, clinging to his precarious perch on the wall by his fingernails. Looking over his shoulder, he watched the demon cross the expanse of the hall below, heading to join the guards in the corridor. He hung on—hung on—his arms aching, his muscles beginning to quiver with the effort. He feared he would lose his grip and drop right into the winged demon's path.

But now Reza entered the corridor and moved out of sight. Rick quickly scrambled down the wall—dropping the last few feet to land quietly on the edge of a rug.

The moment his sneakers touched down, he spun and started running—running for the double doors that had been left unprotected. That was the way into the domed room. He knew he needed to get there fast, get out of sight before the guards started pouring back out of the corridor and spotted him. But he was amazed at just how great this Great Hall was. It must've been as far across as a football field at least, maybe two. By the time he got to the other side of the hall, he was panting hard.

As his hand closed around the handle to one of the double doors, he glanced back over his shoulder. He couldn't see very far into the corridor across the way. He just caught a glimpse of the demon's lashing tail in there—a glimpse of movement as the alligator guards milled around, looking for him.

Quickly, he pulled the door open a crack and slipped through.

He closed the door. Turned. Looked up.

His mouth opened at the stunning sight. The monumental room. The lofty columns. The statues several stories high. The seemingly endless dome of stars above, its moving streaks of light, its moving lines of darkness that seemed almost alive.

But more than anything, it was the vision at the center of the place that gripped him, held him, made his eyes go wide.

A misty and somehow animated presence hung in the air high above him. Its tendrils reached out across the dome, twining and spiraling in places here and there. And, swimming in the depths of that strange disembodied presence, there were images—the images he had glimpsed from the corridor across the way. Jonathan Mars—sitting in a canvas seat along the wall of what looked to be a plane. He was holding a gun, Rick saw now, pointing it at one of the passengers across from him.

They—the others—were visible, too, in this floating,

living 3-D image. There was a shifty-eyed tough guy with skin like jerky. An elegant woman with swept-back golden hair. And then . . .

"Dad!" Rick whispered.

His father, Lawrence Dial, was there as well! Large as life—or small and bald and yet somehow impressive in his serene and unshakable inner strength. Rick stared up at him, his lips parted, thoughts and emotions twining and spiraling through his mind and heart like the twining and spiraling tendrils of pink mist above him.

He saw his father look across the plane's cabin at Commander Mars and he realized: that gun in Mars's hand—it was pointed directly at his dad!

"What are you going to do, Jonathan?" Rick's father asked calmly—his voice was audible throughout the vast domed space. "You going to shoot me dead in cold blood?"

Commander Mars looked at him for a moment, silent but unmoved.

Then he said, "Yes. That's exactly what I'm going to do."

"No!" Leila cried out over the grinding noise of the airplane's engine. "What do you think you're doing, Jonathan? Put that gun away!"

"I can't do that, Leila," said Jonathan Mars in a steady voice. "The Traveler's program is the only way to destroy the

Realm. Everything we've done has been done to keep the technology out of Kurodar's hands. I'm not just going to let him turn it over."

"You can't just shoot him!"

"Yes, I can." Mars continued to train the gun on the Traveler. The Traveler watched him calmly.

Kurodar's voice came over the loudspeaker. "I'm not bluffing about crashing those jets, Commander. Pull that trigger, and I'll bring them down."

Mars slowly shook his head. "I know you're not bluffing about crashing the jets. I just think you're lying when you say you won't crash them if we hand over Dial and the laptop. Whatever happens, you're going to slaughter all those people and we both know it. Why wouldn't you?"

"He won't, because my work is encoded," said the Traveler quietly. "He has no chance of understanding it without my help, and I won't give him that help until I can see for myself the planes have landed safely."

"All the same," said Mars. "We can't let him have your equations. The Realm would be unstoppable then. The MindWar would be lost. All of us, the whole country, would be lost."

Victor One's mind raced as he watched the confrontation. The ramifications were impossible for him to figure out. If the Traveler refused to hand his work over to Kurodar, then Kurodar would crash the planes into the city, sure. But Mars was right: he would probably crash them anyway. And if Kurodar got hold of the Traveler's equations or whatever they were, he would be unstoppable and God only knew what damage he could do then. At the same time, Victor One had been assigned to protect the Traveler's life. He didn't see how he could just sit there and watch while Mars put a bullet in him . . .

Even though his arm still throbbed from his wound, he went to his hip and drew his weapon quickly.

"I'm gonna ask you to drop the gun, Commander," he called across the plane.

Mars's eyes flashed to him, then back to the Traveler. "Don't be an idiot, Victor One," he said. "This has to happen. We can't let Kurodar get that laptop. I'm telling you: he may kill thousands today, but a lot more—millions more—will die once the Realm is fully operational."

Victor One hesitated. He was a simple guy. He never claimed to be anything else. He couldn't work all this out; he just knew it couldn't be right for Mars to kill the Traveler in cold blood. He just knew it was his job to stop him.

"Listen—" he said.

But before he could finish the sentence, the plane keeled over.

It happened with shocking speed. The engines roared, the nose of the U-28A jerked skyward, the left wing went up and the right wing down, and for a moment it seemed the plane would flip completely.

Mars was thrown forward against the straps of his seat so hard that the gun was jolted out of his hand. It flew across the cabin and landed at the feet of Bravo Niner. But before the wiry bodyguard could grab it, the plane had swerved again, still climbing, and the gun spun away across the floor.

Victor One was hurled back into his seat canvas. He nearly lost his weapon, too. It slipped from his grip, but hit his leg as it fell. He grabbed it, first with his left hand, then with both, and held on. His stomach rolled as the plane leveled out fast.

Leila Kent clutched her stomach. Her high cheekbones had taken on a greenish tinge. Mars's face was red with fury as he watched his pistol skitter across the cabin, out of his reach. Only the Traveler's expression remained the same. He didn't seem afraid. He didn't even seem particularly excited. Victor One wondered if that was because of his faith or just because he had guts of steel—or maybe both.

Kurodar laughed—and his laughter filled the plane.

"So much for your gun, Mars," he said. "Now we continue, and when we reach our destination, Dr. Dial, you will give me what I want and I will safely land those seven planes. Agreed?"

The Traveler nodded once. "Agreed," he said.

Rick saw all of this, playing like a three-dimensional movie in the mist that was Kurodar's mind. As he watched, his thoughts and feelings veered and dove and rose like the plane. Jonathan Mars ready to shoot his father dead in cold blood! His mild-mannered dad, so cool and unafraid. Then the plane going crazy . . . the last-minute rescue that was really not a rescue at all . . . Rick didn't understand everything he was seeing—but he understood enough.

He understood, in a single moment, that he had lived these last months of his life lost in a fog of lies. The lie that his father was unfaithful. The lie that his mother was broken and in despair. The lie that he himself was helpless. It had all been untrue—all of it. In fact, his father had given up everything he loved in an effort to protect his family and his country. His mother had been sorrowful, but faithful and strong. And he, Rick—despite his pain, despite his injuries—he had held the power to help them in his spirit all along.

He had let the lies imprison him. Now, in a moment, the truth had set him free. He had to act. He had to help his father—he had to *save* his father—he was the only one who could. He had to do it no matter what it cost him, no matter what it took—even if he had to sacrifice everything he loved to save everything he loved.

For another second, Rick stood where he was, there on the floor of that soaring domed room, his head tilted back as he looked up into the computerized mind of Kurodar. There was no way to touch that mind, no way to stop what he was doing—not here.

His face set and grim, he turned away—turned to the Sky Room's double doors.

He knew what he had to do.

Pressing his wings down against the air, Reza lifted himself above the crowd of guards milling in the corridor. He glided over them, looking down as they searched for any signs of trouble. He could hear their voices growling and buzzing.

"False alarm."

"No problem here."

"We should return to guard the doors."

"We should return to the cellar to search for the intruder."

Reza considered the situation. The alarm had come from Kaaf—a quick, sharp cry for assistance over the communicator: "Intruder in corridor C." And yet here they were in corridor C and—never mind the intruder—Kaaf himself was nowhere to be found. Where had he gone?

Reza's eyes played over the heads of the alligators. What if the intruder had somehow killed Kaaf? That would explain why the guard-bot was gone. But how could the intruder have gotten away? There were only two exits from this hallway: down the stairs to the cellar, and out to the Great Hall. If the intruder had left in either direction, the incoming guards would have spotted him . . .

Hovering there, Reza lifted his eyes to the wall. It was a rough surface with a lot of outcroppings. He supposed if someone was particularly resourceful and athletic, he could have climbed up the wall somehow, but . . . Well, it didn't seem likely.

He called out to the guard-bots below him: "Return to your stations. Resume patrol."

At once, the crowd of two-legged alligators began to

disperse, some heading down into the cellars again, others returning to the Great Hall to take up their posts by the doors.

Thoughtful, worried, Reza drifted above them. What if the intruder *had* climbed up the wall? He couldn't have reached the stairway from there . . .

Flapping his wings slowly, Reza moved back into the Great Hall. He hung in the air, looking around. The guards were returning to their posts at the various doors. One placed himself before the Generator Room. Another moved to the doors leading into the Sky Room—and just as he did, those doors swung open.

To Reza's surprise, out came Kaaf! The chief guard was not dead at all! He nodded once to the alligator taking up his post and quickly moved away along the wall.

He was heading toward the Generator Room.

Still on the other side of the Great Hall, Reza contacted his minion through the communicator: "Kaaf! What's going on? Why did you raise the alarm?"

But Kaaf didn't respond. He didn't even stop walking. Reza started flying toward him, calling again, "Kaaf. What's the matter? Where are you going?"

Kaaf reached the Generator Room. The guard there stood aside as his superior approached. Kaaf went past him and unbolted the room's small iron door.

Reza flapped his wings and flew toward him more quickly. Overriding the communicator completely now, he simply shouted to him, "Kaaf! Wait! Where are you going?"

But Kaaf did not wait. He still did not respond at all. He ducked into the Generator Room.

A moment later, Reza reached the door himself. The guard there nodded at him. Reza ignored him and flew past. He flew directly through the open door and entered the Generator Room.

At first, he saw nothing. Only the metal walkways winding around the walls. The immense Disperser Wheel turning. The flashes of lightning as the energy fed into the bottom of the wheel three stories down and was dispersed into various outlets on the way up.

And then, startled, Reza saw Kaaf. The chief alligator guard was standing right beside him, right behind the iron door.

"What are you doing?" Reza barked at him. "Do you know how much trouble you've caused?"

Without an answer, Kaaf pushed the iron door shut and threw the inner bolt, locking both Reza and himself inside.

"What—" Reza began.

But before he could finish, Kaaf began to change—change impossibly—before his very eyes.

That was close! Rick thought.

It couldn't have been any closer. He couldn't have kept the Kaaf morph in place another second. Exhaustion and fear had eaten away his energy to nothing. He was sure Reza would reach him before he'd gotten through the door. As it was, the demon-like assassin had come in before he could shut him out.

Now the morph gave way in an instant. Rick's alligator size and shape melted away into his old humanity. He was just Rick again, clothed in the armor Mariel had given him, with Mariel's blade in the scabbard by his side.

He turned from the door to face the creature who hovered in the air beside him. He saw Reza's expression change from one of puzzlement to a look of such red, smoking, offended rage that it would have been almost comical—that is, if Rick hadn't known it could be deadly.

"You!" Reza breathed the word with fury. And then he snarled, the disdain nearly dripping from his lips: "The American."

"My name is Rick Dial," said Rick, and he drew Mariel's blade. "And I'm here to destroy this place."

The demon's face contorted with anger, yet he managed to nod with a measure of respect. "You must be a man of great spirit. You are the first to learn to change shape like that. I congratulate you." He even gave a courtly little bow. Then he said, "I am Reza. And I'm going to kill you."

And without another word, he attacked.

Rick nearly died in that first assault. It was so quick, he could barely react in time to defend himself.

Reza dove at him out of the air—and, as he dove, the

claws of his right hand extended into razor-sharp blades. His long, thin, flexible arm snapped like a whip. The claws snaked toward Rick's head with incredible speed and violence.

Reflexively, Rick threw up his sword and ducked, off-balance. Reza's claws struck Mariel's blade hard. The impact sent Rick sprawling. He stumbled over his own feet, tumbled down onto his side, rolling across the narrow walkway until he hit the walkway's rail. Beside him, above him, below him, the generator's enormous wheel turned and flashed with energy bolts, drawing in the purple lightning from the energy pods below and shooting it forth again into the circuits of the fortress.

Reza came after Rick where he lay. The demon landed on the walkway, drew back his arm to slash again.

Rick kicked out, hitting the creature in one of his elongated legs. His foot caught Reza squarely on the knee and Reza's leg buckled. To keep his balance, the demon had to flap his wings and lift up. He had to draw back before he could strike again. That gave Rick the time he needed to scramble to his feet.

But that was all the time he had. Reza renewed his attack. His arm whipped—his claws flashed—again and again in rapid succession. Backing up along the walkway, Rick turned his sword this way and that, catching the claws bare inches from his face and body, feeling the vicious steel tips brushing past his cheeks.

Panic began to flood through his nerve endings. Reza was a master fighter. His whipping blows came on so fast and furious that Rick didn't have time to strike back. If this kept up, he'd wear out, slow down. Then Reza would move in and cut him to pieces. He had to get away, gather his strength, gather his thoughts . . .

But Reza kept pressing in on him. The air whistled and snapped as he struck again with whip-like speed. There was a clash of claws on blade—and then another and another. Rick backed away . . . backed away . . . blocking . . . looking for a chance to deliver a strike of his own.

There was no chance. Reza moved in closer, struck again—then again—forehand, backhand. Blindingly quick. One blow got past Rick's defenses but by good fortune struck only his breastplate. Still, it sent a jolt through his body and a clang through the air that warned of worse to come.

Rick leapt back, but the claws slashed again and this time sliced across a vulnerable spot on his forearm. He cried out as the steel tips tore through his skin, sending trails of blood spitting into the air. The thin cuts on his arm were like lines of fire burned into his flesh.

Rick stumbled on the walkway. The great generator wheel turned above and below him. The purple lightning flashed everywhere.

Reza saw his moment and charged in. Off-balance, Rick had no chance to fight him. He had to get away. He grabbed hold of the railing and flung himself over.

Reza's claws whipped past him—missing by a hair as Rick went over the rail. Rick held on with one hand, gripping his sword in the other. He dangled over the side, his sword trailing down, its steel blade reflecting the purple flashes that went in and out of the generator wheel.

Reza didn't hesitate. He flew over the side of the railing and began to come down after Rick where he hung.

Rick sheathed his sword—and then let go. He dropped through the sizzling air of the generator pit. His body began to turn helplessly, and he felt his stomach flying up as he fell and fell. He knew the fall might knock him senseless, might even break his legs. But before he struck the bottom, he passed the lower walkway—and with those quick, athlete's reflexes of his, he managed to grab the railing with one hand, then the other, dangling now from the lower walkway as he had dangled from the walkway above.

He looked down. The floor of the Generator Room was not that far beneath him. He could make that drop if he had to.

But right now, he needed a place to stand and fight. Reza was already flying down after him.

Quickly, Rick hauled himself up and dropped onto the walkway, his metal armor ringing against the walkway's metal floor. Then he leapt to his feet, drawing Mariel's sword again as fast as he could.

And none too soon because there was Reza, flying in the air on the other side of the railing, the big wheel turning behind him, the lightning flashing all around him.

The demon's purple face split in a white smile. "Do you understand what's going to happen now?" he said, shouting over the slow grind and buzzing sizzle of the generator. "Death in the Realm is a fearful thing, Rick Dial. It's not like ordinary death. It's worse, much worse. It goes on and on. There's a slow, slow fade into helplessness. Then an endless agony of decay. Your spirit gets trapped in here, you see. It can't free itself to go on to the next life. Death in the Realm is death forever. Think about that, Rick. Think about it hard."

Rick did think about it. He couldn't help himself. He knew that what the demon was saying could not be wholly true. Nothing humans make lasts forever. Even the agony of death in the Realm would end when the Realm collapsed and the spirits trapped here were free to move on. But knowing that wasn't much comfort. He remembered the sight of that poor creature in the spider-snake's tunnel, his skeletal face and the look of pain in his huge, bright eyes. He remembered the terror that haunted Favian, who knew that one day—one day soon—he would be a creature just like that. And now he, too—Rick—would become such a creature, if Reza finished him off in here. He thought about it, and the thought made him feel weak inside.

Which, he understood, was exactly what the demon wanted. Fear. Weakness. An expert killer like Reza understood that ninety percent of any battle is won or lost in the mind. In the mind was where Rick had to fight him. He gritted his teeth and forced the terrifying thoughts down inside him. He gripped his sword tighter, lifted it into the air. He remembered Mariel's courage, how she had given up her own dwindling strength to armor and arm him. He couldn't let that go to waste.

He glared at Reza across the shining blade, trying to look braver than he felt.

"Come and get me," he said.

Reza's smile vanished. He flapped his wings once and shot at Rick through the air like a bullet, snapping his arm, swiping his clawed hand directly at Rick's face.

Rick was ready for him. He blocked the strike with his sword. He spun away. He grabbed the railing. He leapt.

The next moment, he was falling past the great Disperser Wheel, down through the flashing darkness. He hit the floor at the wheel's base. He bent his knees to absorb the impact, but still had to drop and roll, his armor rattling on the cold stone.

He leapt up, his sword gripped in his hand. He looked around him. He was in the heart of the machine. The enormous wheel was grinding above him. The air was filled with noise, the mesh of gears, the snap and crackle of electricity. Everywhere, lines of purple power flashed and sizzled—shot into the spinning wheel—then went dark. There were power outlets built into the stone wall, he saw, each with a metal diaphragm. Each diaphragm in its turn would twist open. There would be a faint hum, the smell of ozone, then the purple burst would shoot out for several seconds, fueling the wheel. Then the diaphragm would twist shut.

Lifting his eyes through the flashing, smoky air, he saw Reza descending after him, the demon's bat-like wings spread wide to steady his descent. Even in the chaotic atmosphere, Rick could see Reza's oversized eyes burning brightly in anticipation. Another moment, and the creature would be on him, slashing at him with those vicious claws.

Rick's mind was working fast, his eyes moving everywhere, even as his heart pumped hard with fear. He saw a spiral staircase against one wall. It led up to the walkways and to the door above, but if he tried to climb it now, if he even tried to reach it, Reza would cut him down. There was no other way out of here, no more railings to jump off, no more quick routes of escape, no place left to run. Rick would have to stand his ground and do battle with the demon. One way or another, this would be the end of it.

He didn't have much hope. Reza was just much better at this killing game than he was. Plus he was exhausted. Mariel's blade was growing heavy in his hand. His lungs were pumping and his muscles growing weak with both weariness and fear.

But even as his shoulders sagged, he felt the hilt of the sword pulse against his palm. He heard Mariel's voice speaking in his mind:

You're going to be afraid, but if you surrender to your fear, you're lost. You might despair, but if you give in to your despair, they'll destroy you. Remember, your emotions are only emotions. Live in your spirit, Rick, however you feel. Live in your spirit and you can defeat them.

He tried. Focusing his thoughts, he tried to leave his weariness and fear behind him. He tried to enter into the clean, cool, shining place of his spirit, to send the power of Mariel's blade flowing down into the deepest part of himself. For a moment, he could almost feel it, could almost feel himself becoming one with the shining steel . . .

And a fresh thought came into his mind, as if someone had whispered to him: a new idea.

At the same moment, Reza gave a wild shout and dropped

like Lucifer out of heaven. He struck at Rick's head with incredible speed. A powerful flash lit his bright eyes and glinted off his whipping claws.

Rick moved as fast as he could, spinning gracefully, swinging his sword. He could feel the power of his spirit coursing all through him. He could feel himself in full control of his body, the way he used to feel when he was on the football field.

The two warriors came clashing together one last time. Reza snarled and slashed with his claws. Rick spun and blocked him—backing away toward the nearest of the power outlets. The wheel turned above them, sending out its flashes of lightning. The purple flashes bathed Mariel's blade and Reza's claws as they struck together, sending up fresh sparks of their own.

The two warriors separated for only a second as Reza gathered himself for the final strike.

Down by Rick's leg, the power outlet hummed. Its diaphragm twisted, getting ready to open. There was the smell of ozone. A sizzle as the energy built to fire. It was going to flash.

This was what Rick was looking for. He knew it had better work or else he was done.

Reza attacked. The demon claws drew back, ready for the killing strike. At the same instant, the air went purple and a bolt of electricity shot out of the outlet toward the Disperser Wheel.

Rick lowered his sword into the bolt.

The purple lightning struck Mariel's blade. The blade glowed bright as the blast hit it, but the hilt and handle blocked the flow, protecting Rick's hands where they were wrapped around Mariel's image. With a great breathless snap, the lightning ricocheted off the blade in a steady stream. Rick adjusted the angle of the sword and sent the blast directly into the onrushing demon. The lightning struck Reza just as he was about to deliver Rick's deathblow. It hit him smack in the center of his forehead.

Reza's mouth went wide in surprise as he was sent flying backward through the air. The creature's thin, whip-like arms flew out as he tumbled wildly across the room. He landed hard on his back, his wings crushed beneath him.

Rick did not hesitate. With a roaring battle cry, he rushed across the space between them. The big wheel turned overhead, its engine grinding. The lightning flashed everywhere. The air filled with smoke. An instant later, Rick was standing over the dazed demon where he lay. He raised his sword.

Reza's huge, yellow eyes stared at the death that hung above him. He was all hatred in that moment, all hatred and rage. He cried out, "No!" not because he was afraid of dying but because it infuriated him to be defeated by this American intruder. The hatred was like a fire inside him.

If Rick had had a qualm about killing something so much like a human being, it left him now. He could see Reza's heart in his eyes and he knew: whatever soul this creature had been given had been withered to nothing, strangled by evil as by a vine. God might forgive Reza—God was God—but there was no place for a demon in the world of men.

Rick drove the sword home. Reza's dying scream was

hellish. It seemed to fill the room, to wipe out every other sound, to grow hollow and huge as if echoing from the furthest canyons of damnation. The winged, purple body flashed and crackled with electricity—but it did not vanish as the alligator's had. Instead, it shrank and shriveled around the point of Rick's sword as if all the fluid were draining out of it, leaving nothing but a shrunken husk. Only the eyes remained huge, staring in agony and terror, staring up from the dead shell of a thing that lay at Rick's feet.

Rick remembered that stare. He had seen it in the spider-snake's tunnel, seen it in the eyes of that poor creature buried in the niche, wrapped in the web. Seeing it again in Reza's eyes—well, it was awful. He drew out his sword and turned away.

He glanced down at his palm. His heart sank. His time was almost gone—under three minutes left! If he did not leave the Realm soon, his mind would start to come apart again. He, too, would die in here, trapped, staring, decaying. He had to move, had to find the exit, reach the extraction point—now.

But he couldn't. Not yet. Upstairs, in that domed room, Kurodar held his father captive, was taking his plane . . . who knew where? It didn't matter. Wherever it was, it was where his dad would die.

Rick could not leave the Realm until his father was free.

He looked around him. He saw a control panel against the far wall, lights blinking on it, gears turning behind glass. This was the center of the Disperser Wheel's mechanism. He rushed for it. A lightning flash cut off his path. He stood back, shielding his eyes with a raised hand as the power sparked and danced into the big wheel.

Then the flash ended and Rick ran forward again—but another aperture in the floor opened. There was another hum, the smell of ozone. It was about to flash again. At this rate, his time would run out before he could reach the control panel.

He looked to the aperture. He saw the flash building. He lowered his sword.

The lightning flashed and hit Mariel's blade, bouncing off it, away from the wheel. Once more, Rick turned the surface of the blade, aiming the reflected electricity at the generator panel this time.

The lightning struck the control panel. The lights flashed rapidly. The inner mechanism smoked. Then the whole thing went dark.

All the lightning died at once. The electricity went off. The great wheel ground to a shuddering halt. The deep pit of the Generator Room was plunged into near blackness, covered in thick, smothering smoke. The engine of the fortress was dead.

I did it! Rick thought breathlessly.

Then the control panel exploded.

For Kurodar, it felt like dying. One moment, he was all power, his mind spread into the controls of seven jet planes plus the Traveler's U28-A. Thousands of lives were his to destroy, an entire city at his mercy, and the only man who could possibly outthink him—the Traveler—was at his command.

The next moment, the power in the fortress went out, and he lost his grip on all of it, on everything. He began to slip back into himself, the disembodied mind tumbling and tumbling down into that hunched ugly little body hidden in the basement of its island fortress, wired into its machines and . . .

. . . Kurodar screamed. The sound filled the airplane—a cry so loud it seemed to blow Victor One back in his seat. Leila Kent covered her ears with her hands. The Traveler and all the others flinched and recoiled as if trying to escape the noise.

Something had happened. Something had changed.

The scream faded. It grew dim. It died.

And then, suddenly, the plane's engine died as well.

In an eerie new silence, the U28-A keeled over slowly like a sinking ship. It went nose down. Its right wing lifted and turned over. The plane began to spin, falling faster and faster toward the earth.

Leila cried out once. Jonathan Mars lifted his arms uselessly, as if he could protect himself from what was about to happen. Bravo Niner and Echo Eight braced themselves, their faces grim and resigned. The Traveler's lips moved silently as he prayed.

Then, there was a weirdly soft sound, like a man coughing. Quietly, the engine started again. The propeller took on speed. For another moment, the plane kept falling out of the sky. But Victor One could feel the power surging into it again. The spin stopped and the wings leveled. There was another long, breathless second.

Then the plane's nose lifted. The U28-A straightened.

A new voice came over the loudspeaker.

"This is the pilot. We have the plane again. It's back under our control."

Slowly, the plane turned upward toward the open air. The U28-A began to rise.

The passengers looked at one another. Leila Kent's elegant face was streaked with mascara and tears, but through the tears, she began laughing. Bravo Niner and Echo Eight were grinning, too. Even Jonathan Mars smiled.

Victor One turned to the Traveler—to Dr. Lawrence Dial. For the first time, he saw real passion in the absentminded professor's face. The mild eyes behind his glasses were brighter than the bodyguard had ever seen them. The professor lifted a fist in front of him and shook it at Victor One in triumph.

"Rick did that," he said, his voice trembling with emotion. "That's my son. He's beaten them!"

Not far away, in the glassed-in tower that housed the GTD Terminal Radar Approach Control Facility, the calls began to flood the controllers' headsets. Controller William Lasenby heard the first one:

"Tower, Air East 2612 is under pilot control again."

And then another: "TRACON Approach, Jet Tomorrow 151 is in control."

More voices joined the others. All seven jets were coming back under pilot control. As Lasenby looked around him, he saw on the faces of his fellow controllers what he knew was on his own face. The pallor of fear was giving way to a rush of color and relief. As another pilot called in and another, Lasenby lifted his hand in the air. The other controllers did the same.

Then they all began cheering.

The first blast from the short-circuited control panel knocked Rick off his feet. He dropped down onto the flagstones hard. Mariel's blade was jarred out of his hand and clattered to the floor.

Rick lay dazed, staring blankly into the darkness, shaking his head. He saw zigzagging lines of purple energy running up the body of the great wheel above him. Flames spouted from its energy receptors, and the flames began to spread around its circumference. A section of the wall above the generator panel—blackened and weakened by the explosion—began to crumble. A large flagstone came loose and tumbled down through the air. It crashed to the floor at Rick's feet, breaking into pebbles and dust. The room grew steadily brighter with a wavering orange light as the flames spread around the great wheel. There was a grinding, tearing sound as the wheel began to wobble on its moorings.

Rick blinked, stunned. He looked around. Smaller stones dropped like dust from the ceiling.

The Generator Room was falling apart. The walls were crumbling. He was going to be buried alive in here.

He swept Mariel's blade off the ground. As his fingers wrapped around her image on the hilt, he felt fresh energy flow through him. He heard her voice in his head:

Hurry, Rick. Go.

He climbed to his feet. He caught one more glimpse of Reza where he lay, of Reza's agonized and tragic yellow stare, his desiccated husk of a body. With a shudder, he tore his own gaze away. Looked to find the spiral staircase. There it was, through the smoke and flame, a curling shape against the wall. It was quivering and rattling as more stones began to drop out of the wall to which it was anchored.

Rick ran for it. The wheel was now bright with dancing fire. A burning piece of the mechanism dropped off and fell through the air to crash at Rick's side. Rick kept running, went past it. A hunk of stone crashed in front of him, missing him by inches. He dodged around the fragments. He reached the spiral staircase. He grabbed the iron banister. He flung himself up the first two steps and began a running climb.

Another flaming hunk of the wheel dropped past him, sizzling as it fell through the air. There were more tearing noises. More dropping stones. The iron of the spiral staircase trembled beneath his feet as he climbed. He reached the first walkway. He had to run around the arc of it along the wall to reach the next flight of stairs—the stairs that rose to the door. As he took his first step, the room—the air—the flames—reality itself—seemed to zoom away from him, out of focus. The Realm seemed to dissolve into the energy at its source: snaking, hissing lines of power.

Rick reeled, dizzy, on the walkway, grabbing blindly at the rail. He knew what this meant: his time was up. His mind was beginning to disintegrate.

He forced his consciousness to steady. The world came back into focus. He found he had stopped for a moment on the walkway. Ironically, that pause saved his life.

Because just then, another flagstone came loose and plummeted off the wall directly above. It crashed into the walkway just a few yards ahead of Rick—just where he would've been standing if he hadn't stopped. The stone crashed right through the metal, tearing a hole in the path, leaving a dead drop into nothingness between Rick and the stairs. The walkway wobbled from the blow, and Rick clung to the railing to keep himself on his feet.

He was scared now, good and scared. Everything was coming down around him—his mind was going—he was out of time. And he did not want to die in this place—to die Reza's death, that death that wasn't death, but nothingness and slow decay. He sheathed his sword. He gritted his teeth as he looked across the broken walkway to the stairs on the far side. Then, without another thought, he raced forward, charging at the gap.

In the moment before he jumped he thought: *It's too far! I can't make it!*

Then he jumped. He flew through the air between one jagged edge of the walkway and the other. His arms pinwheeled. His feet sought purchase on the emptiness. But he was right. The gap was too wide, the leap too far. He couldn't make it. He dropped. He screamed. He reached out desperately. His wrists smacked painfully down onto the edge of the walkway—and slipped off as he kept falling . . .

But somehow, with one hand, he managed to snag a loose bar of metal. He held on with the top joints of his fingers.

His body dropped and swung. His own weight nearly pulled him right off the walkway, but still he held on. He dangled there above a fatal fall, the big wheel flaming right beside him, the fire licking at his back. He shouted with effort and pulled himself upward. He grabbed hold of the torn metal with his other hand. Another armload of stones dropped off the walls above him and fell all around him, peppering his face and hair with flecks of rock.

He dragged himself up onto the walkway. Pushed off his knees and stood. There was the stairway, right ahead of him. He rushed for it.

All around him, the Generator Room was now in flames and crumbling. The fire shot up to the ceiling and the stones rained down from the flames as he climbed the spiral staircase's final flight, two steps at a time. He reached the iron door. Threw back the bolt. He heard a loud rending noise above him. He knew the wall was about to come down on top of him.

He hauled the door open and leapt through just as the rocks crashed into the stairs and tore the entire staircase from the wall with an almost human screech. The structure plunged into the flames below as Rick stumbled out of the Generator Room and into the Great Hall beyond the door.

An alligator guard was waiting to meet him there. He nearly ran right into it.

Rick cried out at the sight of the creature. It stared at him, its reptile eyes only inches away, its fierce teeth visible outside its snout. Rick spun to the side to avoid crashing into it. His sword gave a long, metallic whisper as he drew it from its sheath, ready to strike.

But the alligator didn't move. It stood where it was, staring, its enormous hands at its sides. Another moment and Rick realized it wasn't budging at all, wasn't alive at all. In fact, he noticed that, here and there, other guards were also standing lifeless around the Great Hall. The animating force seemed to have gone out of them—out of all of them.

Kurodar is gone, he thought. Kurodar had left the fortress, had maybe even left the Realm—for now, at least—and he had taken his life force with him.

Rick turned to the double doors that led into the domed room where he had seen Kurodar and his father. He wanted to go back there now, to make sure he had set his father free.

But once again, as he gripped his sword's hilt, the energy seemed to travel up his arm from where his hand held the image there—the energy and a voice. Mariel. Whispering in his brain:

Your father's safe now. You've won, Rick. Go.

Rick nodded. Prepared to obey her, he took a step—but as he did, his vision fizzed and blurred again. The world began to fragment. Rick stumbled.

In confusion, he thought: *My mind . . . going . . . have to get out . . .*

He managed to steady himself again by force of will. He recovered his feet. Just as he did, there was another huge blast from behind him in the Generator Room. Stones flew from the wall above him. Flames spat out of the iron door. Across the hall, he saw water flooding out of the corridor, spreading across the rugs. And now the glass in one of the immense rosette windows shattered and came raining down in sparkling shards, making a chandelier swing and flicker.

The whole fortress was coming down.

Dizzy and sick, Rick pushed himself forward. He could see—way, way down at the other end of this enormous hall—a towering front door. He ran toward it on wobbly legs, shaking his head as he went, trying to keep his mind in one piece, feeling it collapsing inside him, even as he saw the Great Hall begin to collapse around him.

Another rosette window shattered. Another storm of glass rained down. More of the stone walls began to crumble, too. A rock fell from somewhere, smashing into an enormous statue. The statue wobbled on its base and then pitched forward, crashing face-first to the floor, the marble head breaking off the neck and rolling over the rug.

Rick reached the door, panting, dazed. Two alligators

flanked the exit, but both stood frozen, lifeless, staring. Rick was still afraid—he still wanted to live—but weariness and confusion were beginning to eat into his willpower as his consciousness began to decay. Still he managed to throw up the bolt on the front door. He yanked it open.

There was a courtyard beyond. The walls, the ramparts, the big front gate with the winch and chain that lowered it. The night seemed to be bleeding out of the sky above, and the yellow color was seeping back into it. The red of the courtyard grass was becoming visible.

Rick ran into the yard. To his left, a section of the fortress wall collapsed and spilled forward, spreading across the grass and dirt, burying the frozen alligators standing on the ground beneath it. Rick reached the winch, knocking yet another alligator out of his way as he went. The guard toppled over like a rotten tree. Rick sheathed his sword to free his hands. He grabbed the handle of the big wheel and turned it quickly. The gate began to lower slowly. He felt the pressure of its descent. He let the handle go, and the gate came crashing down.

Something exploded in the fortress behind him. Rick looked over his shoulder and saw flames shooting out of the rosette windows. Another section of wall collapsed.

He ran out the door, through the outer walls, into the courtyard before the moat. There were more alligators standing here and there, frozen, gazing into empty space.

And there—there, finally—he saw the purple diamond of energy floating near the border of the silver water. The portal point. The way home.

He started moving toward it. But just then, a powerful wave of nausea went through him. Everything around him became energy and light. Reality—or what passed for reality in the Realm—quickly sank into a vague dream. Rick barely knew where he was. He barely knew who he was . . .

When he came around this time, he was on one knee. Sick, exhausted. He wasn't sure what was going on—what he was supposed to do. And then, in a distant sort of way, he remembered. The portal point. The glowing purple diamond . . . He was supposed to do something . . . Oh yes. Reach it! Get out!

He was beyond fear now. Beyond everything but exhaustion and nausea and dissolution. Only a will he did not know he possessed made him push himself to his feet. He staggered toward the diamond out of sheer ornery stubbornness—the native grit that made him almost impossible to stop on a football field, a sort of physical faith that still upheld him when even his mind was nearly gone. He went forward. But it was like pushing through mud now, the mud of his own dissolving personality. His steps grew heavy and slow. His thoughts grew vague. His knees began to buckle.

He came to a stop.

He stood there, staring stupidly, blinking stupidly, his arms hanging loose at his sides. As his fading consciousness flickered back in him a little, he realized he was going to die like this, lifeless on the spot like the alligators around him. Except they were merely bots. He was a living soul. They would feel nothing in their death. He would die and die for a long time before his spirit could get free.

And yet, for all his fear, for all his will, for all his strength, he couldn't bring himself to take another step. He didn't have the power. He stood there helplessly as his mind went to pieces.

He had only enough mind-energy left to think one word. He thought: *sword.*

He lifted his hand. He laid it on the hilt of his weapon, on the image of Mariel.

His whole body straightened as a burst of clarity went through him like an electric jolt. A voice spoke inside him:

Live in your spirit, Rick! Go!

Rick shook his head, uncertain.

You . . . What will happen to you? he thought. *To you and Favian . . . If I leave you . . . What . . . ?*

The voice didn't answer him. It just repeated, *Go!*

But Rick would not. There was something else he had to do. One last thing. What was it?

His hand.

He looked down, confused, at his left hand. He saw the red light flashing beneath the skin. He remembered: the program Miss Ferris had embedded in him. Energy for Mariel and Favian. To keep them alive a little while longer. Until he could come back. Until he could free them.

Now, using all the strength he had left—not much—Rick drew his sword. Its energy pulsed up his arm, pulsed through him.

Go, Rick! Spirit, Rick, Mariel commanded him.

I will not leave you here, he told her.

You have to. Go.

I will not.

He lifted the sword. He set its point against the flashing red light on his palm. He plunged the blade into his hand.

He screamed with the pain. But at the same time, he felt the energy pod burst out of his palm. The red force ran out of him, ran into Mariel's blade, charging it with fresh power.

Go! said Mariel.

The silver blade was now pulsing with red light. Rick could feel it. It was making him stronger.

But now, he drew back his arm and with a mighty effort, he hurled the sword through the air toward the moat.

"I will come back for you!" he shouted.

The silver-red sword flashed over the silver water. The water rose up to meet it in a sudden wave. As Rick watched through unfocused eyes with fading vision, the rising water took the shape of a womanly hand. The hand caught the sword in midair. The red light flashed from the sword into the hand.

Thank you, Rick! Now, go!

And still gripping the sword, the hand sank down and vanished into the liquid metal.

The water closed over the sword and was still, as if nothing had happened.

Mariel was gone.

The burst of energy from the sword had given Rick a little more strength, just a little. Slumped, weary, he forced himself to shuffle forward another heavy step. Another blast of flame flew up over the fortress ramparts as something within exploded. He took one more step toward the portal point and then one more. He was almost there.

At last, nearly dead on his feet, he stood before the purple diamond. A thunderous blast made him turn just in time to see the fortress walls above him beginning to crumble and tumble down. He faced the purple glow of the portal point and marshaled his will. Lived in his spirit. The deepest part of himself.

I'm still here, he thought up into the heavens. *Always here.*

And from the heavens, the answer came back to him: *So am I. Even in the Realm.*

That still, small voice seemed to inspire him with the last strength he needed. He took the final step toward the portal. He willed himself into it.

There was a great liquid rush. The exploding Realm melted around him. He flowed into nothingness.

CUT SCENE:

AFTERMATH

31. HOME FRONT

THE LONG BLACK limousine traveled smoothly over the curling country lane. Forest stood close to the road on either side, the late autumn trees nearly empty, the stark branches lacing the air with the pale and sinking sun peeking through them.

The massive bodyguard Juliet Seven drove the big car. Miss Ferris sat beside him. The Dial family—Rick and his mom and Raider—sat in the backseat.

None of them spoke. Even Raider had finally fallen silent after jabbering like a squirrel for over two hours. His mother had her arm around him now, and he was leaning against her, half asleep. As for her, Mrs. Dial, she gazed out the window, staring into her own reflection on the tinted glass. Her face looked tired, but her eyes looked excited and bright.

Rick sat next to Raider, his crutches propped on the seat between them. He looked out his window, too—excited, too, in a quiet, satisfied way. He gazed out at the passing trees and at the sun gleaming and fading as it appeared and disappeared behind the branches. He was thinking . . . well, he was thinking a lot of things. So many memories and plans and hopes and worries were flitting through his brain that he could barely sort them out. They flashed on the screen of his mind like random scenes from a half-finished movie. Mariel. When would he see her again? The MindWar. His fight with Reza. His father. Jonathan Mars with a gun in his hand. Favian. His good-byes to Molly. Kurodar's fortress exploding. His workouts with his training weights. Mariel . . . Would he get back to her in time . . . ?

It had been over a month since he had fought his way out of the nightmare that was the Realm. The first three days after his return were lost to his memory. Apparently, for most of that time he had lain insensible in a hospital bed in the MindWar compound. When he spoke at all, it was gibberish. He did not remember who he was. He did not remember where he had been. He was so weak and wounded that, at one point, the doctors almost despaired of his recovery.

But he did recover—not slowly either, but suddenly, all at once. Suddenly, he sat up in bed. His mother was sitting beside him.

"Mom?" he said.

She grabbed his hand with both of hers. Her eyes filled with tears. "You remember," she said.

She made him lie down again. He gazed at her face. He did remember. Her. The Realm. Everything but the last few days. "What are you doing here?" he asked her.

"They thought you might die, so they brought me in. They told me everything."

He nodded wearily. He was glad she knew. He hated

keeping secrets from her. He was beginning to hate secrets altogether.

It seemed to him that the next week or so was one long argument. Mostly, he argued with Miss Ferris. He wanted to know about Mariel and Favian. Who were they? How had they gotten stuck in the Realm? How long did they have before their strength ran out and they died? He wanted to go back into the Realm to try to help them. He shouted at Miss Ferris.

"Tell me what you know!"

Miss Ferris would tell him nothing. She only said over and over that he could not return to the Realm—not yet. The energy pod she had given him would buy Mariel and Favian some time. In that time, they would try to find some way to rescue them. They would try. That was all she would say. The expression on her face barely changed when she said it.

Rick finally despaired of getting anything more out of her. He moved without pause into the next argument. He wanted to see his father. And not just that. He wanted his mom and Raider to see his father, too. He wanted the whole family reunited. The government had no right to keep them separated. He understood why they'd had to keep his work top secret. He understood why they'd had to hide him away from everyone and all forms of communication: to keep him out of the reach of Kurodar and the Realm. But no matter how important his work was, no matter how urgent it was to keep it secret, it was not right to separate a man from his family forever.

Miss Ferris did not change the expression on her face

during this argument either, but Rick thought he saw some sympathy in her eyes this time.

One day, as Rick lay in the bed in his hospital room, the hologram of Jonathan Mars appeared. It stood glowing in the corner.

"I want you to understand," Mars said. "We've won a battle, but the MindWar continues. Kurodar escaped the fortress. He's going back before the Axis Assembly to ask for more money so he can stage a larger attack next time and with more security. If the Assembly agrees, if they give him the funding he wants, the danger will be even greater than before."

"Yeah?" said Rick sharply. "So?"

"So if we agree to bring you to your father, you'll have to stay with him. You'll be in a compound we've built for him especially. The compound is designed to thwart the Realm. That means a lot of time there'll be no Internet. No phone service. We can get you to school, but you'll need a bodyguard. It won't be much fun on date night."

Rick shrugged. "You've had people watching us all this time anyway," he said.

"That's true," said Mars. "I just want to make sure you understand what you're asking."

Rick considered him for a few seconds. "You know," he said, "I saw what you did. When you pulled that gun on my dad, I saw that."

Mars drew a breath. "I know. I'm sorry."

"You were ready to shoot him. Weren't you? You were ready to kill him right then and there."

Commander Mars nodded, his craggy face set as always in a frown. "I was. To protect his technology. To protect our country."

"You're a patriot," said Rick.

"I am."

"Well, good for you. But if you ever pull a gun on my father again, I will hunt you down. I will rip your arm off and then beat you to death with it. Do you believe me?"

Jonathan Mars did not answer for a long moment. Then he said, "Yes."

"Good," said Rick. Then he turned his face away and waited for the stupid hologram to vanish.

Soon after that, Rick went home. He talked things over with his mom and Raider. They all agreed. They wanted to be with Dad again. They wanted their family together. They would deal with the problems of living in the compound as they came up.

It took three more weeks for the powers that be in the MindWar Project to arrange the transfer. In the interim, Rick returned to his room. This time, however, he did not close the door and play video games. This time, he kept the door open. And he worked out. He worked his legs. He worked his arms. He worked his core. He worked with weights. A lot. Every day. For hours. It hurt. Also a lot. Sometimes it hurt so much Rick could hardly believe it. When it hurt that much, he would tell himself: *Live in your spirit, Rick.* Sometimes that helped. Sometimes it just went on hurting. But he kept working out. A lot.

When word came that the transfer to the compound had been approved, Rick drove over to Professor Jameson's house. The Jamesons had a gazebo in their backyard. Rick and Molly went out there and sat together on one of the cushioned sofas. Molly was wearing a pink knit cap against the autumn cold and it looked great on her. Her pale cheeks were also pink, and also looked great. Rick found it painful to look at her, especially when her eyes teared up. He did not know how long he would be gone. He did not know when he would see her again.

He told her what he was allowed to tell her: his father had been doing secret work for the government; the story about him running off with another woman had been a lie. He told her that he and his mom and Raider were going to join his dad, but that he couldn't tell her where or how long he would be gone.

"I'll still be able to get e-mail sometimes," he said.

"Great," Molly said flatly. "Nothing I like better than e-mail. Especially when I'm writing to a guy who doesn't write back. That's the part that makes it really special." She angrily knuckled a tear from the corner of one eye.

"I'll write back," Rick said.

"You better. You're on crutches and I'm in great condition. If you ignore me again, I will bounce you around the room like a basketball."

"I'll remember that."

Then they sat there awhile without saying anything. It was hard. Too hard, after a while. Rick said, "Well . . . ," and he grabbed his crutches. He pushed himself up on his legs—his aching legs. He worked himself down the steps of the gazebo. When he reached the lawn, he turned in a small circle, working the crutches around, and looked back up at Molly where she still sat in her cute knit hat, knuckling away the tears.

"I'll see you, Molly," he said.

"Will you?" she asked him.

He said, "I don't know. I don't know what's going to happen next."

She nodded. "That's an honest answer, at least. I hate those."

"Me, too. But it's all I got."

She nodded. She smiled. It wasn't much of a smile. Rick turned away and hobbled away from her across the lawn.

That had been four days ago.

Now, the limousine came around a slow bend in the road, and the compound became visible in the distance. It was a drab and unimpressive place: a large dusty lot surrounded by a chain-link fence with barbed wire around the top. Guard towers with soldiers in them. Soldiers at the front gate.

After the limo passed through the checkpoint, they could see the buildings. There were a lot of them. Barracks mostly. One line of single-story cabins like a country motel. And the central structure—a three-story edifice of concrete and glass that looked like it belonged in some suburban office park somewhere.

Miss Ferris turned around in the front seat and faced them. "You won't be here too long," she said, trying to sound reassuring but mostly sounding like her usual emotionless self. "When your father's project is done, you can all go home."

Rick nodded. "It'll be fine," he said.

"It'll be fine," his mother added.

"I think it's cool!" said Raider.

The limousine pulled up in front of the central building. Looking out the window, Rick saw soldiers in uniform moving toward them. He turned in his seat. He looked at his mom. She looked at him and gave a small smile. Raider's smile was enormous, gleaming. Still, none of them spoke.

Finally, Rick said, "Well, I guess we're here."

And for some reason, his mother laughed out loud. And Raider made a fist and said, "Yes!"

Soldiers opened the car doors. Rick's mom and Raider got out on one side; Rick got out on the other, dragging his crutches after him. Miss Ferris and Juliet Seven got out and stood by the car.

Miss Ferris nodded at Rick with that blank expression of hers. Rick nodded back. He looked down as he worked his crutches under his arms.

And when he looked up, his father was there.

Lawrence Dial—the Traveler—had stepped out the front door of the central building. He was wearing a homey cardigan sweater over his button-down white shirt. His glasses were pushed up onto his balding head. He was blinking mildly into the light of the late sun, as if he had been indoors a long time and had to adjust his eyes to the light. And he was smiling brightly.

He came forward a few steps, but by then Raider was tearing across the lot to him. He hit his dad hard enough to drive him back half a step and wrapped his arms around his legs and held on fast.

Rick's mom laughed as she followed after, but there were tears on her cheeks, too. And soon she was wrapped around her husband as well, holding on to him and rocking herself against him. Rick could see his father's face over her shoulder. He could not remember the last time he had seen his father cry.

Rick watched his dad hugging his mom and Raider. Miss Ferris and Juliet Seven and all the soldiers were looking on, so Rick pressed his lips tightly together, trying to control his emotions—though some of the soldiers looked pretty tearful themselves.

Rick glanced over at Miss Ferris. She nodded at him and gave him something that might have been a small smile. Rick nodded back. He took his crutches out from under his arms. Standing unsteadily, he handed them to her. She took them—but for another moment, Rick held on to them, too.

Rick's legs still hurt. Every day, all the time. But they were much stronger now than they had been. And, after all, it wasn't that long a way.

Rick let his crutches go, and walked toward his father.

ACKNOWLEDGMENTS

MY SPECIAL THANKS to Flight Instructor Andrea Read of Spitfire Aviation and to the staff of the Terminal Radar Approach Control Facilities at Santa Barbara Airport for their assistance with research. I'm also grateful to my truly exceptional editor, Amanda Bostic, and my wonderful agent, Alyssa Eisner Henkin. My wife Ellen Treacy, as always, helped with everything.

READING GROUP GUIDE

1. Rick's life is centered on football. When the car accident takes that from him, he feels like his life is over. Have you ever lost the one thing you cared about most? How do you start over when you lose your center?
2. Some religious philosophies claim that God is responsible for everything that happens, good and bad alike. How would Rick have felt about that concept after his accident? Does your church teach this kind of theology? What do you think?
3. Rick hones his reflexes by playing video games. Do video games actually sharpen your mind?
4. Video games are unique from movies or television in that they are totally interactive: nothing happens without you. Do you think this kind of entertainment is more or less valuable than those that can be enjoyed passively? More or less addictive?
5. Some people become addicted to the fabricated digital world of video games or the Internet. What is the attraction to an alternate reality? Is it fundamentally different from the compulsion toward reading books or listening to music?

6. If you were given the opportunity to relive former glory, but only in a digital reality with a digital body, would you take it? Why or why not?
7. *MindWar* is thick with paranoia. How much stock do you put in conspiracy theories about the government and its clandestine agencies? Do you trust the federal government?
8. Would you have agreed to enter the Realm like Rick did? Why or why not?
9. Rick believes his father abandoned the family for an old girlfriend. He is understandably furious with him. Do you think experiences like this make kids more or less likely to adopt the same behavior in their adult lives?
10. As a side effect of his father's abandonment, Rick loses his faith. How do individual Christians' choices effect others' perception of the religion as a whole? Are we responsible for being *representatives* as well as *followers* of Christ?

ABOUT THE AUTHOR

PHOTO BY MEREDITH W. WALTER

ANDREW KLAVAN WAS hailed by Stephen King as "the most original novelist of crime and suspense since Cornell Woolrich." He is the recipient of two Edgar Awards and the author of such best sellers as *True Crime* and *Don't Say a Word*.

CENTRAL ISLIP PUBLIC LIBRARY
3 1800 00307 9247